PENGUIN BOOKS

THE
DARKEST
DUET

CONNIE GLYNN

Books by the author

The Rosewood Chronicles

UNDERCOVER PRINCESS
PRINCESS IN PRACTICE
THE LOST PRINCESS
PRINCESS AT HEART
PRINCESS EVER AFTER

The Cursed Melodies

THE CURSED MELODIES
THE DARKEST DUET

THE
DARKEST
DUET

CONNIE GLYNN

PENGUIN BOOKS

PENGUIN BOOKS

UK | USA | Canada | Ireland | Australia
India | New Zealand | South Africa

Penguin Books is part of the Penguin Random House group of companies
whose addresses can be found at global.penguinrandomhouse.com.

www.penguin.co.uk   www.puffin.co.uk   www.ladybird.co.uk

First published 2026

001

Text copyright © Connie Glynn, 2026
Sheet music copyright © Thomas Clarke, 2024, 2025. All rights reserved.
Cover illustration copyright © Fernanda Suarez, 2026
The moral right of the author and illustrator has been asserted

Penguin Random House values and supports copyright.
Copyright fuels creativity, encourages diverse voices, promotes freedom
of expression and supports a vibrant culture. Thank you for purchasing
an authorized edition of this book and for respecting intellectual property
laws by not reproducing, scanning or distributing any part of it by any
means without permission. You are supporting authors and enabling
Penguin Random House to continue to publish books for everyone.
No part of this book may be used or reproduced in any manner for the
purpose of training artificial intelligence technologies or systems. In accordance
with Article 4(3) of the DSM Directive 2019/790, Penguin Random House
expressly reserves this work from the text and data mining exception.

Set in 11.52/14.4pt Goudy Oldstyle Std
Typeset by Six Red Marbles UK, Thetford, Norfolk
Printed and bound in Great Britain by Clays Ltd, Elcograf S.p.A.

The authorized representative in the EEA is Penguin Random House Ireland,
Morrison Chambers, 32 Nassau Street, Dublin D02 YH68

A CIP catalogue record for this book is available from the British Library

ISBN: 978–0–241–64620–5

All correspondence to:
Penguin Books
Penguin Random House Children's
One Embassy Gardens, 8 Viaduct Gardens, London SW11 7BW

Penguin Random House is committed to a
sustainable future for our business, our readers
and our planet. This book is made from Forest
Stewardship Council® certified paper.

For anyone who ever searched for fairies in the garden

The Cursed Melodies world

Characters
Residents of Faymore Manor

Astrid and Jonas Bunting
Bloom Blooded teenage twins who were brought up in Red Blooded society. Due to their connection to magic, they were isolated, deemed psychologically unwell, and kept under treatment for much of their adolescence. They can wield Ancient Magic and communicate with and control nature, making them valuable assets to the Order of Pendragon. They also have a mysterious connection to Gwendolyn Chatterjee: they feel an overwhelming need to protect her.

Gwendolyn 'Gwen' Chatterjee
A teen Bloom Blood with a magical anomaly. Her powers seem to be connected to the Shadowling and the book of Cursed Melodies. She only recently discovered that she can perform Ancient Magic and feats of extraordinary strength.

Magnus Faymore
A Rapscallion and the last surviving Faymore. He has dedicated his life to solving the mystery of the Grim. He and his

husband, Elijah, have become surrogate father figures to the inhabitants of Faymore Manor.

Elijah Faymore (né Ackerman)
Magnus's husband and the only other surviving member of the Rapscallions. He loves to bake.

Lorelei Murphy
A powerful and beautiful young woman with a mysterious past. She is Magnus's research assistant for investigating all things relating to the Grim.

Thomas Murphy
Lorelei's younger cousin and an apprentice in the Order of Pendragon.

Janaki 'Jan' Chatterjee
Gwen's older sister and an apprentice in the Order of Pendragon.

Buttonbug
A magical creature known as a felimoth that the twins found in a cave, and have kept as a pet. She has the appearance of a midnight blue kitten with moth wings and antennae.

The royal family

Prince Theodore Dora
A handsome and charming young royal who is next in line for the throne of the United Kingdom, and will inherit the Magister of the Western European Faction of the Order of Pendragon title. He is also the bane of Jonas's existence.

Magister (Queen) Beatrice Dora
Queen of England and the United Kingdom as well as Magister of the Western European Faction of the Order of Pendragon. She is a venerated and powerful woman.

Princess Alice
The queen's wife and Ambassador of Magical History at Fountains Abbey.

Other notable characters

Ambassador Harriet Loupe
Ambassador of Potions and Charms. She can be prudish and rude but is a loyal servant to the Order of Pendragon.

Sister Seraphina (deceased)
The previous Ambassador of Ancient Magic before she revealed herself as an instrument of the Shadowling. She was eaten alive in service to him.

Rupert Faymore (deceased)
Magnus's younger brother and a member of the Rapscallions. He was infected with the Grim, but was able to fight it long enough to ask Magnus to kill him before it took hold completely. Before dying, he gave Magnus his Savonnette and told him to find the missing pieces of its lid.

Rani Chatterjee (deceased)
Gwen and Jan's mother and a member of the Rapscallions. She seems to have understood that Gwen was special and had a connection to the Grim – something she didn't want the Order to find out about, for fear it would put Gwen in danger.

The Shadowling
An ancient monster from before the magical dark age, and the most evil and hateful being in all of history. He holds a searing disgust for humankind and will stop at nothing to wipe them off the face of the earth. With the Grim, he can possess magical creatures and darken their hearts. He has the form of a white-and-gold dragon.

The Order of Pendragon's hierarchy

Magister
The primary authority of each magical faction around the world. Together, they make the Grand Coterie. They meet at the Shadow Library to address matters of global interest.

Ambassador
Second-highest position below Magister. Every faction has five ambassadors for each area of study who typically reside in and teach at the main academy of their faction.

Custodian
A full-fledged member of the Order of Pendragon. A custodian typically dedicates their life to one area of magical study or a specific role in Bloom Blooded society. Their Savonnettes are gold.

Apprentice
One step below Custodian, they usually spend time shadowing Custodians and helping with research while figuring out what vocation they would like to fulfil once they pass their final exams. Their Savonnettes are silver.

Pledge
Young Bloom Bloods who have pledged themselves to the Order of Pendragon and are only beginning their magical studies. Their Savonnettes are bronze.

Locations

Enchanted Quarter
A protected and hidden area of potent Bloom managed by Custodians. It is populated by magical creatures who have been collected by the Order of Pendragon. There are Enchanted Quarters by Faymore Manor and Fountains Abbey Academy.

Faymore Manor
Perched on a Devonshire cliffside, Faymore Manor is the home of the Faymore Cluster. The estate is comprised of three buildings – the main estate, Windyside Cottage and the stables – and vast gardens, a graveyard and a strip of beach with a dock.

Fountains Abbey Academy
The main Order academy of magical research in the Western European faction, although Bloom Bloods from factions all over the world come to study and work there.

Fountains Vale
The surrounding area of Fountains Abbey Academy, where many Bloom Bloods live and work. It is hidden from the Red Blooded world.

The Shadow Library
The headquarters of the Order of Pendragon. Situated on Lake Geneva, it is the greatest bastion of magical knowledge that remains on earth since the magical dark age.

Key terms

Ancient Magic
Extremely powerful magic from before the magical dark age. Little is understood about it or why such powers were lost.

Bloom
The melodic make-up of the entire universe and the source of all magic.

Bloom Blood
A person with magic in their blood who can hear and manipulate the melodies that make up all things.

Cluster
Similar to the concept of a witch's coven, a cluster is a group of Bloom Bloods who work and oftentimes live together.

Deliverance
A spell used to contain magical creatures inside a Savonnette, so they can be moved to a safe location – in most cases, an Enchanted Quarter.

Faction
A subsection of the Order of Pendragon, organized along geographical lines. Its equivalent in the Red Blood world is a nation.

Grim
A terrible curse that possesses magical creatures and Bloom Bloods. It corrupts their hearts, turning them hateful and cruel, and submits them to the Shadowling's bidding.

Instrumentation
The practice of channelling Bloom into music to perform magic.

Magical creature
A creature made of Bloom. It may be harmless or extremely dangerous. The Order of Pendragon's main job is to capture magical creatures and move them to Enchanted Quarters out of sight of Red Blooded humans. Examples include the felimoth, rusalka, Nure-onna and Kelpie.

Magical dark age
A period of time between the fifth and sixteenth centuries in which Red Bloods turned on Bloom Bloods and magical creatures. During this time almost all magical knowledge was lost, and many sentient magical creatures vanished or were forced into hiding.

Old kings
Legendary rulers from before the magical dark age.

Order of Pendragon
A secret society dedicated to the conservation and study of magic and magical creatures. Established in the sixteenth century by Lady Jane Grey, it has factions all over the globe and holds tremendous power.

Rapscallions
A group consisting of Rupert Faymore, Magnus Faymore, Rani Chatterjee, Elijah Ackerman, Abigail Bane, Francis Bane and Quin Larkspur. Their sole mission was to uncover the secrets of Ancient Magic using the book of Cursed Melodies as a guide. They were responsible for releasing the Shadowling and the Grim back into the world and have since dedicated their lives to reversing this strange curse.

Red Blood
A human being who cannot perform magic.

Rupert's Savonnette
An ancient Savonnette found by Rupert Faymore. It once held the Shadowling's soul until it was shattered by the Rapscallions during a summoning ritual. Rupert, for reasons unknown, collected and mended all the pieces of the Savonnette – except for two shards from the lid that were later found as pendants belonging to Astrid and Jonas.

'Sanguis Noster, Officium Nostrum'
The greeting used by Order members. It means *'our blood, our duty'*.

Savonnette
An enchanted pocket watch carried by every member of the Order of Pendragon. The more advanced types are used to perform Deliverance, a spell that can pull a magical creature into the Savonnette so it can be released into an Enchanted Quarter for protection and study.

The Cursed Melodies
A book of seemingly indecipherable spells, history and artefact. It is forbidden, as it is considered to be evil and dangerous by the Order of Pendragon.

Twelve Spells
The main melodies that every Bloom Blood must master in order to be able to perform instrumentation. The term is also occasionally used as an expletive.

Ward
A powerful charm whose melodies confuse, cover and contain. It is usually placed around Enchanted Quarters to keep magical creatures in and Red Bloods out.

1

The Earth and the Water

Sometimes, when Astrid couldn't sleep, she liked to watch her. She'd hum to the vines under her window, curling them round her wrists and ankles. They'd rustle, delighted, lifting her up so she could see her through the glass, sleeping, peaceful and safe. Gwen. She looked like royalty, dark skin glowing blue in the moonlight, wrapped up in her velvet bedspread, her inky hair pooled over the pillow like a crown.

Tonight was freezing, a midwinter blanket of pure-white snow covering the Faymore Estate. The earth beneath was sleepy and slow to respond, with all the little napaea and tree spirits slumbering until spring. Still, Astrid went out, wrapped in her cloak and hat, leaving a trail of footprints in her wake to where she was about to scale the old brick wall.

'You're being a weirdo.'

Astrid turned, sighing.

'Hello, brother mine.'

Hands on his hips, Jonas sniffed the icy air, Buttonbug on his shoulder. The little felimoth's whiskers were frost-tipped, midnight-blue wings twitching against the cold. Jonas's nose and cheeks were pink as polished apples, his hair shining white in the starlight. Astrid didn't need a mirror to know she looked the same, for the twins always matched.

'And what are *you* doing out here?'

This time, Jonas rolled his eyes. He didn't answer, but Astrid knew. He was here for the same reason – Gwen.

Their magic was tied to her, for reasons they didn't know, and that night, they'd heard the trees whispering. Something had disturbed the peaceful winter night and called them to her window.

It was January, months since their fateful encounter with the Shadowling, and since the twins had started calling Faymore Manor their home. Now they had grown attached to the estate and its inhabitants, and they would protect them at all costs.

As winter had crept in, so had a heady and deceptive calm. Tucked away safe here, the twins had learned much more of magic, the Bloom that coursed through their veins.

While Gwen tried (and mostly failed) to figure out *her* new power of unusual strength, the twins spent their days practising spells and music under the tutelage of Lorelei and Magnus. They learned potions and charms, and melodies to stitch cuts back together and soothe burns. In lessons with Elijah, they were taught every ingredient and how to procure it, from moon tonic to nixie hair. Some mornings they'd ride down past the Valley of Rocks to their Enchanted Quarter for supplies, slowly becoming accustomed to the magical biome. There, Astrid and Jonas were free to meditate amongst the trees, at one with the land, were able to flex and train that hidden muscle inside themselves that let them communicate with and control nature – the same one that told them they were different from other Bloom Bloods. That they could perform ancient and unknown magic.

Yet beneath this peaceful life they'd all cut for themselves, everyone knew: the Shadowling was out there, waiting.

Every day they anticipated news from Magister Beatrice or the Ambassadors of the Western European Faction of the Order. It never came, and neither did the danger. But it was coming; Astrid could feel it in the restless soil, hear it in the whispers of the trees. They had to be prepared.

Which was precisely why she had taken to going out into the vast gardens of the Faymore Estate, and, just as a sheepdog watches his master's flock, she would watch Gwen through her window.

'Honestly, I don't know why you don't just peek through her bedroom door like a normal stalker,' Jonas said, placing his palms against the ivy and moss like a concert pianist placing his fingers on the ivories.

Astrid came to join him, and the vines wound round their limbs.

'You know as well as I do that our powers are stronger outside. And besides . . .' Astrid hesitated. 'The door creaks.'

'Ah.' Jonas needed no further explanation. Astrid was in love, and the twins had always had peculiar ways of handling their emotions. Like how Jonas was currently keeping a particular black-heart lighter under his pillow, which he didn't know she knew about – and he would probably wring her neck if she mentioned it.

Still, she could feel that he understood. Jonas always understood, for they were the same, one half each of the same soul. It was reflected even in the pendants they wore round their necks, two shards of an ancient Savonnette that had once held the evil they were now preparing themselves to face once again.

Together, the twins hummed, the edges of their vision turning green. It was second nature now, like blinking or breathing. The earth responded, the ivy and moss lifting them up to the window.

On the way up, Jonas said, 'I'm sure the whispering was nothing. She's probably fine.'

He immediately ate his words.

Peering through the window, they saw the bed was entirely empty. Not only was Gwen missing, but the whole room was in disarray: sheet music of spells strewn across the floor, potion ingredients turned over, cupboards and drawers opened and spilling over.

Buttonbug hissed, her fur spiking up. And then they heard it: a high-pitched alarm of panic. The earth screamed a single warning.

Danger.

Dropping back down from the window, they hit the ground running. Jumping over roots and weaving through trees, they didn't need to go far, for the second they arrived at the back door of the main estate, they saw footprints in the snow. Footprints that headed to the rocky sea path.

'You go get Magnus,' Astrid instructed, her breath coming out hot and panicked into the cold air.

Nodding once, Jonas took off up the trail to Windyside Cottage, where the adults slept. Astrid went to the beach.

This is it, Astrid thought. The danger they'd been anticipating.

Even in the milder months, the path down to the beach was perilous. Steep, with rocks and roots waiting to trip, now snow hid these obstacles, and ice created new complications. Taking a deep breath, Astrid quietened her rabbiting heart, placing her palm in the snow, her skin connecting with the ground, asking the earth for guidance. It was something she and her brother had been practising. *Thud. Thud.* There it was. Footsteps. Distant, already stepping on to the sand. *Gwen.*

Astrid ran. Whenever she slipped, she called upon the earth to steady her. The earth listened, roots squirming out of her way, grass lying flat. At the halfway point, instead of following the path sideways and down, she jumped straight over the edge. Reaching her arms out, Astrid sang the earth to her, and just before she hit the beach, it reached back. Weeds and roots along the crag grabbed her, cradling her down to the sand.

Nature fell behind her as she followed the fading footsteps away from the cliff path. Now she was on her own, with just the snow-covered beach and the freezing water.

'Gwen!' Astrid called. But it was difficult to see in the dark, and the haze seemed to be growing. Tendrils of air, salty and sweet, thick as smoke. Where was it coming from?

'Gwendolyn!' Astrid called again.

And there she was. Just a flash of white in the dark, until Astrid ran closer.

She looked like a ghost. A figure, barefoot, in only a white nightgown, her black hair flowing over her shoulders as she slunk down the jetty towards the sea. If she reached the end, there would be nothing Astrid could do. Astrid couldn't swim.

'Gwen!' Astrid screamed. But Gwen kept going, inching further into the haze, and closer to the end of the jetty. *Why couldn't she hear her?*

It was as though Gwen were possessed, something calling her out into the ocean.

Even though the waves were calm that still winter night, only lapping at the shore with a soft *hush hush*, Astrid saw them as monstrous. She remembered what it had felt like to drown months ago, and she would never – must never – let that happen to Gwen.

You must protect her, the earth sang.

Astrid didn't hesitate, not for a second, her feet pounding on the rickety jetty.

Gwen was just in front of her now, and Astrid could clearly see the delicate shape of her small frame. Could almost smell the orange tang of the incense Gwen favoured for her room.

Reaching out her hand, Astrid had less than a second, less than half, before Gwen would step off and into the ice-cold water. Her fingers brushed the back of Gwen's nightgown, closing tight round the fabric. She didn't think, she just pulled. Then Astrid saw, just as she threw Gwen behind her, that her eyes were glowing gold.

Stunned, Astrid tried to commit the image to memory. It was as if a star were shining inside Gwen's head, bleeding light into her pupils.

There was little time to make sense of it. Gwen came hurtling backwards, Astrid flinging her down hard on to the wood of the jetty with a thud. Astrid toppled forward from the sheer force of the action, her toes nipping the end of the jetty; there was no stopping the motion.

Instead of Gwen, it was Astrid who went stumbling into the water.

Astrid almost laughed, except she was quite sure she was about to die.

The shock of the freezing water was immediate. She felt an all-consuming cold like needles in her skin, as though the water were injecting ice into Astrid's heart. She was sinking into it, her arms flailing, her mind submerging as much as her limbs. Even if she had known how to swim, there was no way to fight the icy pull of the water.

Then, hands came down from above, delicate fingers wrapping round Astrid's wrists. They were so warm, grasping with fierce determination. Astrid trusted these hands implicitly, her own fingers clasping and tightening like a vice around them.

Pulled by a strength too great to be human, Astrid shot out of the water and found herself landing on the jetty. Sodden wet, shivering and too shocked to even gasp for air.

'Breathe, Astrid.' Gwen's voice came through like a beacon, but Astrid was still choking on her own panic.

Then came a mighty slap across her cheek. 'Breathe, you fool!'

With one great gasp, Astrid sucked air into her lungs. *Relief*.

'Queen's mercy!' Gwen all but screeched. 'What in the Twelve Spells is going on? Where are we? Why were you in the water? You can't swim, for heaven's sake.'

Astrid grabbed Gwen's chin, turning her head to the side to check her eyes. They were fine, back to their regular molten brown. Gwen barely even had a hair out of place with the air so still.

'Hey!' Gwen protested, trying to bat her away, but Astrid caught her hand in her own.

Looking around, the sea was calm, the shining gibbous moon bouncing off the water.

'You were sleepwalking,' Astrid told her, surprised to find her voice tight, until she remembered that she'd just been saved from drowning. Again.

'I was *what?*' Gwen looked incredulous.

'One second.' Closing her eyes, Astrid reached into her own Bloom, feeling the magic course through her as she summoned the spells of Fire and Wind. She couldn't get it to dry her completely, the way she'd seen Lorelei do, but she was able to warm them both up.

'Gwen! Astrid!'

It was Magnus, calling from a distance, his long, heavy night-robe dragging patterns through the sand and snow. Lanterns floated around him, lighting the path – and the thick lines of worry etched on his stark, pale face. Behind him, Astrid could make out Lorelei, Jonas and Elijah – whose feet were bare, a nightcap dangling from his head.

'Come on,' Astrid said, standing up and stepping forward, bringing Gwen with her. Together they greeted the others, Astrid keeping her sights on Gwen's eyes the whole time.

'We're OK,' Astrid huffed.

Unconvinced, Lorelei and Magnus grabbed them both by the shoulders, appraising them. Lorelei was fully clothed, in a long black dress and a leather apron covered in burn marks and grass stains. There was an ash mark on her cheek, the white powder shining bright against her dark brown skin. She'd been awake, working on potions perhaps.

'Hardly,' Gwen protested, rubbing at her arms. 'Astrid nearly drowned. I had to pull her out of the water.'

At this, Lorelei muttered something under her breath, fixing one of her fierce mother-hen expressions on the twins. She said with a huff, 'That's it. The second this weather gets warmer, I'm teaching you two landlubbers how to swim.'

Jonas shrugged off the comment, coming to Astrid's side. A wordless exchange passed between them: she was fine. Gwen was fine.

'Gwen was about to go over the edge of the jetty,' Astrid explained. 'She was sleepwalking. Like she was under a spell.'

'Sleepwalking? Good heavens,' Elijah gasped, clutching his chest as if clutching pearls.

Now they all turned to Gwen. She stared back, her mouth opening and closing like a fish on land.

'Gwendolyn?' Magnus probed gently. 'Can you remember what you were dreaming about?' He was wearing his most common expression, that of patient curiosity. With his jet-black hair and night-robe, he bore an uncanny resemblance to a crow tilting its head in interest.

'I . . .' Gwen's brow furrowed, her nose scrunching up in thought. 'I think . . . I think something was guiding me into the water.'

'The Shadowling?' Astrid hissed, Bloom sparking at her fingertips. 'He's in your mind again.'

Gwen shook her head. 'No, no, it was something else – someone trying to show me something. Something important.' Gwen blinked, her eyes going wide. 'I think the person guiding me in my dream . . . was me.'

2

Dream-Walking

Gwen stared down the strange drink as though it might bite her. It was the watery brown of weak tea, but with silvery, constantly moving swirls. It made a sound different from regular Bloom, a soft clicking, like a foreign birdcall.

'Draumrum,' Lorelei said. 'To help you remember your dreams.'

'I've never heard of such a potion,' Astrid interjected into the conversation, sceptical.

'They don't teach this stuff in any Order textbook,' Lorelei replied cryptically, then turned back to her chopping board.

Gwen swallowed the tonic hard, ignoring the fuzzy feeling it caused on her tongue. Then she sat, waiting.

Like a stereogram coming into focus, her memories turned sharp at the edges. But when she tried to remember last night, the vision remained hazy, like trying to hear words underwater. There had been something she needed. Something that belonged to them, to her. Something that had shone gold and sung sharp.

And then she'd woken up.

Once again, like a knight in shining armour, Astrid had thrown herself head first into danger to protect her. This time, to protect Gwen from her own dreams.

'It's not working,' Gwen said, pushing the cup away. 'All I can remember is that there was something they . . . *I* was trying to show myself.'

'Then perhaps it was not a *dream*,' Astrid and Jonas said together, contemplating the word like they were dissecting a frog.

Sitting at the side of the table closest to Gwen, they looked as perfect as porcelain dolls. Gwen used to find it creepy, how clear their skin was, like glass, and their pristine white-gold hair. Even now, not a single strand of it was out of place after the excitement of the night.

'Maybe you were being lured by mermaids,' Thomas offered. 'Grim-possessed mermaids would be a frightening thing.'

Astrid smirked. 'Then we'll kill them.'

Jan gasped, nearly dropping her tea. 'The Order doesn't deal in death,' she reminded them sternly.

But Gwen only snorted. The twins were just making one of their usual inappropriate jokes . . . probably. Astrid caught Gwen's eye, the small smirk spreading over her lips, as if pleased with Gwen for laughing. Gwen looked away, embarrassed, biting down hard on a strip of bacon to avoid making any more eye contact. She knew how Astrid felt about her – possessive, protective . . . and something else. Something Gwen wasn't ready to grapple with.

What did surprise her, though, was Lorelei's response.

'Mermaids are hard to kill,' she said. Her back was to them as she laid out knives to be sharpened on the thick butcher's block. 'They're not the pretty things the Red Bloods tell fairy tales about.'

With the fog gone, they had a clear view of Wales across the sea. While Magnus and Elijah scoured the library for possible causes of Gwen's sleepwalking, Lorelei had dished them all up a very late breakfast. Jan, Thomas, Gwen and the twins sat round the old elf-wood table chewing over the information, the scent of bacon and fresh bread filling the crowded room.

Buttonbug, used to such excitement by now, was already perched on the Aga stove, playfully batting at the mugs and utensils hanging above. Thomas poked her on the nose as he passed by, stopping her from knocking over a container of elderberries.

'I think we all know what it *really* is,' Jan said, her face grim as she stared down at her porridge and jam. 'I don't know why you're pretending it's something else, Gwenny.'

Gwen rolled her eyes at her sister, her temper rising. She could still feel the chill of the ocean air, still see Astrid slipping away in her mind.

'It wasn't the Shadowling,' Gwen snapped.

Jan muttered disapprovingly.

'It's not a dirty word, you know,' Gwen shot back, the Bloom in her fingertips tingling. 'Shadowling, Shadowling, Shadowling,' she barked.

Jan didn't react, only taking a slow breath.

In all her life Gwen had never been able to understand how her sister could be so calm about everything. They were different in every way – Jan tall, Gwen short; Jan with her long face, Gwen with her round one; Jan with one plait, Gwen favouring two; Jan who had known their parents well, and Gwen who had hardly known them at all.

Putting a gentle hand on Jan's shoulder, Thomas tried to defuse the situation with one of his cherubic smiles. 'I think your sister is just worried about you.' His voice was calm, but his smile was twitching. 'And I'm sure the Order of Pendragon will be able to help.'

'Yeah, because they were so trustworthy and helpful before,' Gwen grumbled. The truth was they didn't even know whom they could trust in the Order. *Anyone* could be under the Shadowling's spell. He wanted to end humanity, and they had no idea how many people Sister Seraphina might have rallied to his cause before he had eaten her.

'It wasn't the Shadowling,' Gwen insisted. 'I would know.'

When Gwen looked up, she expected the twins to be scrutinizing her. Only, their icy-blue eyes were firmly on Lorelei.

She was still facing away from them, sharpening a knife by the sink. The metallic swish of the blade was like the rhythm of the tide.

'You know something, don't you?' Astrid said.

Silence filled the kitchen, the blade going still in Lorelei's hand. Even Thomas seemed surprised that his older cousin didn't immediately deny it.

'There's old folktales about dream-walking,' Lorelei eventually said. 'Old magic, from long before the Order. Some Bloom Bloods believe it's how people communicated with their own spirit, or even the dead.'

Gwen nearly choked. 'The dead?'

The thought made her dizzy.

'I've never heard of such a thing,' Jan said, glancing at Thomas warily. He only shrugged, equally baffled by the tale.

'The old ways of magic are not practised by the Order of Pendragon; they are only studied.'

'And yet –' Astrid had that look in her eye as she lifted her tea to her lips, like a predator picking up a tantalizing scent – 'it almost sounds like you've experienced it firsthand.'

Jonas had a sly look on his face, too. 'Though, of course, that would be impossible, right?'

Lorelei sighed. 'All I'm certain of is that if something inside you wanted you to go to the ocean, you should pay attention.'

'Hmm, maybe the Shadowling is hiding at sea?' Thomas pondered. 'If I were an ancient evil dragon trying to destroy humanity, it's what I'd do . . .'

Lorelei bopped him on the back of his head. 'It's no laughing matter,' she scolded, pouring a potion over one of the knives until it sang a piercing and dangerous melody, one that would keep it sharp. 'The ocean is an entirely different world.'

Frowning, Thomas gave his cousin a sideways look, the clouds of vitiligo on his cheeks scrunching up in confusion like a brewing storm.

'How do you know all this?' he asked, a nervous laugh escaping him. 'Did you study marine magic?'

Gwen paused in her thoughts: it had never occurred to her that she didn't actually know anything about Lorelei's life previous to her joining the Faymore Cluster and becoming Magnus's research partner. Lorelei was much younger than Magnus and Elijah, with not even a speck of red in her nearly black eyes – the red being a telltale sign of age in Bloom Bloods. With her lithe build and high cheekbones, she was obviously beautiful, and she was also extremely proficient with her Bloom and knowledge of spells and potions. She could have achieved any powerful position in the Order, studied anything she wanted. And she hadn't been a member of the Rapscallions who'd unleashed the Shadowling in the first place all those years ago, so why was she also burdened with the Faymore responsibility of stopping the Grim? And why had she brought Thomas here?

Lorelei cleared her throat, wiping her hands on her apron.

'You lot mind your business,' she said cryptically.

'OK,' Jan said, putting her mug down, her usually serene features turning serious. 'Change of subject. Thomas and I have an announcement: we're going to accept the Order's offer to enlist in their new defence programme.'

'Wait, what? Defence programme?' Gwen blinked in confusion, sure she'd heard her sister wrong.

'I'm not going to finish my Apprenticeship; the Shadowling needs to be defeated now.' She spoke decidedly, like she'd been rehearsing the words. 'So, we're going to help the Order stop him. We're going to fight.'

Gwen nearly choked, dropping her fork on her plate. It was like Jan was talking in a whole other language.

'Fight? What are you talking about? The Order doesn't fight. You're going to study tree spirits and newborn magic, remember? You can do that here.'

'I've already sent an acceptance letter to Ambassador Loupe and the Magister. This isn't up for debate.'

It didn't make any sense. How could Jan – sweet, soft-spoken Jan – be expected to fight the Grim? The very idea of it made the Bloom in Gwen's blood start to bubble, her palms tingling with unpredictable power.

'This isn't your problem, Jan,' Gwen said, a growl creeping into her voice. 'I won't let you. The Shadowling is my responsibility.'

Jan only sighed, something desperate entering her eyes.

'Exactly. You're special. Mum and Dad died protecting you. And now it's my turn to keep you safe.'

Gwen's vision split – a flash of memory. No longer was she in the overcrowded kitchen full of pots and pans, with the scent of breakfast; she was outside, in a courtyard, with the sweet fragrance of pansies.

But the same conversation was happening.

'We have to keep you safe.'

Then she blinked and it was gone, lost like a dream.

Standing up, Gwen slammed her hands down on the kitchen table, Bloom burning in her throat. Her vision flashed gold.

'No, I have to keep all of *you* safe!'

Silence filled the kitchen, Gwen's fork clattering on to the ground.

Jan clutched her chest in shock while the twins stared up at her with icy fascination.

'Whoa!' Thomas breathed, staring down.

It was only when Gwen looked down too that she saw the crack. A jagged thing in the table like a lightning bolt, right under her left hand.

She'd split the heavy wooden table in two.

'I . . . Sorry,' Gwen gasped. She couldn't make sense of what had happened. It was like her mind wasn't her own. Her thoughts fragmented and mixed up. 'I didn't mean to . . . Sorry. I don't know what happened, I –'

'Gwen,' Astrid began. 'It's OK –' She stopped short.

The cups and utensils on the table were shaking, *clink clink clink,* in time with a growing rhythm. A shadow crept in from the windows. Something was coming down from the sky. Something big.

Heart beating frantically, Gwen ran to the front

door and pulled it open, followed closely by the twins. She took a step back, staring up, sure for one dreadful moment she was seeing the terrible white-gold wings of the Shadowling. But it was not a dragon at all – or any magical creature – and as realization dawned, Gwen almost wished it had been.

'Well, this is that last thing we need,' Jonas groaned behind her.

A carriage hung in the sky, better known in Bloom Blooded society as a Cloud Skimmer – the most powerful means of magical transportation, reserved almost exclusively for Ambassadors, Magisters and royals. This was the biggest one Gwen had ever seen. As it got closer, it rang with commanding magic, a combination of Wind, Push and Pull spells like a symphony above their heads.

The three ran and huddled together to greet the gold-ornamented carriage as it landed in the open meadow. Wind blew around them from the residual magic, hair and snow flying everywhere and forcing them to shout over the noise as if they were caught in a storm.

'Who is it?' Gwen bellowed, covering her face against the wind.

By then everyone else was running to join them – Lorelei and Thomas and Jan, with Elijah and Magnus rushing down from the cottage.

The Cloud Skimmer landed and the music of the spell slowed. Then, with a hiss of air, the door opened, and a familiar figure appeared, flanked by two attendants in standard Order-issued black suits and cloaks, with simple silver Savonnettes hanging on chains round their necks.

The boy in the middle, by contrast, was dressed as if he were heading to a ball, all crisp lapels and tailored silk, the stark white of the fabric bringing flattering focus to his bronze skin and matching his dazzling smile.

Gwen immediately turned to Jonas, to see his expression. He looked ready to throw himself off the nearby cliff.

'Eh-ehm.' One of the attendants stepped forward to speak. 'It is by decree of Magister Beatrice that the following members of the Faymore Cluster are to be escorted to a secure location: Magnus Faymore, Lorelei Murphy, Gwendolyn Chatterjee, Astrid Bunting and Jonas Bunting. As a gesture of goodwill and a token of trust, I have sent my son, Prince Theodore, as an escort. You are to pack a single bag and leave with him immediately. *Sanguis Noster, Officium Nostrum.*'

3

A Reunion of Sorts

They had thirty minutes to prepare. Elijah and Lorelei tried to reason with the Custodian attendants who had brought the prince, but they were under strict orders not to share any further information.

Magnus, on the other hand, was oddly silent. The silence of acceptance.

Cutting through the chaos, he said loudly, 'Get your stuff, quickly, and meet us back here.'

Lorelei frowned, clearly ready to argue more, but Elijah put a soft hand on her elbow. With a huff, Lorelei stormed off. If even she couldn't argue them out of this, no one could.

'This is madness,' Gwen hissed, stomping back to the manor.

'Surely they can't plan to take you away for too long,' Jan said, her voice uncertain.

'Surely,' Thomas repeated.

'Jan, Thomas, could you please go get our instruments from the music room while we pack our things?' Astrid asked.

The two gave her a wary look but acquiesced. They couldn't argue that there wasn't much time.

Astrid eyed up the Custodians from the doorstep. Two of them. She and Jonas could have had them tangled in vines with a single melody.

Except they couldn't. There were people in the Order looking for any excuse to bring the twins into the fold, to deem Magnus a bad mentor and strip him of their wardship.

'Why is he coming this way?' Jonas suddenly asked, panic in his voice as they watched Prince Teddy traipsing towards them through the snow. His shoes were wildly unsuitable for the icy paths, so he skidded about, looking like a pampered dog discovering snow for the first time.

'Distract him,' Astrid whispered to Jonas. 'And make sure you get the Savonnette.'

Jonas balked. 'Wait, what?'

Ignoring her brother, Astrid grabbed Gwen's hand and made a run for it through the corridor, dodging instruments and loose potion bottles until they escaped through the back door.

'Where are we going?' Gwen whispered.

'I want to know what Magnus is planning,' Astrid replied. 'He must have something up his sleeve.'

They ducked low, Astrid easily guiding them over the slippery rocks and roots. Like snakes in the grass, they weaved across the overgrown path and through the woods up to Windyside Cottage. When they got close, the trees whispered a melody of caution, and Astrid pulled Gwen low behind a holly bush.

There was a shed next to the cottage, full of charms and antique weapons. The door creaked as someone appeared in the doorway from inside.

It wasn't Magnus. It was Lorelei.

She looked about, checking the coast was clear. Then, satisfied, she stepped out, tucking something into her satchel. Astrid barely caught a glimpse of it, a pale instrument of some kind.

'It's a fife,' Gwen said. 'Just an instrument.'

'So why is she hiding it?' Astrid wondered.

Both girls startled at Elijah's voice coming from the cottage. 'Lorelei!' he called, bounding through the snow in his thick winter coat.

The girls crouched lower, barely breathing.

'I found your potion holster – what are you doing out here?' Elijah gasped, his pink cheeks turning pale as the snow. 'You're not . . . Lorelei, *you can't.*'

Grabbing him, Lorelei held him against the stone wall of the cottage. She spoke in a hushed tone, one they could barely hear over the distant sea.

'It's only a precaution,' she told him. 'If my commitment to helping the Faymores means anything to you, you won't tell Magnus. You know what he'd say.'

Elijah's doe eyes gazed at her. He was larger than Lorelei, with fiery auburn hair, but he looked helpless as a field mouse in her grip. Eventually he sighed, an almost desperate sound.

'I trust you, Lorelei,' he said earnestly. 'Just promise me you'll keep them all safe.'

Lorelei stepped back, her expression softening. 'I'll do whatever I have to do. Now come, before Magnus gets suspicious.'

Lorelei and Elijah followed the path through the snow and disappeared into the cottage.

The moment the door shut behind them, Gwen stood up and threw her arms out incredulously. She was furious, her anger dripping off her like lava. 'What the bloody hell was *that* all about?' she hissed. 'Now *Lorelei's* keeping secrets?'

And suddenly, whatever Lorelei was up to was the least interesting thing to Astrid, because she was quite sure that just for a second Gwen's eyes had flashed gold.

'Stop,' Astrid said simply. She stood over Gwen, and before the girl could protest, she cupped Gwen's cheek in her hand, the skin of her face warm and soft, like fresh bread. Astrid tilted her head gently to the side. Inspecting.

'Hey, what are you –'

'There's something different about you,' Astrid mused. 'You feel it too.'

Gwen went quiet, staring back.

Up close, Astrid could smell the raspberry jam from breakfast lingering on Gwen's breath. Astrid's favourite. But the most curious thing was under Gwen's skin. She could always feel it: Gwen's Bloom, that shining, triumphant magic, always simmering below the surface. Astrid's own Bloom called to it, seeking it out. And now there was something else. No – that wasn't right: there was *more*. It was as if Gwen held the magic of more than just herself.

Astrid leaned in further, scrutinizing Gwen's eyes. They were back to their usual brown. Strange.

'I'll have to keep an eye on you,' Astrid said. Then she let her go.

Gwen stumbled away from her, directing her indignant expression towards Astrid. She looked like she was about to explode or faint.

'You are so . . .' Gwen scrunched up her nose, searching for the word. 'You're *impossible*.'

And without another word, she marched off back the way they'd come.

'Didn't you get my letter?' the prince asked, lingering over Jonas's shoulder.

'Yes, I got your ridiculous letter,' Jonas hissed back. 'I'd assumed it was some stress-induced hallucination.'

Jonas was in his room frantically packing bags for himself and Astrid while she was off spying on someone, no doubt. And, apparently, the prince had decided this should be a group activity.

Buttonbug, the little traitor, was curled round the prince's shoulders, nuzzling at his cheek for attention, which the prince gave generously. Jonas imagined how all the Red Blooded teens would react upon seeing their prince cuddling her; even if Buttonbug had been a regular cat and not a magical flying one, it would probably still have been headline news in a tabloid.

'So, this is where you sleep?' Prince Teddy asked, running his fingers along the vines curling round the bedposts. There were flowers and creepers everywhere; they grew in the night while the twins dreamed.

Trying to suppress a shiver, Jonas swatted at the prince's hand. 'Get away from there.' Mary forbid Teddy should know that Jonas could almost feel the touch of his fingers through the ivy.

'Touchy, aren't you?'

He didn't have time for this.

He needed to find Rupert's Savonnette.

Jonas tried to ignore him as he rifled through Astrid's bedside table until he found the old thing – the remains of a centuries-old white-gold Savonnette. It had once imprisoned the Shadowling that now threatened to destroy the world. It was different from the Order-issued ones: there was no clock inside, and etched on the cover, instead of a sword rising from ocean waters, a sword rose from intricate spirals.

It had been Magnus's brother Rupert's, and somehow, for some reason, the twins had been given the broken pieces.

Jonas was so distracted staring at it, he didn't notice Prince Teddy getting dangerously close to things he most certainly shouldn't.

'What's this?' the prince asked, a smirk pulling at the edges of his diabolically handsome smile.

Jonas looked up and nearly passed out from embarrassment.

Prince Teddy was holding up Jonas's pillow, and underneath where it had been was the charmed black-heart lighter Teddy had given him.

'Oh yes, I heard this saved your life,' he drawled, grinning over at Jonas in a way that made Jonas want to jump out of the window.

Jonas marched over and snatched the lighter away.

'And it'll be the end of yours if you're not careful,' he said, then quickly turned his back before the prince could see the red creeping into his cheeks. 'Where are we going, anyway?'

Prince Teddy hesitated.

'I can't say.' At least he had the decency to seem remorseful about it. Jonas grabbed the broken Savonnette to shove in his bag. He took a second to eye up the missing chunks of the lid. He had one of those pieces round his neck now, as did Astrid. No one had figured out why they'd been left these pieces as babies – what plans Rupert had had for him and his sister, or the purpose of this broken shard of magic metal.

Jonas sighed. 'Well, what good are you, then?'

Without another word, Jonas whistled Buttonbug to him and stormed off with the bags to join Astrid outside.

The prince, of course, followed behind.

The others were all ready to go, with Magnus saying his goodbyes to Elijah, Lorelei ruffling Thomas's hair, and Gwen making one final plea to her sister. It wasn't going well.

'Jan, you have to promise me you'll be smart. I don't need you to fight this battle for me.' Gwen looked even smaller than usual next to the huge carriage of the Cloud Skimmer. The landscape around them was still and pure white, and Gwen stood out in her red coat, like someone had dropped blood on to the snow.

'We're going to stop the Shadowling, OK?' Jan replied. 'I'm going to finish what our parents started.'

'Jan, please . . .'

'I'll see you when you're back.' Jan pushed Gwen towards the door of the Skimmer. Then she turned to the twins. 'Keep her safe,' she said. Not a request, an order.

Astrid and Jonas nodded.

In the hullaballoo of goodbyes, Jonas leaned over to his sister.

'What happened?' he asked under his breath.

Astrid did a sweep, making sure no one was listening.

'Lorelei,' she replied, not needing to elaborate.

Jonas recalled what she'd termed them the previous night. *'Landlubbers'* . . . It was seafaring slang.

'Should we be worried?' Jonas asked.

Astrid considered the question.

'No, not yet. Did you get the Savonnette?'

Jonas nodded, but his eyes were on the manor.

'I don't want to go,' he said. He could feel the wave of heartache crashing over Astrid, mirrored in himself.

'Neither do I,' she replied.

Magnus clapped his hands, holding his cane under one arm like a ringmaster.

'Well, come along, then, everyone!' he instructed. Whether his too-broad smile was for the prince or for their sake, it was hard to tell.

The twins paused, taking one final look at Faymore Manor. Hidden away in the woods, its stark silhouette was softened by the thick blankets of ivy that climbed its walls. They could sense wildflowers poking through the cracks in the stone pathways under the snow, and, distantly, they could hear the horses neighing in the paddock. The manor was like them, at one with the earth, and the twins had formed a deep bond with its old brick bones; they ached at the prospect of separation. Beneath their feet, the earth was lamenting, willing them to stay.

It felt as though they'd only just accepted this unusual place as their home. Now they had no idea where they were going, or when they'd be returning.

'We'll be back,' Magnus said softly beside them. 'I'll make sure of it.'

The interior of the Cloud Skimmer was comfortable and deceptively spacious. From the constant melodic drone, Jonas could tell it must have taken a remarkable amount of Bloom to power, not to mention to keep it warm and hidden from mundane human eyes. The Skimmer was comprised of two carriages, and the Faymore Cluster was seated in the back, away from Prince Teddy and his attendants. The door between their compartments was wrought iron, like a prison cell.

'Do you have any idea where they could be taking us?' Astrid asked.

Magnus shrugged while Lorelei went through her bag for the umpteenth time, taking inventory of all the potions she'd packed – and not much else, it seemed.

'For certain rituals and honours that involve the Magister, it's not unusual to be whisked away in such a fashion.'

'Do you think this is one of those cases?'

Magnus chuckled, then said, 'No.'

Eventually the blue hues of twilight crept in. By the time they landed, the sun had nearly set entirely, and they stepped out of the carriage on to an open field, the wind roaring in their ears.

In the dying light, Jonas could make out clumps of purple scattered about the large stretches of green.

Buttonbug scurried out from the neck of his shirt. She was purring nervously, peering at the landscape with equal caution.

Inhaling the salty air, Jonas centred himself, placing his palm against the bitterly cold ground.

Heather, the earth hummed to him. *Bog myrtle, Scottish primrose.*

They were far north, in Scotland. A dozen metres away the land dropped off, and they could hear the howl of the sea below, but these were not the familiar cliffs of Faymore Manor.

Jonas approached the edge and peered over: waves spat up white horses of foam, lapping at sand dunes below like a battering ram trying to break through a castle door.

'Follow me! It's not far,' Prince Teddy called above the wind, his hair flying about his face as he led them to a gated path along the shoreline. He hummed a quick tune, and two lanterns on either side of the gate lit up and proceeded to follow him like well-trained dogs. When Jonas looked back, the Cloud Skimmer was taking off again. They had nowhere to go but with the prince.

Pushing against the wind, their troop eventually came to the beach below and an old rickety shack built against the cliffside. The place looked one strong breeze away from collapse.

After three quick then two slow knocks at the door, the prince stepped back and waited.

Then waited some more.

And some more.

He turned back to them and smiled awkwardly. Jonas noted that even his awkward smile was unfathomably charming.

'Shouldn't be long,' Teddy promised.

Magnus approached the door. 'May I?'

Prince Teddy hesitated. 'Umm, it's a secret code, it can't –'

But Magnus didn't wait for permission; he simply performed the same knocking sequence, but with slightly different timing. Three quavers, then a dotted half, then another quaver.

The effect was immediate.

The door swung open hard and fast, and with it a flood of potent Bloom was released. The view through the doorway glistened like a mirage, like it would be wet to the touch.

Without another word, Magnus beckoned them forward, then vanished out of sight as he stepped into the doorway.

'Sometimes I really hate magic,' Gwen groaned, then she too stepped through and vanished, followed by Lorelei, who looked equally displeased.

The twins took a glance back at Prince Teddy, who was gaping at the door, still trying to make sense of how Magnus knew his super-special secret code.

'Need to practise your dotted rhythms, it seems.' Jonas smirked, then they too walked through.

They should have braced themselves first, because the force drawing them was enough to nearly knock them down. Melodies of Push, Pull and Chaos interwove, creating a sound like the clang of a shield, as if they were being jostled about on a battlefield. With a gasp, the twins stumbled forward, then warmth and firelight washed over them as the space changed. It was no longer a dingy, crumbling shack: instead, it was a charming cottage.

'Gwen!' Astrid called, looking about.

'I'm fine,' she called back, and she was, albeit also rattled by the pull of Bloom. She was standing unsteadily by a fireplace, which was lit and had creepy porcelain dolls lining the mantle. A large round table dominated the small room, with two of the chairs occupied by people drinking tea from floral bone china.

Jonas recognized one of them immediately. Strawberry-blonde hair, a thin, pink smile – Harriet Loupe, Ambassador of potions and charms.

At first Jonas thought the other lady was a stranger – but he quickly realized this woman was someone the twins had seen many times before, when they were still part of Red Blooded society. Because there, sipping tea like it was just an ordinary Sunday afternoon, was Queen Beatrice Doria, Queen of England and Magister of the Western European Faction of the Order of Pendragon.

4
Get That Thing Away from Me

The queen put down her teacup, pushed back her chair and stood. She was shorter than Astrid had imagined, not much taller than Gwen.

The whole Faymore Cluster bowed.

'Hello, Mummy,' Prince Teddy said, coming to kiss her on the cheek.

Astrid stole a peek up at them from her bowed position, and she wasn't the only one. Jonas was staring too.

The two royals had the same copper-toned skin, the same dark hair. They even had the same lopsided smile and acne scarring along their jaws.

As the history books will tell you, Princess Alice had married the queen a few years after Teddy was born, and no one knew who Teddy's father was; it had been a great mystery in the Red Blooded world. It was clear now, though, that whoever Teddy's father was, he would likely have little resemblance to him. Teddy was his mother's child.

'Hello, darling,' the Magister said. 'Well done on getting them here promptly.' Her voice was rich, and as warm as the fire when she spoke to him. 'Could you head over and prep the others for our arrival?'

'Of course, Mummy,' the prince responded, then turned to head back outside. He paused briefly to run his gaze over Jonas, who, still bowing, seemed to ignore him, although Astrid could feel the prickles the attention sent over Jonas's skin.

The queen addressed their troop, her warm voice turning suddenly icy: 'Up, all of you.'

Standing straight again, Magnus smiled fondly at Magister Beatrice, entirely disregarding her cold welcome. 'It's a pleasure to see you again, Bea.'

'Don't lie, Magnus,' she shot back, then turned and walked towards Gwen. Both Astrid and Jonas instinctively moved to flank her.

'You,' the queen said. 'You're the one who punched an unspeakably evil dragon with your bare fists.'

Gwen simply stared back at the woman, uncomfortable with the sudden appraisal. Then she spluttered, 'Well, what else was I going to punch it with?' Both twins had to resist snorting, and, seeming to remember herself, Gwen quickly added, 'Your Majesty.'

Magister Beatrice continued to loom over Gwen, which was not an easy feat when they had barely an inch of height difference between them.

Then the Magister fixed her gaze on each of the twins in turn. 'You two. I can hear the unruly, untamed Bloom pulsing under your skin. Is it in response to my being so close to Gwendolyn here?'

Glancing at each other, the twins weighed an appropriate response, which Astrid then entirely disregarded. She said, 'It'll stop if you step away . . . Your Majesty.'

Ambassador Loupe gasped, utterly scandalized, her tiny nose wrinkling in disapproval. 'It seems you still haven't learned any manners.'

Magister Beatrice held up her hand, commanding everyone to silence. Again, she appeared to consider the trio, her face clear of any perceivable emotion. 'Your Bloom compels you to protect her?'

The twins nodded.

'Very well. Come on, all of you,' she said abruptly, gesturing for them to sit at the table, the lot of them crowding in round the doilies and sugar bowls.

Harriet gave the twins a wary look. The last time they'd sat round a table for tea, she'd ended up with cake all over her face. Astrid chuckled at the memory.

'Hello again, Ambassador,' the twins said in unison, voices sweet as honey.

Ambassador Loupe gave them an annoyed sideways glance as she pulled a parchment out of her purple robe. Then she cleared her throat and spoke, her voice coming out nasal and pitched like a mosquito: 'What happened to Gwendolyn last night was not an isolated event.'

Magnus cocked an eyebrow from his position in the chair closest to the Magister. 'You've been spying on us,' he said.

'Naturally,' she replied, then whistled a quick tune that caused a newspaper to float over and land in front of Magnus. It was a Red Blooded one, and Astrid craned her neck to read the headline: *Second Mysterious Drowning in a Month: Authorities Probe Latest Incident at Beach Resort.*

'A man was found dead on Blacklands Beach, a strange black ooze covering his skin,' the Ambassador said.

'Red Blooded casualties,' Lorelei said gravely.

'The Order has been kept very busy covering all these up,' the Ambassador continued. 'The Shadowling is targeting all our oceanic research facilities, and it's not just the Western European Faction. Other Magisters have been reporting unsettling incidents. There was a mermaid attack on the Coral Arcana Research Vessel in the Great Barrier Reef, and numerous sea monsters have been drowning divers studying at the Borealis Sanctum north of Iceland. All reported discordant, nauseating music.'

'The Grim,' said Gwen, sitting very still.

The twins, meanwhile, were thinking about the name of the research institute, reminded once again of just how expansive and powerful the Order of Pendragon was. Regular humans had no idea what was right under their noses . . . or how much danger the world was in.

And yet, Gwen had been adamant it wasn't the Shadowling or the Grim that had led her to the ocean. But surely the two must be connected.

'But why would there suddenly be all this focus on the sea?' Magnus asked.

Astrid glanced at Gwen, who was staring at her hands with a pained expression, the kind they'd seen on kids at their Red Blooded schools when they'd been told to solve a particularly difficult maths equation.

'There's something in the sea,' Gwen said, so quiet everyone almost missed it.

'Excuse me?' Ambassador Loupe asked, the room going silent.

'He's trying to keep us away from the sea,' Gwen repeated, her eyes still cast downwards. 'He's trying to keep *me* away. It's what my dream was trying to tell me.'

A log in the fire snapped, understanding settling over the group – except, not the Magister. No, she looked pleased.

'I was hoping you would say that,' she said with a surreptitious smile.

Lorelei narrowed her eyes. 'What are you planning?'

Instead of answering, Magister Beatrice clicked her fingers at the Ambassador, who quickly got up and left the room.

'The incidents of the Grim have predominantly occurred around unusual artefacts, or people.' She cut her eyes at Gwen as she said this. 'We did not understand this fully until you three stole one of those artefacts from our research facility and used it to heal a page of *The Cursed Melodies*.'

Gwen bristled at the book title, as did Magnus. The mysterious tome of cursed magic that had started all of this.

'What have you done, Bea?' Magnus asked, his voice serious.

'The Shadowling is clearly plotting something, biding his time while he gains his power back, and we need to strike first. He wants us to be wary of the ocean, and we have a vague idea of the area he is particularly keen to keep us away from, so the question is . . .'

'What is he hiding?' Astrid finished for her.

'Precisely,' the Magister said. 'And we think we have a way of finding out.'

Ambassador Loupe returned with a bundle of cloth that must have been charmed, as the Bloom emanating from it was rich with the melodic spells of Lock and Conceal. The Ambassador held it cautiously, as if it were a venomous animal.

Perhaps, Astrid thought, a dangerous creature would have been better – because it was instantly clear to her what was hidden beneath the fabric.

Even through all the Bloom, the effect on Gwen was instant. 'No!' she cried, panicked. She threw her hands over her ears, trying to block out sound that only she could hear. 'Get it away from me!'

Ignoring Gwen's protestations, Ambassador Loupe unwrapped the bundle. Even Buttonbug began to flutter, emerging from Jonas's pocket to hiss at the object as it was slowly revealed.

Red scales, yellowed pages, a burning, terrible pull of Bloom. It practically glowed in the firelight.

The book of Cursed Melodies.

Except – it looked different from how they'd first found it in Rupert Faymore's pile of things, battered and worn. Now it appeared to be brand new. It had been healed.

The Magister took it from the Ambassador and gently laid it in front of Gwen, as if handing her a gift. 'We found all the missing parts of the book in Sister Seraphina's belongings,' she said softly.

Astrid stiffened at the mention of Seraphina. She only regretted that she was not the one who had brought about that traitor's demise.

'It appears, when Seraphina originally gave the book to Rupert, she failed to mention the parts that had been removed. Gwendolyn, we've spent the last months tirelessly working to heal this book, but only you can unlock its power. We brought you here for a very important mission. But first,' the Magister said, her voice turning hard, 'we need you to read it.'

Fury. It radiated off Gwen's skin like a rolling mist. And not just anger, but fear also. Astrid could hear her Bloom, that inhuman strength simmering.

And there it was, so quick that Astrid guessed only she had seen it: Gwen's eyes flashed gold.

'What in the Twelve Spells do you mean, *"read it"*? You know I can't read it,' Gwen growled, her fingernails digging into the table. 'Even if I were willing to touch that evil book again, the language in it is ancient. How would I make sense of it?'

Beneath Gwen's fingers, the wood had fresh grooves. She'd damaged a table again. The Magister was staring at the fingernail marks with wide-eyed fascination.

'With all due respect, Your Majesty.' Astrid chose her words carefully, the temperature in the room rising. 'My brother and I tried to make sense of the text numerous times, but it was impossible.'

Astrid imagined herself like ice, cooling the fire burning inside Gwen. Whatever was going on there, she highly doubted Gwen would want it to happen in front of the Magister and Ambassador Loupe. She needed to calm the situation, but before she could do anything, Lorelei interjected.

'You put that thing away,' she snapped, pointing a finger at the Ambassador, then she turned to the Magister. 'Can't you see it's distressing her? You have no right to do this, to always ask these things of us.' There was something there, the flicker of an old argument.

Curious, Astrid thought. Perhaps Lorelei and the Magister had history?

Magnus cleared his throat, patting Lorelei on the shoulder. The intention was clear: he would handle this. 'Gwen is quite right,' he said. 'It's not readable. Even the extremely limited passages my brother and I were able to decode were thanks to the pictures inside, and context pulled from other works from the same era.' He turned to look at the Magister directly – his ancient eyes with a tinge of red, hers still a clear brown. 'And I need not remind you it was a catastrophic decision to do even that. We're still presently dealing with the consequences of it.'

Ambassador Loupe's lip quivered with outrage, and she looked ready to call them all to heel. But she was interrupted:

'Have you tried?' the Magister asked, looking only at Gwen, as if no one else were in the room.

Gwen froze, the question catching her off guard. It caught the twins off guard, too.

'What – I . . .'

'Have. You. Tried?' she repeated slowly, her voice like gravel. 'And I don't mean just looking at it – have you actually tried sitting down and *connecting* with the book?'

Gwen's mouth opened and closed, her expression lost.

'No, she hasn't,' Astrid said, because it was true. And for a moment, Astrid's stomach stirred, her heart and mind at odds. She could feel Jonas next to her, willing her to say what needed to be said, to do what needed to be done. For Gwen. 'So she should try.'

The twins were never ones to shy away from the truth, and sometimes the only way to be kind was to be cruel. Even to the ones you loved.

'The book responds only to you, Gwen,' Astrid continued coolly, trying not to react to the hurt on Gwen's face. 'The contents don't even appear without you touching the pages. Somehow, for some reason, this book of cursed magic is yours. And it might be our only chance at stopping the Shadowling.'

Gwen's eyes shimmered, and then she slowly sat down in her seat, the fury of her Bloom extinguished. She looked like a scolded puppy, and it made Astrid's chest ache.

'I don't know how to read it,' Gwen insisted, her voice soft.

This seemed to satisfy the Magister.

'Well, when you're ready to try, we'll be waiting.'

'We need her to do it now, Beatrice,' Ambassador Loupe protested.

'She'll do it when she's ready,' the Magister repeated calmly. 'Based on his pattern of attacks, the Shadowling is most keen to protect an area in the north, at the Borealis Sanctum. We can start there. Cloud Skimmers can't travel over the ocean. They guzzle too much Bloom for the distance, and there's a lack of cloud cover, but we have a workaround, one we think the Shadowling would never expect and therefore will not be prepared for. The Magister of the Arctic Sector has been notified and is expecting your arrival in fourteen days. I will have someone report in every three days, and I expect you to at least make an attempt to learn from this book what it is that the Shadowling is so keen to hide from us. Is that understood?' Magister Beatrice gave Gwen and the twins a stern look, and they each nodded. 'Excellent. Then it's time to meet the crew who will be escorting you on your journey.'

'Crew?' asked Gwen.

'Yes,' she replied. 'You're setting sail tonight.'

5

The *Tidebinder*

'This is a terrible idea,' Astrid hissed.

'I know. They want us to head *towards* the danger?' Gwen whispered back as the group grabbed their bags.

'Not that,' Jonas said. 'The idea of stepping foot on a bloody *BOAT*.'

Gwen blinked at the two of them, realization dawning on her. The twins could not swim, nor could they wield their Ancient Magic away from land. They were doomed.

'Oh, for Mary's sake,' Gwen groaned into her hands. 'We're going to die at sea, aren't we?'

'Well, to avoid that, our only option is to find whatever it is they think the Shadowling is keeping from us,' Jonas said pointedly. 'Fast.'

'Yeah, yeah,' Gwen grumbled. 'Just drop it.'

But the twins would have to convince her soon. She needed to read that book.

They had been led through a hatch in the floor of the cottage, and now the Magister and Ambassador were escorting their group through a winding, damp tunnel. Poking out of the dirt walls, between the roots and stones, were chunks of white that whispered, voiceless, as they passed. Bone.

'What is this tunnel?' Astrid asked, both twins bracketing Gwen protectively from the weird walls.

'It's the work of ancient beldams, masters of blood and bone, and it's far older than the Order of Pendragon,' Lorelei told them, then stared ahead. 'The Order have taken control of many things from the golden age of magic.'

The Magister turned back, frowning, but didn't say a word.

At the end of the tunnel was a stone door that, subjected to the same knocking sequence as before, obediently rolled away. The sky beyond was black as coal, the stars hidden behind undulating clouds, with the sound of crashing waves in the distance.

'Best of luck on your mission, Pledges,' Ambassador Loupe said, waving the lot of them off with her tight-lipped smile.

They scowled at her. The lucky wasp got to stay on dry land.

Outside, the wind was silent and still. Astrid heard other strange sounds – creaking and groaning in chorus with the waves.

'Queen's mercy,' Gwen gasped, her jaw hanging loose.

They were on a sequestered section of beach, looking at a jetty stretching out into the ocean – a hidden port. The beach was closed in by two giant rock formations that had statues of ancient deities carved into the sides. They stood decapitated, worn down over time to lumps of shaped stone with limbs. And between them, towering over the shore, was a ship.

A titan of the seas, it was less a ship than a monster. Its dark hull had a rich, dusky purple sheen, like the bruised sky before a storm. Stitched into the rippling sails was the Order of Pendragon sigil, a sword rising from the sea. And the ship was singing, a soft, meandering melody with the occasional sharp note – like wind moving across the ocean. The vessel had magic woven into its timbers and would carve through the sea like the moon through the night.

Together, they walked down the jetty to the gangway. Pausing with her hand clasping the wooden rail, Astrid looked back at the grassy clifftops behind them. The twins felt their grasp on nature slipping painfully out of reach with each step, and it was only going to get worse.

Two men dressed in smart maritime uniforms greeted them, bowing low. Then they took their belongings from them as they entered, as though the Faymore group were about to embark on a luxury cruise; indeed, the interior was more like a lavish hotel than an ancient magical ship.

'Welcome aboard the *Tidebinder*,' the Magister said.

Inside, the air was thick with the scent of polished mahogany, burning incense and the faint, metallic tang of seawater. Charmed candles floated above in wrought-iron chandeliers, throwing green-and-red light over the carved woodwork everywhere.

Astrid paused at one of the large windows. The glass panels were adorned with intricate filigree patterns, and she noted there were similar markings etched into the wood all around them. There was something strange about the magic emanating from them – an odd, winding melody.

'Counter Melodies,' Magnus said at the same time as Lorelei, before he continued, 'Those rune marks above the window. They're to ward off magical creatures of the sea.'

'So Gwen will be safe on this ship,' Astrid said, mostly for her own peace of mind.

Up on deck, stars gleaming above them, the true nature of the ship was revealed. There were iron panels embedded into the walls, reinforced with runes for both protection and attack. Brass and obsidian cannons were subtly integrated into the ship's structure, their sleek, intimidating designs suggesting both beauty and destruction.

Everything sang like the thrumming drums of battle.

'Oh,' Jonas breathed, both twins looking over to see Magnus's reaction.

This was a ship of war. An odd thing indeed for an Order dedicated to conservation and research, an organization which strictly forbade killing anything, for any reason.

Magnus, of course, did not look pleased.

As they stepped forward, a chorus of '*Sanguis Noster, Officium Nostrum*' rang out. A whole crew – there had to be more than forty of them in total, each dressed impeccably in navy – stood at attention for their Magister.

'At ease.'

They lowered their hands, still rigid as rakes.

The Magister led the Cluster to two people at the helm. 'This is Captain Fenwick Bellamy. I will be leaving you in his capable hands.'

A giant of a man lumbered forward, dark curly hair pouring out from under a cocked hat and over his hefty shoulders. Gwen and the twins had to lift their heads high to get a good look at him. He spoke in a gruff voice, a few gold teeth flashing in his mouth.

'It's an honour to meet you three. The lieutenant and I will do our utmost to protect you on this journey. Your safety is the most important thing in the great service of stopping this evil.'

At this, a lean woman stepped forward. Hair long and black like an oil spill, thin eyebrows, and skin as pale as the whites of her eyes. She was frowning, and the rigid lines round her mouth suggested this was her usual expression.

'Lieutenant Isobel Thorn.' She announced her name with pride, as if it were a very serious matter indeed.

Jonas leaned over to Astrid. 'Do you think if we jump overboard, they'll have to jump in after us?'

Astrid giggled under her breath. 'Perhaps we should try it.'

Astrid's smile was quickly wiped off when she noticed the Savonnettes at the captain and lieutenant's breasts. They were not the usual bronze, silver or gold of a standard Savonnette: theirs were an oily-looking obsidian, like the black skin of a spitting cobra.

'You have a keen eye,' the Magister said, noticing Astrid's line of sight. 'These are our new, specially crafted Savonnettes. We have had a team working on their design since we first understood how serious a matter the Grim is. They are given to all high-ranking members of our new defence forces.' The Magister's eyes narrowed, staring at the twins. 'They have the power to neutralize *any* Bloom Blooded threat.'

Astrid bit her tongue, suddenly understanding that this defence force Jan had been talking about joining was more of an outright army. Magnus, though, had no such qualms.

'Magister Beatrice,' he said, his voice low like a rumble of thunder and his usually pleasant smile replaced by an expression of barely suppressed fury. 'Do you mean to tell me that this defence force you've lured Jan and Thomas into joining is in fact an army, and that the Western European Faction of the Order of Pendragon is crafting magical *weapons?*'

Defiant, the Magister held her ground.

'It's necessary, Custodian Faymore,' she said, almost flippantly. 'And our faction is not the only one. The Magisters have been working together to build a covert army. Our soldiers have been instrumental in controlling the ever-growing cases of the Grim. This here is but a small part of it, should we have to face the Shadowling in battle.'

Magnus looked like he might either be sick or explode.

'Do I really need to remind you, Beatrice, that the Order does not and must not ever deal in death? We are to keep peace in the magical world. Death, destruction, cruelty – it could bleed into the Bloom; it could plunge the world into a new magical dark age.'

Magister Beatrice spoke, cold as ice. 'Sometimes it's unavoidable. You should know that better than anyone.'

The reference to Magnus's brother, Rupert, left the Faymore Cluster winded, but the Magister was not done yet.

'I shall leave you all now in the capable hands of Captain Bellamy and his crew,' she told them with finality. 'The next time you report in, you're going to have found what the Shadowling is trying to hide, and we're going to use it to destroy him.' Her gaze turned sharp. 'I will have someone keeping an eye on you to make sure this is a smooth journey. Is that understood?'

There was no room for an answer, as the Magister simply left them where they stood on deck. Then the Faymore Cluster was escorted officiously to their cabins. Magnus, rather concerningly, had little to say to them all; he and Lorelei spoke in hushed tones as they walked, then they turned off at a corridor junction and disappeared together. Worse, the swaying ship was already starting to make the twins queasy, and they hadn't even hauled anchor yet.

As they neared their cabin, Astrid was ready to be done with the whole cursed day, just wanting to go to bed. After some sleep they would figure out a way of getting themselves and Gwen out of this dreadful situation and back on dry land.

Unfortunately, they had an uninvited guest at their cabin door.

'You have got to be joking?' Gwen said.

Prince Teddy stood leaning against their cabin door like he owned the whole ship. Actually, maybe he did, Astrid realized.

The prince turned to them, grinning. 'Sorry, my mother can be quite the bitch.' The twins found they couldn't disagree. 'I think she's just worried the world is going to end.'

'Why are you here? The boat's about to leave, if you hadn't noticed?' Astrid asked, crossing her arms.

'Although you *could* always jump off and swim to shore, something I for one would love to see,' Jonas chimed in. Then, slowly, realization dawned on them. 'No . . .' Jonas breathed.

'What?' Gwen demanded, not understanding.

The prince only continued grinning that terribly handsome grin of his.

'He's coming with us, Gwen.' Astrid sighed. 'He's the one the Magister has assigned to keep an eye on us.'

'I did tell you I'd be joining your Cluster,' Prince Teddy said, and winked. 'We're going to have so much fun.'

6

Knows All Your Secrets

The *Tidebinder* set sail for the Borealis Sanctum at the witching hour, with its course set for a fourteen-day journey. Melodies crept through the cabins, emanating from the bowels of the ship – magic at the oars, pummelling forever onwards into the vast sea. This did not agree with the twins at all: that much was immediately clear.

But this was not what woke Gwen up. Someone was calling her.

Confused, Gwen tried to follow the voice. She was lost, a golden light guiding her like a north star. There was something emerging, an image she knew well, one she saw almost every day.

Wake up.

Something was itching in the corners of her mind. Spirals and waves. Clues she almost understood.

A sword rising from the sea.

WAKE UP!

Gasping, Gwen opened her eyes.

Freezing cold. Wind and sea spray spat at her face. Her nightgown was drenched. Waves roared against the ship. She looked down and nearly collapsed in shock. She was right at the edge of the deck, staring into the ocean.

'Oh, mother Mary!' She gulped, stumbling back. 'Not again, not again,' she mumbled, disorientated.

She'd been dream-walking.

The memories of her dream slipped just out of reach, and all that remained was the knowledge that she'd been shown something important. Something she recognized, if she could only remember what.

The sun was only just beginning to rise. Panting and confused, Gwen nearly tripped over herself getting back to the stairwell. Her fingers were already chapped from the cold, and she dreaded what Astrid would say when she found out. She couldn't stand that constant look she'd adopted recently, that analysing stare. It made Gwen's heart skip in a way she refused to acknowledge.

Suddenly furious, Gwen stopped and marched back to the edge of the deck.

'Whatever the bloody hell is going on, just stop it!' Gwen hissed at the sea. 'Just tell me what you want. What are you trying to show me?'

'Hey!' a sharp voice called. 'Who's out there?'

Gwen went very still. By now her hair was soaked, the strands at the front sticking down like black liquorice. Ignoring the discomfort and cold, Gwen tiptoed barefoot, crouching down by some barrels.

'I know you're out here,' the voice called. Gwen took a peek from her hiding spot.

Dark hair pin-straight from the sea spray, it was Lieutenant Thorn. She turned sharply, a silver flame in her hand lighting a line just shy of Gwen.

Gwen held her breath, terrified to take her eyes off the frightening woman.

Then something barked – an odd, wet sound – and

Lieutenant Thorn seemed to collect herself, muttering under her breath as she went to calm the unseen dog. Gwen let out a low sigh of relief and noted she'd have to find it later, to thank it.

She was readying herself to sneak back to her cabin and forget this whole thing ... when she saw it. Winking in the moonlight just for a second as the lieutenant turned round: the Black Savonnette, that mysterious weapon. But it wasn't its purpose that had Gwen's heart jackhammering. Like being violently awakened, she remembered.

She remembered what her dream had shown her.

Astrid and Jonas woke up at the exact same moment, entangled in the blankets and pillows of their shared bed like baby birds in a nest. Buttonbug hissed and ruffled herself, annoyed too at being disturbed from sleep.

Someone was knocking on the door.

'I feel like death warmed up,' Jonas groaned.

Usually, when Astrid awoke, the earth greeted her, and by synching with the rhythms of nature she'd have a grounding sense of the weather and the time of day. Now there was nothing but the nauseating sway of the ocean.

'We need to get off this ship before I murder someone,' Astrid said, not even sure if she was joking. The constant movement of the floor and the outside view of miles of ocean made the twins feel dizzy and displaced. It was like they were missing an entire sense, or as if a limb had been severed. At least when they'd been locked up by their Red Blooded doctors for being 'crazy' they'd stayed on dry land.

Opening the door, she found a very wet Gwen, who looked about, as if expecting to have been followed.

'Hi.'

Without question, Astrid moved aside to let her in.

As Astrid shut the door, she could hear the sounds of the ship, crew members busy starting the day.

'Went for a morning swim, did you?' Jonas asked.

Ignoring him, Gwen made straight for their still-unpacked backpacks strewn on the cashmere carpet. 'Where's your Savonnette?' she asked, pulling out clothes. 'The one that belonged to Rupert.'

Intrigued, Astrid came to assist her, kneeling down and opening up the pocket they'd stashed it away in. There it was, white-gold, a jagged break where a chunk of it was missing, those lost fragments that had never left the twins' necks as they'd grown up.

'This,' Gwen said, nearly breathless. 'This is what I've been dream-walking about.'

The last of the sleep vanished from Astrid. Her look of concern must have registered because Gwen said, 'I'm fine.'

Stretching, Jonas heaved himself out of bed and came to join them on the carpet, Buttonbug curled on his shoulder.

'The Pendragon sigil?' he asked.

Gwen shook her head, water dripping down her plaits. 'No, not the sigil, this exact image. The sword with the spiral etchings behind it. The dream, the voices – they've been trying to lead me to it.'

'Could it be, just like we thought before . . . a weapon that can defeat the Shadowling?' Jonas said, excited. 'A sword!'

Gwen grinned. 'The question is, how do we find it?'

In the silence that followed, Astrid let her mind sort through the information. And then, like finding a missing puzzle piece, she could see all the connections they'd missed.

It wasn't just on the Savonnette. This image, this blade, had kept appearing to them. 'You know, we saw a sword before,' Astrid said. 'Under Windsor, in the ancient temple. You remember it. We told Magnus about it.'

Gwen swallowed. 'Yeah, the one with a silver pansy at the hilt. I remember.' Gwen had been the one to reveal the etching from millennia ago, the temple answering only to her. It depicted a man with a sword, defeating an evil dragon.

Jonas's eyes lit up; he too now following the same trail of breadcrumbs.

'Then, do you also remember that we saw that same sword and this image too –' Astrid stopped to tap the Savonnette – 'somewhere else? Somewhere we have very easy access to right now.'

Gwen stared at her, deadpan. She knew exactly what Astrid was talking about.

'No,' she exclaimed, her nose scrunching up.

'Yes,' Astrid insisted. 'It's in the book of Cursed Melodies, and you're going to read it.'

'No, I'm *not*.' Gwen stamped her foot, and for a split second that ring of gold entered her eyes again. 'The book is dangerous. Need I remind you it lured my mother and the Rapscallions into releasing the Shadowling? Who knows what it might manipulate us into doing if we let it.'

They were staring each other down, sparks of anger practically flying between them, when there was another knock at the door.

'Don't tell anyone about this,' Gwen hissed at the twins. 'I'm going to figure this out myself, without the book.'

Astrid refused to answer. In her mind, Gwen was being painfully naive. Why couldn't she just do what Astrid said?

She just wanted to keep Gwen safe, to help her unlock whatever power was hidden in her tiny frame.

Peeling himself away from the awkward stand-off, Jonas answered the door.

'Good morning, Jonas,' Magnus said, looking far too chipper. He was dressed in his usual quirky attire – a velvet cloak and top hat, like the ringmaster of some gothic circus. 'Oh, and Gwen . . . why is your hair wet?'

'I went for a swim.' Gwen said, crossing her arms.

Magnus blinked, then chuckled as if it was a funny joke. 'Well, I was hoping I could borrow Astrid and Jonas? I want to have a word with them over breakfast.'

Gwen scowled at Astrid, clearly still sour about their disagreement over the book.

'Fine by me,' Gwen declared, then stormed off back to her own cabin.

Astrid watched her leave, thinking, *This conversation is not over.*

The dining hall was a wide, orderly space. Long tables with blood-red runners were lined with rows of rigidly seated sailors, their peacoats neat despite the early hour. To see Custodians in a military setting was strange, and wrong.

They caught sight of Lorelei first, sitting on her own at a porthole, staring dreamily out of the window – which was very unlike her. Astrid was tempted to ask Magnus about it, to spill that she'd seen Lorelei hiding the fife and Elijah hatching plans with her that they intended to keep from Magnus. But Astrid knew she'd be betraying Lorelei in doing so, and she needed to understand more about what was going on.

And, really, what harm could a little fife do anyway?

Across the hall, they caught sight of someone else – Prince Teddy. He was seated at a table with Captain Bellamy and Lieutenant Thorn. He winked as they passed, earning a groan from Jonas.

As they carried their plates through the room, a Custodian would occasionally break rank and peer over at them.

'Is it just me or are you starting to feel less like a person and more like a rare animal in a zoo?' Jonas murmured as they sat down.

Astrid couldn't disagree.

Magnus considered the room of Custodian soldiers with a sombre look. 'The unfortunate price of having the fate of the world on your shoulders . . .' he said gravely. 'Now, I wanted to show you something. Elijah and I were sorting through old Rapscallion memorabilia and we found some photos you might enjoy.'

Carefully, Magnus placed the images on their table amongst the teacups and pastries. Around them, the quiet clink of utensils mingled with an easy hum of melodies, magic filling the air to heat and cool, push and pull, disciplined and measured. Ready for anything.

Magnus pointed to one of the photos: a fresh-faced young woman grinning with a gap-toothed smile, and a man with dirty-blonde hair and the kind of facial features to make you swoon. 'These here are Abigail and Francis,' he explained, then moved to the next one, an image of a woman who looked just like Gwen. 'This is Gwen's mother, Rani.'

Then a wistful look overtook Magnus as he pointed to the last one.

'And that's Rupert, as you know. Next to him is our old friend Quin Larkspur.'

The twins paused, leaning in. Rupert looked like Magnus, only a little younger and a little more muscular. Quin, on the other hand, was waifish, with dark hair and grey eyes that held a perceptive glint, like he knew all your secrets.

'Looks like a fun group,' Astrid said, pushing the photo of Quin across for Jonas to look at.

Magnus's face turned grave as he spread some jam on his toast. It felt like he was preparing himself.

'You know, when Seraphina first put the Cursed Melodies in our hands, we had tremendous fun,' he admitted, and the confession surprised both twins. 'Sometimes it felt like the book was almost a friend. Like it wanted us to solve its secrets. We really felt like we could bring Ancient Magic back, that we could make the world as it used to be, with Red Bloods and Bloom Bloods living together in a world of wonders.'

Astrid imagined it too, how incredible it would be to bring back that lost time of magic. For the whole world to be full of miracles again, not just in this shadow society of Bloom Bloods. But Magnus's expression darkened once more.

'Quin was the first to be tainted by it,' he said, putting his knife down. 'He was obsessed with the book, more so than the rest of us. We'd find him poring over it late at night, for hours. It changed him – do you understand?' The twins nodded, listening intently. 'Eventually his obsession consumed him.' Magnus sighed, staring off into the distance through one of the portholes. 'He left us, even before we so foolishly awakened the Shadowling.'

The way Magnus said the words *'left us'* made it clear what he meant. And it was also suddenly clear to Astrid why he was telling them all this.

'You don't think Gwen should read it,' she said.

Magnus shook his head. 'No, I don't.'

Astrid couldn't help but feel frustration rising. 'But Rupert charmed the book *for her*,' she reminded him. 'He left it to her. He thought she was meant to find it. We need to figure out why.'

'I cannot speak for my brother; I can only agree with Gwen in her reluctance. The risk of more disaster is too great.'

Astrid went to say more, but felt Jonas's hand gently rest on her knee under the table. The familiar cool skin was calming, and she took a deep breath.

'I think what Astrid is saying –'

But Jonas could not get another word out, because just then there was a harsh squeak and the clatter of chairs being knocked over.

On the other side of the room, a person screamed. Prince Teddy.

Something smashed into the table in front of him, something big, wet and fast – and clumsy. It knocked all the food off with a great crash, and before anyone could react, the *thing* lunged at Prince Teddy.

7
Wouldn't Hurt a Fly

'Argh!' Prince Teddy shouted, falling backwards on his chair. He was moments away from bashing his head into the sole – the wooden planks beneath their feet – and was only caught by a whip-sharp spell from Lieutenant Thorn.

The twins had rushed across the room, jumping over the mess. The hall was in chaos, with food strewn everywhere, the prince down on the floor, and every sailor on their feet, seemingly paralysed with uncertainty about what to do.

The cause of this pandemonium was not what either twin had expected.

Half-otter, half-dog, with giant paws that were clawed, its wide mouth sprinkled with whiskers, the creature's tail wagged back and forth, still knocking the plates and bowls around on the floor. It also smelled terrible, like brine and bad breath. The twins had seen its kind in books: Dobhar-chú, King Otter, except this one was collared and currently slobbering all over Prince Teddy like he was a fresh slab of meat.

'You're an odd thing, aren't you?' Astrid marvelled. The creature's tongue lolled, wet nose sniffing at Jonas's hand. He turned his palm upward, allowing it to get a good whiff.

'Oh, Queen's mercy, I'm so sorry, uncle,' a voice huffed from the doorway. He was a dishevelled, red-headed boy with a lead in his hand. 'He got away from me again.'

'Eddie, my lad.' The captain's voice came out in a boom. 'What do we call me when on board?'

'Sorry, uncle – I mean, Captain.' The boy tripped over his words. He certainly was a meek little fellow, compared to Captain Bellamy. 'Biscuit was just having a swim, you see. I took him off the side of the boat like you said, but he didn't want to go back to the cabin. Something's got him all restless after last night – there was someone on deck, we never caught them, and then . . . and then . . .'

Blink and Astrid would have missed it, but just after Eddie mentioned someone being on deck, Lorelei chose that moment to slink away, out of the room. *Weird*, Astrid thought.

Eddie looked out over the mess hall, his cheeks going pink as peonies.

Now the room was totally silent but for the wet slapping of Biscuit's tail, and everyone turned to stare at the prince. Slowly he stood up, looking – well, looking like someone who'd just been knocked over by a slimy sea-dog.

'Captain, what are you planning to do about this?' Prince Teddy asked, his voice calm despite the disarray.

Tense, everyone waited for the captain's response. His eyebrows were knitted together, his beard still covered in crumbs from the bread rolls he'd been digging into. Things were not looking good for the ugly dog-thing.

Then Captain Bellamy let out a great bellowing laugh, one so loud it could be felt through the wooden floor.

'Nothing like a little salt and saliva to wake you up in the morning, hmm?' he hollered, coming to give Biscuit a good pat-down as the rest of the sailors joined in laughing. 'Who's a funny boy?' The otter-dog opened its sharp-toothed mouth wide in an unsettling grin as its tail smacked even harder at the sole.

'You're all in one piece, aren't you, lad?' Captain Bellamy said amiably, clapping the prince so hard on the shoulder that he stumbled forward. 'Come on, then – let's get to work, everyone. Enough fun.'

Jonas looked to his sister with a raised eyebrow. So the captain wasn't just a giant, war-hungry seafarer after all.

'Well, wasn't that exciting,' Magnus said, smiling merrily and tucking his photos of Rupert and Quin away. 'But, if you'll excuse me, I need to go and have a word with Lorelei.'

So, Astrid wasn't the only one who had noticed Lorelei's strange departure.

With them gone, Astrid would take the opportunity to investigate other matters. She tipped her head towards Eddie, and Jonas followed.

All the sailors had begun restoring the room to its previous pristine condition, filling the space with the clang of metal tableware and the scraping of shifting furniture. The boy, meanwhile, was clipping the lead onto his sea-dog. When he looked up, the twins were standing over him.

'Oh my, it really is you!' the boy gasped, doe-eyed with awe. Up close, Astrid could see constellations of freckles dotting his face. He must have been about the twins' age, or maybe a little older based on the silver Savonnette at his chest, and yet he had a babe-like quality to his face – cherubic, even. 'You're the twins, aren't you?'

'We are twins, yes,' Astrid said. 'And you are?'

'Eddie Clam.' Standing up slowly, the boy couldn't take his eyes off them, especially the shards of Savonnette round their necks. 'I heard about what you two did, and that girl . . . fighting that . . . that . . . shadow thing.'

'The Shadowling,' Jonas corrected.

'Is it true you can do . . .' He leaned forward to whisper, '. . . *Ancient Magic?*' The twins shrugged, and Eddie nodded soberly. 'My uncle thinks you're going to change the whole Bloom Blooded world. I can hardly believe you're real . . . I mean, you hardly look real. You look sort of like my sister's dolls but . . . scary. Sorry, I'm so sorry, I didn't mean it like that –'

There was a great heaving groan, and the prince sauntered over.

'Do you always talk so much?' he asked, and although it was rather rude, neither twin could blame him for asking. This boy clearly had no filter.

'Sorry, I . . . well, yes. Sorry, Your Majesty.' Eddie bowed low, clearly embarrassed. By now the other sailors had filed out of the mess hall and it was only the four of them left.

Prince Teddy rolled his eyes. 'It's *"Your Royal Highness"*, actually. *"Majesty"* is for kings and queens.'

Eddie looked like he was about to combust with shame; the twins were sure they could see his heartbeat through his shirt.

'I'm so sorry, Your Highness, and I'm so sorry about Biscuit. He's actually very sweet. He wouldn't hurt a fly.' Biscuit's tongue lolled out in response, apparently happy as a clam. 'We rescued him as a pup, actually; his back leg was broken and he was in danger of getting caught in lobster lines, which would have caused all sorts of problems for the Order of Pendragon, so I raised him myself –'

'What's your job on this ship, anyway?' Prince Teddy interrupted. 'Other than to cause a nuisance.'

'Oh, I . . . Let me show you.'

Without another word, Eddie jogged off with Biscuit, leaving the three of them to catch up. He took them through the corridors to one of the large windows near the cabins. It had rune marks etched into the surrounding panelling, exactly like the ones Magnus and Lorelei had pointed out the night before. Astrid guessed that if she looked, she'd find them everywhere on board.

'Counter Melodies,' Astrid recalled. 'Magnus said they protect the ship. We can hear them in the back of our minds constantly.'

'That's right,' Eddie said, clearly impressed. 'I manage the protective runes that emit the music. Biscuit here is trained to scent out anything that's not supposed to be on board or to hear any changes to the melodies. He's got all of your individual scents, too. We go round ten times a day to check and make sure none of the runes have been tampered with.'

'So . . . don't touch the runes,' Jonas confirmed.

'That would be grand, thanks.' Eddie beamed at them, revealing a charming gap tooth. 'It would take some seriously powerful magic to damage them, but they're the only thing stopping magical creatures from attacking the ship. And with the rise of Grim-possessed creatures, we would probably all be mermaid food without the runes.'

'And your uncle put *you* in charge of them?' The prince chuckled in disbelief, and although neither twin could fault him for asking such a thing, Astrid and Jonas suddenly felt a fierce need to defend the poor boy.

'Odd that Biscuit made a beeline for the prince, isn't it?' Jonas pondered aloud. 'Perhaps he doesn't *trust* you.'

'What exactly are you insinuating?' Prince Teddy asked, narrowing his eyes.

Jonas shrugged. 'Nothing.'

'Well, it's a very rich *nothing* coming from a boy who sleeps with my lighter under his pillow.' The prince's words had an edge now, that lopsided smirk turning sharp. He was enjoying this.

Eddie blinked at the two of them. 'Is that some sort of land-slang I don't know?'

Jonas huffed, looking about ready to cast a spell on the pompous prince, but a thought had just occurred to Astrid, one that was far more important than her brother's little flirtatious squabble.

'You said there was someone on deck?' she asked Eddie.

'Oh, yeah,' Eddie said, thinking to himself. 'I summoned Lieutenant Thorn because I thought there was someone traipsing around in a suspicious way on deck. You see, I'd heard a strange melody, possibly from a flute.' Astrid bit her tongue to stop her expression betraying her.

A flute . . . or a fife?

Eddie went on: 'Now we think it might have been two people, because Biscuit couldn't figure out which direction to chase in. Lieutenant Thorn thinks it was probably one of your lot,' he admitted sheepishly.

Astrid remembered how Lorelei had slunk away not long ago. Like she hadn't wanted Biscuit to catch hold of her scent, perhaps? But what would she have been doing playing a fife on deck before sunrise – what kind of magic was she making?

'Knowing their track record, it definitely was,' the prince said, rolling his eyes. 'And might I remind you both that we're trying to avoid you getting in any trouble.' He was looking at Jonas as he spoke, having dropped his usual cocky attitude; his tone sounded almost concerned. 'Everyone on this ship is just trying to keep you all safe.'

Astrid suddenly felt incredibly stupid – a very rare feeling indeed. There was clearly a plot of some sort going on under her nose. Lorelei was up to something suspicious, and Magnus had probably now figured out what. Meanwhile, what was Astrid doing? Talking back to Magnus and fighting with Gwen, the girl she'd burn the world to ash for? Each moment was precious, and she needed to do everything in her power to keep Gwen safe. She couldn't very well do that if Gwen wouldn't even talk to her.

Oh god, Astrid realized . . . she needed to apologize.

'Jonas,' she said, biting her lip – a thing she was sure she'd never done in her life.

'Yes, yes,' he said gently, already having reached the same conclusion. 'We'll sort it out.'

'It was lovely to meet you, Eddie,' Jonas said for both of them. 'We'll see you at dinner, perhaps?'

Eddie, rather adorably, bowed, and his otter-dog followed with a similar gesture.

'Hey, come back here!' Prince Teddy called after them, but it was useless. Astrid needed to go figure out exactly how one apologizes to the girl one is in love with.

Gwen spent the whole day avoiding the twins, which was no easy task on a ship in the middle of the ocean. She refused to answer the door to them, and by the time evening rolled around, she'd snuck out of her cabin only a few times to stock up on food, avoiding the inquisitive stares of all the sailors and ignoring how they carefully made way for her. They were treating her like some kind of precious cargo.

She supposed that's what she was. She was the thing they were transporting, the purpose of this whole mission.

She bit off a chunk of an apple from the fruit bowl on the polished rosewood table in her cabin. The room was irritatingly luxurious. Chandeliers, views out to sea, crystal bowls and glasses. She wondered how many people on board had ever even seen the Grim in person. If any of them had any idea of the utter horror that was the Shadowling. She was sure none of them would be able to enjoy any of the ship's luxuries either if they knew what was out there. They were completely unprepared for the horrors awaiting them. Horrors it would fall on Gwen to put a stop to, at whatever cost.

Now, with the sun setting, a thick fog had enveloped the boat, making Gwen feel even more trapped. And, worse, she wasn't alone. She was trapped in this cabin with that damned book.

She vehemently refused to think about it, instead trying to draw the spiral patterns from the Savonnette in a notebook. It should have been hard to do from memory, and yet her hands seemed to know the patterns. A fact she didn't want to dwell on. There were so many details to keep on top of. The silver pansy image that kept reappearing, the sword, the spirals . . . the voices. It would be so convenient if someone or something would just explain it all to her. What she was, what this all meant.

The book could do that, of course.

But she wouldn't.

She couldn't.

She was not going to look at the book. Nope, nope, nope. Astrid was just going to have to deal with being disappointed. Nothing good could come from such a thing.

She sketched harder, until – 'Urgh!' Gwen cried out, her pencil slicing through the page.

Shuddering, for a second she thought she felt hot breath up her back, and turned violently.

'Hello?' she called out.

Directly behind her, stashed under the bed, was the charmed cloth hiding the book.

Needy little thing, she thought.

'You're not mine,' she insisted aloud, and almost gasped in shock when she thought she felt a shift in Bloom . . . like the book was protesting.

The thought had her shuddering again, but the Bloom didn't stop. It was a gentle whispering sound, like many voices at once. Even through the cloth, it was trying to speak to her.

And worst of all, she felt it again – the sense that she recognized these voices . . . almost like . . . they were the same ones from her dream-walking.

Gwen spoke out loud again, hesitantly: 'It couldn't be?'

Before she could lose the dream-memory, and before she chickened out, she marched up to the bed and yanked the cloth bundle out from underneath. She stared down at it, ready to rip the whole thing apart if there was even one second of funny business.

Swallowing her reservations, she very carefully peeled back the fabric. She caught a flash of crimson, the scales on the leather-bound cover almost glowing molten red. The book seemed to sigh in relief as it was exposed to light – hissing, like a hot pan under cold water.

She went very still, listening.

'Oh no,' Gwen said then, dread settling into her stomach. 'I do know you.'

Gwen almost gasped as the book practically preened in her hand, the whispering Bloom rejoicing.

With the same voices as from her dreams.

And one of them was her own.

8

Over-Dramatic Little Pest

Standing outside Gwen's cabin door, Astrid took a deep breath. She'd let Gwen cool off over the day, but this had to be done, now. It was an hour past dinner, and most of the crew were getting ready for bed or a night shift.

'Will you knock, or shall I?' Jonas said, a mocking lilt in his voice.

'Give me a second,' Astrid hissed.

Astrid lifted her hand to knock, but the door suddenly swung open.

'Argh!' Gwen nearly tumbled right into her. 'Holy mother Mary,' she exclaimed, clutching her chest. 'I was just coming to find you both.'

'Gwen, before you say anything, I'm here to apologize,' Astrid said firmly. She had to get all the words out before she overthought them. 'You don't have to read the book if you don't want to. We won't force you.'

Gwen gaped up at her, astonished by the apology. Astrid chose not to be offended that she'd be shocked by this.

And then Gwen said the very last thing Astrid would have expected: 'Oh, well. Umm, I kind of . . . already started.'

The twins froze, a million and one questions poised on their lips. They settled on the most important one.

'Without *us*?' they spluttered.

Gwen rolled her eyes. 'Just get in here.' She pulled them in and shut the door with a bang.

Inside, there was a healthy assortment of empty plates and discarded fruit peels scattered about, thanks to her day of hiding. On the bed, sitting in the middle of a nest of charmed fabric, was the book of Cursed Melodies – and it was open.

The delicate script of runes and indecipherable language had been brought back to life by Gwen's touch, looking so perfect it practically glowed: the Magister had done a miraculous job of restoring it.

It drew them in, even as Jonas eyed it warily, and Astrid could feel that thrill, the promises radiating from it, of power and knowledge.

'Gwen,' Astrid said cautiously. 'What happened?'

'OK, so, I don't know how, or why,' she began, her voice wavering, 'but the voices in the Bloom that I can hear from the book?' Gwen gestured for them to sit round the table while she brought the book over. 'One of the voices is *my* voice. I can't explain it. It's the same as for the voices I heard in the dream-walking. It's like . . . a part of me is inside it.'

The twins glanced at each other, apprehension creeping over Jonas's shoulders that Astrid could feel like pins on her own skin. Astrid, on the other hand, was having to quell her excitement.

'Does that mean you trust it now?' Jonas asked.

Gwen nearly choked on her indignation. 'Heck, no!' She scowled at the book like it had insulted her. Almost the look one might give someone they were squabbling with.

'But I'll do it. I'll try and read it,' Gwen said resolutely, 'if it gets us out of this whole situation quicker. I'll . . . I'll try. I just . . . I need you to be patient, and if I . . . if it . . .'

Even saying the words out loud clearly made Gwen uncomfortable, so Astrid knew she needed to be careful not to push her too hard. So she said, 'I'll destroy it before it can harm a single perfect hair on your head.'

'No need,' Gwen growled, and Astrid caught that fire in her eyes. 'Because I will.'

This was it: they were really going to read it. All their questions could have their answers.

But before Astrid could get another word out, there was a great banging at the door.

'Hello?' It was the prince, because of course it was. 'I know you're all in there. Open the door immediately.' His voice had the same easy confidence as if he were simply speaking to a palace hound.

Jonas ran his hands over his face, exasperated. 'Just what we need.'

There was another barrage of knocks, and it was clear Prince Teddy was not going away.

'If it's patience you need, the little princeling is going to be a problem,' Astrid whispered to Gwen. 'We won't have long until he's barging the door down.'

Gwen nodded. They needed to get rid of him.

'We need something to distract him,' Astrid said. 'Or . . . someone.'

Gwen and Astrid turned to Jonas expectantly. It took a second for him to catch on, and when he did, he looked like he'd been slapped in the face with a wet fish.

'What? No, you can't be serious,' Jonas all but spat. He turned to his sister. '*Et tu*, Astrid?'

Astrid put a delicate hand on his shoulder. 'See if you can find Magnus and Lorelei while you're out there.'

Another furious knocking came from the door. '*Hellooooo?*' the prince called.

Jonas huffed, levelling them both with a look that could have turned blood to ice. 'I'm going to make you both pay for this.'

Then, right in front of their eyes, his expression turned saccharine – sweet, almost – as he walked to the door. He opened it only a fraction.

'Oh, Teddy,' he said, voice hushed. 'Could you keep it down a little? Girl troubles – you know how it is.'

Gwen had to cover her mouth to stop herself laughing, while Astrid, used to his antics, only rolled her eyes.

'Really?' Prince Teddy's voice was quiet now. 'You're not lying, are you?'

'Of course I'm not,' Jonas hissed. 'Now, do you want to help me find some potions for my sister and Gwen, or do you want to keep banging at this door and asking rude questions?'

The rest of the conversation became muffled as Jonas shut the door behind him.

Gwen was staring wide-eyed at the door.

'You two lie like it's a competitive sport,' she mumbled.

Astrid smiled. It was a rare moment: she had Gwen alone, and she was going to savour it.

'Are you ready, Gwen?'

'Are you ready, Gwen?'

Gwen startled at the sound of her own name. With the eerie fog building outside, suddenly the room was very quiet but for the constant hum of runes and the endless swish of the sea. Astrid was sitting at the table, serenely poised apart for the glint in her eye, that sharp desire for knowledge. Now it only just occurred to Gwen that she was alone in her room with Astrid. Not with her and Jonas, just Astrid. The thought made her breath catch in her throat. Astrid always made her strangely nervous in a way she didn't completely hate.

'Shall we begin?' Astrid asked, licking her lips.

Gwen hesitated, unable to keep her eyes off the ethereal girl. Astrid had that hunger about her, and Gwen suddenly felt like she had become a piece of cake.

And also watching her was the book, humming impatiently on the table.

'Gwenny?'

'Yes, yes, OK,' Gwen grumbled, fighting off the growing feelings of panic and unease. 'I'm ready.'

She should have known Astrid would always get her way in the end, and the book seemed utterly pleased with itself over the outcome.

'You and the book are both so pushy,' Gwen muttered.

Astrid eyed Gwen with that same intense curiosity, her golden hair falling in soft curls round her face. 'You seem to have developed an interesting relationship with it,' she said.

Gwen did not like that at all.

'Don't say that,' she muttered. The thought made her stomach turn. If *The Cursed Melodies* could help them defeat the Shadowling, so be it, but she wanted nothing else to do with it.

With the book spread open on the round table, it almost looked like they were about to perform one of the old rituals – a seance, perhaps. Like they were about to communicate with the dead.

Gwen didn't realize her hand was shaking until Astrid carefully placed hers on top. The feel of her cool, milky-white skin, the buzzing of their Bloom mingling together, soothed something in Gwen.

'It's going to be OK,' Astrid said, and she sounded so sure. 'I'll protect you, always.'

She spoke like it was her calling, her solemn duty, and Gwen remembered what Astrid had said all those months ago: that she wanted to serve her, like a loyal subject. It should have flustered Gwen, made her embarrassed, but it didn't. It felt right. Perhaps that's what frightened Gwen most of all.

And yet Gwen couldn't find it in herself to ask the one question she most needed to know the answer to:

What was Astrid to her?

Instead, taking a centring breath, Gwen pulled the book towards herself, peering down at the strange symbols on the ancient parchment. As her fingers glided over the images of the sword and flowers, her skin sparked.

Recognition.

It was just like before: when she looked at the pages, the whispers grew, the book trying to get inside her head. Except this time, she didn't shy away from it. She scrutinized each scrawled line of text, until the whispers flooded her ears. At first nothing happened but the growing crescendo of voices, each desperate to be heard but unable to communicate. She was about to cover her ears, tell them to shut up – when all went quiet.

Her vision split, the room skewing.

She felt it: her Bloom, that golden thing inside her. It was in this book too, only somehow tainted, like an eclipse of the sun.

'Gwen, what's happening?' Astrid asked, her voice oddly distant.

Gwen blinked down at the book. Except, suddenly she wasn't sure that Gwen was her name, nor where she was. She was vaguely aware her lips were moving. She was singing. The pages were stirring.

Her vision was blurred, only the sword visible in her mind. The scent of pansies filled the air.

This has happened before.

She saw the sword in her hands, but they were different, driving the blade into the Shadowling. One last desperate attempt.

You have to use it right.
Find it in the spirals.
The locket is a map.

She wasn't sure if the thoughts were her own, or someone else's.

No – not a thought, a memory.

See this spell. See our magic, the voice called. *See the horror.*

The words were gnarled at the edges, a prickly feeling like breath on her back. Like the Shadowling was watching.

'Gwen!' Another voice broke through. Angelic. She knew that voice; she'd know it in every lifetime. It had changed now, but she'd trust it with her life.

'GWEN!'

Gasping, Gwen nearly choked, violently coming back to herself in her cabin aboard the *Tidebinder*. Astrid was holding her shoulders and staring at her, those icy-blue eyes wide and frenzied. She put her hand to Gwen's cheek, leaning in close, and Gwen could smell the earthen scent, like spring rain, that followed Astrid everywhere.

Gwen saw it then – the room, the chaos. The heat.

The crystal fruit bowl had been smashed against the wall, while everything else – the fruit, the papers, even the carpet beneath her – was scorched as if the room had been struck by lightning. Under Gwen's hands, still sizzling, the table had burned nearly to dust.

Astrid sucked in a breath, and she looked almost excited. 'That was incredible,' she whispered.

Gwen swallowed, pushing her away in panic. 'What the hell happened?'

'You,' Astrid said, marvelling at the room. 'You don't remember? You connected with the book and turned the pages on your own, and then you started singing a spell. You should have seen yourself, or heard it – it made you light up! At first it was like angel song, almost heavenly, and then, well . . .' She gestured to the room. 'If the book can give you this kind of power, you'll be unstoppable.'

'No,' Gwen whispered, shaking her head. She was disorientated and confused. She glanced down at her fingers. At first it looked like soot was caught under her nails, except it wasn't soot at all. They were stained black, the magic tainting her under the skin. 'Argh!' Gwen cried out, shaking her hands. The darkness recoiled, vanishing, but she could feel it, her body fighting off the evil residue of the spell like it was a parasite.

One thing was abundantly clear. They couldn't use that spell again, whatever it was. Or any of the spells in the book.

'We can't. This is wrong – something's wrong with this magic.'

The book sat entirely unharmed in the centre of the burnt table, the whispers now calmed to near silence.

'But I got what we needed from it,' Gwen explained, trying to calm her own thrumming heart. 'The sword – it *is* a weapon we can use to defeat the Shadowling. It was forged to stop him, and it nearly ended him once before; we just have to find it and finish the job.' Gwen closed her eyes, trying to grab on to the memories before they faded. 'We need your Savonnette. It's a map!' Heart still thudding in her chest, she remembered the last bit, the terror. 'But this . . . the spells in here? They're not to be used.'

The voices – they'd made her cast this spell to show her the damage such spells would inflict. To show her the memory, yes, but also to warn her off.

' "*See the horror*" indeed,' Gwen muttered to herself as she stared at her hands again. The black marks were gone now, but she could still feel the taint like worms in her blood.

Astrid blinked, the excitement still not leaving her eyes. She was almost salivating. She hadn't seen the marks. She didn't know.

'The book told you all that?'

Gwen shook her head, lunging up to grab Astrid's hand. She knew that hungry look in Astrid's eyes.

'Listen to me, Astrid,' she beseeched, squeezing her palm. 'You have to promise me – that spell you just heard? You can never, ever repeat it. Please. Promise me.'

Astrid opened her mouth to speak, but instead she went very still, her eyes darting to the side.

Gwen squeezed her hand harder. 'Do you understand –'

'Wait.' Astrid's other hand shot out, her finger covering Gwen's lips. 'Do you hear that?'

Startled, Gwen could scarcely move as Astrid leaned in very close.

'What?' Gwen whispered. 'I can't hear anything.'

Astrid's eyes went wide. Gwen could tell she was frightened, something that was alarming enough on its own.

She whispered back, 'The runes that protect the ship – they've gone quiet.'

Gwen blinked, not following.

'What does that mean –'

She didn't have a chance to finish the sentence because they heard an ear-splitting sound, a *crack* like an explosion that rattled their bones. Alarms, shouts and screams – all hell broke loose. And there, in the centre of all the noise, was a sound they knew well now.

The Grim.

It was time.

The Shadowling had finally come for them.

9

Going Under

The fog, somehow, was growing thicker. Traipsing the many corridors of the ship, with all the sailors going about their assigned tasks, Jonas scowled at the windows. Nothing but thick grey. He tried not to look, the view too reminiscent of his and his sister's time spent in confinement. Grey everywhere, as far as the eye could see.

This was bad enough, and that was not even accounting for the fact he was currently babysitting Prince Theodore Doria.

'We can try the apothecary; I'm sure they'll have something useful in there . . .' Prince Teddy was all business, leading the way as if he were spearheading an important mission. It was charming . . . in a way. *Queen's mercy*, Jonas thought. He needed to touch some grass. Soon.

Jonas hummed absent-mindedly at Teddy's suggestion, keeping an eye out for Magnus or Lorelei as they navigated the maze of corridors. All he had to do was keep the prince occupied for an hour or so; that should easily give Gwen and his sister enough time to try reading the book.

Licking his lips, Jonas imagined what they might find, what it could mean if Gwen really was able to read it. All the mysteries surrounding where Jonas and Astrid came from, their Ancient Magic abilities. Yet part of him felt deeply guilty at the thought. Magnus had been adamant that they mustn't consult the book, and he was rarely wrong. Jonas just had to trust his sister to stay wise, even with the tantalizing book in their clutches.

Jonas felt himself becoming frenzied, his thoughts of the book almost feverish. Hot and itchy, he didn't feel like himself, and he knew Astrid must be feeling similarly. They needed to get back to land.

'Are you unwell?'

Jonas blinked up at the prince where he'd stopped in a long, somehow even more ornate corridor. They were alone. Through a large window at the far end, Jonas could see the carved wooden hems of the maiden at the bow who guided the *Tidebinder*. There was an odd smell in the air, almost herbal. And something else – an ever-so-quiet hum of Bloom.

'Where are we?' Jonas asked, ignoring his question.

Prince Teddy ignored Jonas's question in turn. 'Usually there's this delightful pink tint to your cheeks, like a ripening rose, but you're all pale . . . well, more pale than usual.'

'I'm going to pretend you didn't say that,' Jonas replied. 'What's behind all these doors?'

The prince grinned, practically dancing as he stepped further ahead into the corridor.

'These are the Captain's Quarters,' he explained.

As they walked through the hall, the hum of Bloom grew louder, a melody tickling the back of Jonas's mind. If only he could locate its source.

'. . . and his apothecary is just through this door up here . . .'

Jonas stopped dead in his tracks. *There* it was. The sound was coming from behind the door, a sound he'd never thought he'd hear on a ship. He stepped closer, hardly believing his ears.

Plants, alive, growing and *singing*.

Jonas's mouth filled with saliva. A need as pure as hunger. Prince Teddy reached for the door handle, but Jonas pushed past him, an animal springing from its cage.

Jonas all but stumbled through the door, and there it was. Green, so much green. Rare and magical plants spilling over the walls and shelves in glorious cascades of viridescence. The energy in the room was a balm on his feverish skin.

'Thank the heavens,' Jonas said, unable to stop the smile spreading over his face.

The apothecary was a life-sprouting haven on the sparse, earthless hellhole that was the *Tidebinder*. A gentle ringing of Bloom greeted them, the air dewy and fresh from melodies of mist-making. Jonas inhaled a long, deep breath. His muscles untensed, his face softened.

Welcome, welcome, the plants seemed to call, excited by his arrival. Jonas brushed his fingers against one. Merriwort – a plant he'd never seen before.

'Well, look at that, back from the dead.' Prince Teddy chuckled behind him, slowly closing the door.

'Excuse me?' Jonas said. Only Prince Teddy could find a way to ruin his mood.

The prince smirked. 'Your cheeks – they're pink again.' His stare was intense, and Jonas felt heat in his face. The prince caught it. 'And here they go again!'

Furious, Jonas turned back to the plants, scowling at them as they trilled with Bloom. The little devils were giggling.

'If you must know, it's this ship,' Jonas huffed, trying to change the subject. 'Astrid and I aren't comfortable being this far away from land.' He rubbed at a leaf to find some comfort in the texture. 'It's like we're being starved.'

The prince's boots made soft clicking steps on the wooden floor. He was pacing, thinking, then he stopped.

'I was wondering,' he said in a careful tone, 'how did you survive all that time when you were living in Red Blooded society? When they locked you up?'

Jonas gritted his teeth, turning sharply to face the prince, only to find he was much closer than he'd expected.

'Let me guess – another thing you read in one of the files the Order keeps on us?'

Prince Teddy only shrugged, utterly irksome.

Jonas glared up at him. 'I don't know why you're so obsessed with me, but –'

Jonas didn't have a chance to finish before Prince Teddy leaned towards him. His words dried up in his mouth and suddenly he was entirely distracted by the soft brown of the prince's eyes and the pebbledash scarring along his jaw. Teddy leaned in even closer, analysing Jonas like a rare gem. The prince smelled like apple cider and gunpowder, and, for a split second, Jonas was even sure he could hear the melody of the Bloom in his blood – a crackle of fireworks. Jubilant.

'What are you –'

'You really have no idea, do you?' Teddy cut him off. There was no smirk now, only his captivating eyes like a lit bonfire. 'You and your sister and Gwen are the most important thing that's happened to the Bloom Blooded world since the Order was established all those hundreds of years ago. And it goes far beyond whether you can stop that damned dragon or not.' His voice was softer than usual, like he was recalling a fairy tale. 'They tell stories of the old times, before the magical dark age, when fairies roamed and witches and sorcerers could move mountains with their powers. Now we have nothing but old songs as a tiny glimpse of the magical world. The Order of Pendragon can only do so much with the information we have. We built academies and rewilded Enchanted Quarters, but the truth is we're still in the dark. We can achieve only a fraction of what we know magic is capable of.' He chuckled softly, his expression turning reverent. 'And then you came along. You, who can perform the magic of an ancient, lost time. You, who can speak to the earth itself. You, who were kept hidden from Bloom Blooded society and nobody knows why.' Jonas was frozen in place, his heartbeat wild as he stared up at the prince. 'Don't you see? You are the most fascinating thing in the world.'

Lost for words, Jonas could do nothing but stumble backwards into the plants. They weren't giggling now; no, they were bashful.

Jonas cleared his throat, schooling his expression. 'Did you memorize that whole speech just for me?'

The prince let out a loud laugh and, thankfully for Jonas, took a step back.

'Well, of course. I needed to give your sister and Gwen enough time to do whatever secret thing it is that you're trying to distract me from.' That smirk was back, and for a second it was so disarming that Jonas nearly missed what the prince had said.

'They're only . . .'

He cut Jonas off. 'Please, you can't lie to me. I happen to be an expert.'

Incensed, Jonas's palms began to tingle, Bloom burning in his throat. What was the prince planning? What on earth did he want from him?

'Then what in the Twelve Spells are we doing here?' he demanded.

Every plant in the room was poised and ready, responding to his emotions. Prepared to strike if given the command.

Prince Teddy only smiled, something almost sweet entering his eyes.

'Getting you alone,' he said, the smile reaching his voice. 'Obviously.'

Prince Teddy stepped forward again, carefully leaning down. There was the scent of smoke and apples, his lips getting closer. Breath catching in his chest, Jonas suddenly realized what was happening. Right there, amongst all the strange and beautiful flowers, in the middle of the ocean, Prince Theodore Doria was going to kiss him.

How dare he.

'Stop that!' Jonas spat, stepping backwards with a decisive flick of his wrist. Bloom flooded through him, the plants reacting to his voice and the gesture. Before Prince Teddy could even open his eyes completely, he was swarmed by green. Vines circled his wrists, holding him back as he let out a confused yelp.

'Hey, what the –'

'You can't just *kiss me*,' Jonas said, crossing his arms with an exasperated eye-roll.

'Wait, I didn't . . . I thought . . .' Prince Teddy stumbled over his words, something close to genuine surprise falling over his features as he dangled in the grasp of the vines. But Jonas had been through this before. He knew how deceptive Prince Teddy could be. He was a master of deceit; he'd just said so himself.

'Don't you think we have more important things to be

concerned about right now than this little game you're playing?' Jonas said.

The prince tried to squirm free, but Jonas only tightened his hold. Beautiful prey caught in his web.

'That is, unless *you're* the one trying to distract *me*. Like you did at the palace last year.' He narrowed his eyes, daring Prince Teddy to protest.

He said nothing, which was answer enough for Jonas. The prince could not be trusted. That was all there was to it.

'I'm not falling for your tricks again.' Then, with a gentle hum, Jonas twisted the plants tighter to hold the prince in place and made for the door.

'Hey, you can't just leave me here –'

On second thoughts, Jonas added some vines over his mouth for good measure. Without his hands and voice, the prince shouldn't be able to cast any spells. The petals and stems trilled, enjoying the mischief.

He looks good like that, Jonas thought. Happy with his work, he dusted himself off and left the room to hunt for Magnus. He was dizzy with what he'd done, rejuvenated from reconnecting with nature.

The prince had tried to kiss him. Absurd.

When Jonas reached the top deck he could see how thick the fog had become. Even the moon could scarcely break through. Floating through milky grey, the ship seemed like it was suspended in nothingness.

Then someone shouted and Jonas ducked, barely missing a boom as it swung by. He jumped over buckets and ropes, trying to steer clear of the crew and their busy work.

He was about to ask a crew member if they'd seen Magnus or Lorelei, but then he spotted them – and it sounded like they were arguing.

'Lorelei, is this you?' Magnus was demanding.

They were standing right at the edge of the deck, looking out at the grey air.

'The fog is nothing to do with me,' she countered. 'I only used the fife.'

Magnus swore under his breath. 'Confound it! We need to find Gwen and the twins at once. We can't know when –'

Taking a step forward, Jonas was about to interrupt them when, on the starboard side, the red-headed boy, Eddie, and his strange otter-dog went barrelling towards Lieutenant Thorn. When he reached her, he had to hunch over, panting, as he gestured wildly. Biscuit was next to him, barking loudly. They were too far away for Jonas to hear a word above the noise of the ship, but it was clear as day that Eddie was frightened.

And more worrying still, whatever he had just told Lieutenant Thorn had an immediate effect. She turned, sharp as a whip, her pin-straight hair twirling around her. Her piercing eyes landed on Jonas at the same time as the lieutenant's hand reached for the Black Savonnette at her breast. Jonas took a cautious step back as she began marching towards him, the obsidian weapon cocked in her hand. Was she heading for Magnus, or Lorelei, or Jonas? He couldn't tell. But she looked poised to kill.

She opened her mouth, and Jonas wasn't sure if she was about to let forth a barrage of spells or shout an order.

And he would never find out, because just then there was a deafening crack like thunder. It shook the boat to its very core, the sound alone sending all the crew to the deck.

Then, muffled at first, Jonas could hear it. Discord. Mayhem. The Grim.

Jonas grabbed on to a crate of cannonballs, winded by

the force of whatever the hell had just hit the ship. There were screams, shouting, people yelling instructions.

Jonas blinked to clear his mind, the world coming into focus again through the terrible discordant melody of the Grim. His body was charged with panic. He could hardly make sense of the shouting and chaos around him. Melodies overlapped, spells being fired in every direction. He stumbled to the side of the ship, sure he was about to throw up.

Below him, something came into view beneath the waves. Black, a circle of darkness. It shimmered under the sea foam.

And then it blinked.

Amongst all the chaos, one word came out clear. A single shriek of terror.

'Mermaids!'

10

Last Resorts

The ship was screaming. Astrid could feel it in her bones. Every snap of wood and groan of metal. Another boom. Another crack.

The ship wouldn't last long under these conditions. It was going to sink. Someone, somehow, had destroyed the runes and they were under attack.

'He's here,' Gwen breathed, her hand trembling in Astrid's, from fear but also fury. 'The Shadowling has sent the Grim after me. And now everyone on this ship is going to die.'

'Not everyone,' Astrid swore. There was only one thought in Astrid's mind. *Save Gwen*. No matter what she had to do.

The lower decks were already a deadly hazard. Chandeliers threatened to fall, vases smashed and rolled along their path. With every fresh battering the ship received, Gwen and Astrid went flying into the walls like glitter in a snow globe.

'The lifeboats! We need to get up on deck!' Astrid shouted over the alarms. Beneath the shrill sound, murky through the water, there was a sickening melody of rot and decay, discord and destruction. Hatred in its purest form.

There was another *boom*, a huge mass hitting the port side, and the two girls stumbled backwards just as one of the windows in front of them exploded like a starburst. Astrid took the brunt of it, cradling Gwen.

'Argh!' Gwen shouted. She had the book of Cursed Melodies clutched against her chest, holding it protectively like one might a teddy bear. Astrid wondered if she even noticed she was gripping it so tightly. 'What the hell was that?'

Just as the words left her mouth, there was a fresh wave of ear-splitting discord. The twisted melody rolled through Astrid's stomach and she pushed it down, focusing intently on the thrumming of her own Bloom to block it out.

She turned towards the shattered window and saw it. A shadow through the mist. A spiked tail, bigger than any living thing Astrid had ever seen in her life. It disappeared back into the foggy water with the slippery precision of an eel, but she knew what it was.

'A giant mermaid,' Astrid breathed. Shimmering green, crusted with shells, and marled beyond repair by the slimy rot of the Grim.

'I brought this here,' Gwen said, her voice barely above a whisper. 'They're here for me. The Shadowling must have found me because I read the book.' But Astrid didn't believe it for a second. Someone had brought this evil, all right, but it wasn't Gwen.

They ran down the corridors, hand in hand, until they reached the stairwell leading up to the deck. Above them they could hear crew members shouting and firing spells. Then there was a pained scream and Astrid pulled Gwen out of the way just in time as a sailor came flying towards them down the stairs. He landed in a slumped pile, limbs sticking out at odd angles. They both quickly looked away.

'Hurry,' Astrid said, ushering Gwen upward.

But there was no way she could have guessed at the utter horror waiting for them on deck.

Fog, thick as fat, and inside it could be seen and heard blood, screams, shattered lanterns, raging fires and the creatures themselves. They flew out of the water, sharp-toothed and thirsty for human blood. Sailors clutched their severed limbs, the mermaids wriggling over the deck, slippery and deadly. Those who had been killed lay lifeless, their gills dilating and pulsing, their once beautiful faces mottled by the Grim.

And there was the captain, the giant, jolly man who'd been lenient with the strange otter-dog. Dead on the deck.

It all blurred together hellishly. Over the edge of the boat, patches of water bloomed crimson. As far as Astrid could tell, there was scarcely half the crew left, all of them firing spells into the water at an enemy that simply vanished and reappeared in seconds.

'Turn back!' came a voice they recognized.

He materialized through the mist – Magnus. He clutched Jonas to him, while Lorelei threw out spells to protect them both. They were unharmed, somehow. A miracle.

'Take him down. We will come for you in a minute,' Magnus instructed, steering Jonas towards her. 'We have to aid these people as best we can before help arrives.'

'We'll meet you at the apothecary,' Jonas said, to which Magnus and Lorelei nodded.

'Don't go!' Gwen shouted, but their tutors ran back into the fog, ducking just in time as a jagged chunk of wood came careening towards them from a portside explosion.

Astrid grabbed Gwen and, shouldering Jonas, marched them down the steps again and quickly down the corridor. She got a good look at her brother: he had scrapes all along the left side of his face and was walking with a slight limp.

'Someone did this,' Astrid said. 'Someone tampered with the runes.'

'Wait. We can't just run off, we need to go back for Magnus –'

Gwen was unable to finish when a red-stained hand grabbed her, pulling her back.

Every cell in Astrid and Jonas's bodies screamed. Jonas's injuries forgotten, they turned on their attacker. Astrid hissed like a wild animal, pouncing, and both twins pushed the figure to the floor, holding them down. Except, their attacker didn't fight back; they couldn't. They were too preoccupied holding the gaping wound on their neck.

Lieutenant Isobel Thorn.

She held their gazes, a gurgling noise bubbling from her blood-pocked lips. Even dying, she was fierce. She tried to speak, but no words could come out. Slowly, Astrid and Jonas let her go.

Frantic, Lieutenant Thorn scrambled at her breast pocket, unlatching the Black Savonnette, her weapon. Hands wet with crimson, she shoved it into Jonas's palm, her blood staining everything she touched like some twisted King Midas. Her eyes were wide, desperate. She was trying to tell them something. But what?

'It's OK,' Astrid told her. 'We've got it.'

Lieutenant Thorn blinked, her eyes relaxing. She had completed her final mission.

There was another *boom*, and the three of them stumbled, a heavy brass candelabra crashing to the floor behind them. It narrowly missed Astrid's leg as it landed by the lieutenant.

The charmed candles set the floor ablaze, and Lieutenant Thorn with it. She was gone.

Astrid helped Gwen to her feet and they scrabbled back from the spreading fire. Gwen's eyes were wide, her body quaking as she clutched the book to her chest.

The book. Astrid watched it in Gwen's hands, knowing now the power that one little spell from it could unlock.

And she'd heard the music. She remembered the melody . . .

'This way!' Jonas shouted over the sound of screams, cutting off Astrid's thoughts. 'I know somewhere we'll be safe, at least until Magnus and Lorelei come to get us!' He ushered them through door after door until they reached a luxurious long stretch of corridor directly in the middle of the ship. A window at the very far end was sprayed with blood on the outside.

Jonas slammed the door to the corridor shut behind them. Carefully, he put the Black Savonnette in his pocket and fastened the button to secure it.

Astrid glared at her brother. 'What happened out there?'

'Well, bad news. There are about a million small mermaids and one giant one. They've eaten the lifeboats . . . and most of the crew.'

Astrid swore under her breath.

'Worse news . . .' Jonas chuckled, the feeling not quite reaching his eyes. 'You're both really going to laugh at this.'

'Jonas, what is it?' Astrid demanded. She could sense the guilt oozing from him like tar.

He grimaced. 'I tied Prince Teddy up in the apothecary with some plants. He's probably still there.'

Astrid's ears pricked up. The prince she couldn't care less about, but if there were plants on board, they'd have a shot at succeeding. And if not . . . She looked to Gwen again, who was shell-shocked, muttering under her breath, the book held to her chest.

'I can't,' she hissed. 'I won't.'

There was a frenzied look in her eyes as her fingers tightened round the book. Was it talking to her? Trying to get her to use it?

This middle part of the ship, directly under the horrors on deck, was peculiarly quiet. Charms, Astrid realized; somehow, this place was still protected. There was only the occasional thump and rattling to remind them they were all about to be eaten by mermaids.

Astrid felt it before they even got close – a wash of relief, an oasis in the desert. Throwing the door open, she breathed in the glorious rush of Bloom. The plants were calling to them, beseeching them:

Save the girl.

'Yes, yes,' Astrid murmured, the lot of them rushing into the room. 'We're on it.'

Astrid was so caught up in attuning herself to the plants, thinking of how she could use them to destroy the Grim-infected mermaids, that it took her a second to realize what Jonas and Gwen had already clocked.

The prince was not there.

'I –' Jonas spun around, a dog looking for its tail. 'I left him in here tied up. His mouth was covered. He couldn't have got free.' His eyes went wide, and Astrid was suddenly overcome with a wash of emotion, like an electric current through her spine.

Jonas had just had a revelation. He turned to Astrid, frantic.

'The runes,' he said, grabbing her shoulders. 'I saw Eddie, the boy in charge of them, moments before the ship was attacked, telling the lieutenant something. He looked afraid. What if the person who messed with the runes was –'

'Prince Theodore,' Astrid finished. She felt it like a lead weight in her stomach. Had they allowed him to betray them once again?

'Kids!' they heard Magnus shout. He rushed in, Lorelei at his side, both heavily scratched up and covered in purple powder . . . and slick with so much blood.

'Everyone, hold on,' Lorelei added, checking them over. 'This ship will be going down very soon. But we've got you, don't worry. Help is coming.'

'Help?' Jonas questioned. 'Who's coming?'

Lorelei had a determined set to her brow, glaring at Magnus who *tsked* under his breath.

There was another *boom* and shake, and Gwen's eyes widened.

'We need to run,' she breathed, her voice distant. 'We need to get out of here. Now.'

There was a low creaking, the sound of straining wood, of a ship being pushed to its limits. A snap. A crack like thunder.

The entire ship tilted like a see-saw, everyone crashing to the side.

'Gwen!' Astrid screamed. The plants reacted, a swarm of green wrapping round the poor girl and lifting her up moments before a shelf came plummeting down on top of her.

Power burned through Astrid's limbs, Bloom sparking inside her like neon. Her vision flashed emerald. Gwen would survive this, no matter what.

Throwing out her hand, Astrid summoned the plants to bring Gwen towards her. Jonas appeared at her side. Poised. Ready.

'They're coming,' Gwen hissed.

Another crack, this time visible in the ceiling. The line of the crack divided and grew quickly, inching round them like a parasite. The entire room began to fall away from itself with a desperate groaning.

The ship was being split in half.

'Everyone, hold on!' Magnus shouted.

In perfect sync, the twins honed their power, sending tentacles of green out to wrap round everyone's limbs, attaching them to the sole just as the walls began to break away from them.

The whole stern of the ship fell away and the icy fog poured in. People screamed, bodies fell, the last remaining crew members were thrown into the freezing ocean. The bodies bobbed at first, peacoats and sailor's hats, so many of them, floating in red. Then the mermaids, snaking through the water, feasting.

Then they saw the monstrous queen herself. Cresting from the water just in front of them, sending up sea spray that pelted their skin. Majestic and destructive as a typhoon. A giant mermaid, in all her glory.

Scales dripping rot ran all the way up to her neck, tangled hair spilling over her shoulders. She breached the back of the ship, her emerald tail gnarled with barnacles, the skin round her webbed claws stained dark with blood. And her eyes – black as the abyss, with a single circle of silver, embedded in a face so beautiful it could start a war.

It was a beauty Astrid recognized: that deadly horror that lived in her own blood. The power of nature itself.

And this monster was in the hands of the Shadowling.

Gwen gasped, the sound more like she was choking. She had her eyes squeezed shut, like she was trying to block something out. Like she was in her own world.

'Gwen!' Astrid called out. 'Hold on!'

The mermaid landed, a great crash that sent the water bubbling up like a cauldron. The ship yowled in agony, wood snapping, pipes bursting. Jonas's shoe came loose, splashing into the water below. Everything not held by the plants fell away into the churning ocean.

They caught another glimpse of the spiked tail.

Then that dead stare of the Grim.

The Shadowling had its eyes on them.

'He sees us,' Gwen said, her voice like ice.

The sound of the Grim was nearly unbearable, a bludgeoning force in their heads. Mermaids swarmed like sharks, teeth sharp as needles.

'Brace yourselves!' Lorelei called out – her voice maddeningly calm seeing as they were all about to die.

The ship creaked forward again.

'Gwen!' Astrid shouted, desperate. 'The spell! We have to use it!'

Gwen's eyes turned clear, fury burning through.

'No!' she shouted.

But she had to: it was the only way. That power, that burning light. It could incinerate these creatures.

Nearly frozen with horror and awe, they watched a huge mouth open beneath them. The giant mermaid, ready to eat.

'If she won't use it,' Astrid said to herself, 'then I will.'

She remembered the melody, the feel of it – like holy light, but subtly twisted. Opening her mouth, she let the first few notes pour out, feeling the buzz under her skin, the raw, unnatural power of it.

'Astrid, what are you doing?' Jonas asked, and Astrid forced herself to tune out the panic in her brother's voice.

She leaned into the spell, the way it crawled through her skin like it was alive. Fascinating.

'Astrid, no!' Gwen screamed, her voice like storm fire.

'Stop it, Astrid!' Magnus shouted now too. Angry in a way that was truly rare for him. 'You have no idea what you're doing! So help me, if you let another note of that spell come forth, I'll –'

Magnus was cut off as a sizzling bolt of power dripped from Astrid's fingertips. It landed beneath her, melting through the boat like acid. They didn't understand; none of them did. They had to do everything in their power to protect Gwen, no matter what. She caught a glimpse of Jonas, his eyes wide in horror and fascination at the twisted music and the terrible promise of what it could do.

The spindly edges of the melody were strange. Such an odd sensation, and yet familiar; a thing she knew. She pushed further, focusing on the rotten core of the spell.

It sounded like a memory, but whose?

Just as she had the thought, she heard it. A voice in her head. No, not just a voice – a message.

Remember us.

It was like when the earth communicated with them, except this was no plant or tree. It was a person.

Someone familiar. Someone from long ago.

Oh.

Distracted by her discovery, the spell caught in Astrid's throat. Before she could complete it, there was an abrupt *whip-whip* sound. Then another. The sound of metal, hard and fast, of things flying through the air.

The music was lost on her tongue, but she'd seen it: a flash, something from the past.

When she looked down again, the mermaid had been speared through her head by three glistening harpoons. Harpoons charmed with powerful magic, because just as the boat tipped forward again, the sea sure to claim them, there was a sharp hiss of Bloom, and the mermaid exploded.

11
Captain of the *Sea Reaper*

The world shattered. Sinew and blood, rot and flesh flying everywhere. Gasping for air. Freezing. Fires blazing. Skin like ice. Gwen grappled in the water. The ship was going down, the current pulling her under. She was dragged beneath the surface.

She needed to get Astrid and Jonas.

Astrid, who had tried to use a Cursed Melody. Wait – was that really her name?

Her vision split. Her mind cracked. She had known them by another name once. She blinked, and she was back in the sea.

Glancing down into the bubbling water, she found she was still clutching the damned book, her fingers refusing to let go.

The book, the spell. Was this a memory, or real?

Emerging from the water again, she spluttered, frantically looking around.

In the chaos of the sinking ship – the noise, the flotsam, the scattered bodies and burning wood – she searched for them. Panicking, Gwen thought of the mermaids down there. But the Grim had gone quiet.

'It's OK, Gwen, we're coming!' a voice shouted. Lorelei?

She was disorientated, everything moving too fast.

Her mind was tattered. A quilt, different lives and voices stitched together.

Rope wrapped round her waist, someone hauling her up on to a ship. She wondered if she should fight back, but she didn't have the energy. Flopping over, she coughed down into the wood, the book still clutched in her hand like a lifeline.

'That's it, lassie, get it all out.'

Sucking in a breath, Gwen collapsed on her back, staring up at the sky. The fog was gone. A man leaned over her, wearing a three-pointed hat with a feather, and a golden parrot on his shoulder. His eyes were so dark she could see her own reflection. Gwen almost laughed.

'Astrid . . . Jonas,' she wheezed.

'They're safe, Gwen.' Magnus's soothing voice. He was OK. 'But where did Astrid learn that spell, Gwen? What did you do?'

Gwen coughed, the world fading at the edges, but she clung on to it with the sheer fury in her belly.

'Astrid,' she groaned. How could she . . . How could Astrid do such a thing? 'Astrid!' She shouted this time, fire entering her voice.

'I'm here – get out of my way – I'm here, Gwenny,' Astrid cooed, coming to her side.

In her peripheral vision Gwen could see strange people, gold-toothed people, people with muscles the size of logs and blackened eyes. She ignored them, gripping on to reality, and gripping hold of Astrid's sodden shirt.

'You idiot!' she hissed. 'What were you thinking?'

Gwen's mind cracked again. She'd had this conversation before, in another life.

'Gwen's right,' Jonas chimed in, appearing over Astrid's shoulder. The shock on Astrid's face was immediate. 'That was utterly foolish.'

Gwen's vision flashed again, the air getting thinner. It had all been too much: reading the book, the spell, the attack. The Grim. She was fading, but she wasn't going without a fight.

'Gwen, I had to. I was protecting you all,' Astrid said, blue eyes like ice. 'I need to tell you something.' She paused, squinting down at Gwen, smoke billowing behind her as the *Tidebinder* burned somewhere nearby. 'You hear them too, don't you? The memories.'

But Gwen could hardly focus.

'This is not over,' Gwen breathed. Then, the next words came out of her mouth, but she wasn't sure they were her own: 'We can't make the same mistakes.'

Everything went black.

'Astrid!'

Gwen woke up in a panic, the sheets gripped in her hands. Searching around, she tried to make sense of where she was. They were moving – so, on board a ship. There were two bunk beds along the wall of a small room, the cabin smelled like hay and rum, and the sheets had yellow stains that she decided not to dwell on. There was silver light in the sconces on the wall, charmed. In the distance there was shouting and thumping, the ship alive with activity.

Someone had left a bowl of porridge on an overturned wooden crate next to the cot she was in. Not minding that it had gone cold, Gwen grabbed it greedily. She felt like she hadn't eaten in an elven decade.

There was something else on the crate, red scales glinting in the morning light that shone down through a tiny porthole.

'Why couldn't you have just drowned?' Gwen huffed at the book. The whispers in response were muted, like the book too was exhausted.

It came back to her slowly, then all at once, everything that had led up to the mermaids attacking the boat . . . and Astrid nearly using that spell.

Astrid. She had to find her. Astrid knew something . . . something Gwen wasn't sure she was ready to hear yet.

Some clothes had been left out for her, a heavy wool coat with a hat and scarf. She put them on and prepared to face whatever was on the other side of the door . . .

A riotous rumble of noise greeted her when she left the room. A huge woman with tattoos was asleep against the wall. There were cracked potion bottles lining the corridors, rags lying about and messes uncleaned. The scent of salty meat and spiced alcohol filled the air, and Gwen waved her hand as billows of steam flooded from an open door where she caught a glimpse of a tiny man with pointed ears frying bacon on a singing stove of green fire.

While the *Tidebinder* had been a model of order and luxury, this ship was chaotic as a storm.

Gwen found her way to the deck, where roughened crewmen were tossing barrels as though they were pillows. Someone shouted a command, and a huge man pulled on a rope. The sail fluttered, its cloth depicting a skull with fairy wings.

'You lost there, young lady?' the huge man asked her. When he spoke, Gwen saw that half his teeth were silver – and sharp.

'Gwendolyn, over here!' someone called across the deck. Lorelei.

Gwen did a double take at her clothes – a ruffled shirt with a purple waistcoat, rugged trousers and a huge utility belt. Her braids were pulled back off her face by a bandana, but they hung loose and long over her shoulder. She looked like . . .

Gwen gasped.

'This is a pirate ship!' Gwen said, everything coming together. 'And you . . . you're –'

Lorelei made a prim face. 'What I got up to in my past is neither here nor there,' she sniffed.

The silver-toothed man let out a boom of a laugh. 'So says our Lady Viper.'

Lorelei went rigid as a board, glowering at the man. 'That's quite enough, Silverfang.'

The man – Silverfang – chuckled under his breath and turned back to his work on the boat.

Lorelei gestured for Gwen to follow her. 'Now come along, dear. Magnus will be keen to see you up and about. He's with the captain, and I fear the captain'll want to meet you too.'

'Wait,' Gwen said, standing firm. 'What happened to the twins? Astrid – where is she?'

Lorelei *tsked*, hands on her hips – a gesture Gwen was used to from her, but now seeming so different in those garments.

'They're all fine, Gwendolyn. You'd better believe Astrid got a good talking-to from Magnus. She's in her cabin, waiting to speak to you.'

Gwen remembered what she'd said, just before she'd fallen into blackness. The urgency in her voice.

'You've been asleep for a good twelve hours,' Lorelei told her. 'Come, I'll take you to Magnus. We can explain everything.'

Gwen couldn't get Astrid out of her head as Lorelei ushered her through the boat, scowling at the rest of the crew as they watched them curiously.

'Is this *your* crew, from before? Does Thomas know about any of this?' Gwen couldn't stop herself; the questions kept pouring out even as they hopped over ropes and narrowly avoided flying barrels. 'You called them to rescue us, didn't you? That's what that fife you took with you from Faymore Manor was about, wasn't it – it called them?'

Lorelei paused at this. 'You were spying?'

Gwen nodded.

'Good lass. Yes, I called them. I was going to have them kidnap you and the twins.'

Gwen nearly choked. 'What?'

But there was no further explanation, as they'd arrived at the Captain's Quarters. Inside, it was smoky with pungent incense. Curious treasures covered every wall and surface, the whole place overflowing with gold, like in tales of hoarding dragons.

Here, amongst the treasures, they found Magnus sharing tea with a man at a desk in disarray. It was the man she remembered from before, with the golden parrot on his shoulder and eyes black as outer space.

In the corner sat Jonas in a high-backed chair, with not a hair out of place, thank goodness. It was weird seeing him without his sister, but Gwen couldn't help feeling relieved. She wasn't sure how she would react towards Astrid now. One thing that was welcome, though: Buttonbug was resting in his lap, the poor thing clearly still rattled.

'Thank god you're OK,' Jonas said, sighing with relief as he pushed a chair out for Gwen. 'Astrid's been pulling her hair out. Says she needs you.'

'Good,' Gwen grumbled. Then mumbled as she sat down, 'I'm glad you're both OK, too.'

Jonas's lips twitched. 'I'm sure Astrid will be thrilled to hear it. My foolish sister is currently meditating in our cabin. Won't tell me why, until you're present.'

Gwen raised an eyebrow.

'I have spoken to Astrid,' Magnus said, his voice tight, and Gwen had to wonder how much trouble she'd actually been in. 'She told us you need Rupert's old Savonnette.'

Gwen suddenly realized Jonas wasn't wearing his pendant, only to then spot it on the captain's desk, in its own cleared space amongst the disarray, alongside Astrid's piece of the Savonnette.

'So, what the hell is going on?' Gwen demanded.

The captain chuckled, a hearty sound.

'Quite the introduction!'

Up close, he was obviously handsome, with braided onyx hair and bronze skin kissed darker by the sun. He wore a gold-lined velvet jacket that hummed with protective spells, and when he moved, Gwen saw there was something strapped round his ruffled shirt – a dagger, in a sheath that looked like a snake. More precisely, a viper.

What had the huge man called Lorelei – *'Lady Viper'*?

'I'm Captain Dorian Kane, and this is my ship, the *Sea Reaper*, and you are my prisoners.' This might have been an alarming thing to say, except he winked at Lorelei, who immediately groaned and put her head in her hands.

'Perhaps I should explain,' Magnus said, side-eyeing the captain. 'Captain Kane here was alerted to our whereabouts by Lorelei.' Magnus didn't sound too thrilled about this. 'She was planning on leaving us –'

'Magnus, you know I was getting help,' she interrupted. 'And I think we can all agree it's lucky that I did.' There was an edge to her voice, an old argument dragged back up again. 'There are things the Order simply doesn't know about magic or things it refuses to engage with. If we're going to help Gwen and the twins fight the Shadowling and the Grim, we need to start thinking outside the box.'

While Gwen balked at Lorelei's outburst, the captain seemed to approve, his parrot squawking on his shoulder.

'The Order of Pendragon,' Captain Kane said, his mouth twisting as he spat on the floor. 'They don't hold any power over us out here.'

Now this thoroughly confused Gwen. These people on the ship were definitely Bloom Bloods, so how . . .

'They're Rogues,' Jonas said, a thrill in his voice. 'Bloom Bloods who don't follow the Order . . .'

'. . . or any order at all,' Magnus added, somewhat amused.

'But that's impossible,' Gwen said. 'The Order keeps track of all Bloom Bloods, all over the world.'

Captain Kane guffawed, banging his hand on the table so that all the trinkets danced.

'Not on the seas, they don't. They belong to us Rogues. We don't believe in sectioning off magic with wards or living separately from magical creatures: we follow the old ways. From when humans and magic coexisted. No Magisters or Ambassadors or poncy Shadow Library. It used to be kings and fairies, monsters and men, all living in harmony.'

Gwen, baffled, asked, 'But don't you come across Red Bloods out here?'

'We have our own ways of keeping hidden from them,' he replied, a glint in his eye that Gwen wasn't sure she liked.

'Now, the little blonde changelings tell us you're looking for a sword?'

It took a moment for Gwen to realize who he meant, and when she did, she narrowed her eyes at Jonas.

'Did they?' Gwen said.

'Gwen, dear,' Magnus began, concern wrinkling his face. 'Astrid told us you read the book?'

'Yeah, I did,' Gwen snapped. 'And we won't be doing that ever again.'

The concern melted off Magnus's face, replaced by an almost proud look that made Gwen's cheeks warm. 'I think that's very wise,' he said.

'When I was . . . a member of this crew,' Lorelei began, clearing her throat sheepishly, 'we searched for magical relics and hidden temples. We believe we may have found things that could help you uncover your link to the Shadowling, and the twins' curious powers.'

Gwen listened intently. Her bizarre experience with the book of Cursed Melodies had left an odd, anxious feeling in her chest, knowing she was on the very cusp of understanding what all those weird voices and memories meant.

'So, what we've got here is a broken map,' Captain Kane said, gesturing down at the Savonnette. 'And if we put all the bits together, we reckon they start to look an awful lot like a place called the Spiral Isles, just north of the Borealis Sanctum. That's where we reckon this here weapon must be. So if we fix the Savonnette properly, it could guide you to the sword's exact location.'

Magnus hummed his agreement, his features pensive. 'We're stopping off at a small Rogue settlement, Runefjord. They've told me there's a blacksmith there with the necessary skill.'

'And there's a temple,' Lorelei added, 'that you'll want to visit, Gwen. We've already sent word of our arrival.'

Magnus grimaced at this, but didn't protest.

Gwen tried to follow along, but something didn't make sense.

'What do you get in return for this?' she asked the captain bluntly. 'Why would you help us when we're members of the Order?'

'Because you, dear girl,' he said, a dark spark in his eyes, 'are going to kill the Shadowling, the beast that stole my wife and her family from me.'

A taut silence filled the room, and Lorelei rubbed her arms in discomfort. The captain glanced over at her, his eyes shadowed.

'I have an issue to raise,' Jonas said, interrupting the strange tension. 'Someone on the *Tidebinder* must have broken the protective runes. We need to know who and why, and, on that matter, why on earth Prince Theodore completely disappeared just before the attack.'

The captain raised an eyebrow.

'The Order's princeling?' He said it with distaste. 'You think he might have caused all this?'

'Well, he vanished off the ship,' Jonas explained, stroking Buttonbug's fur as she purred contentedly. 'It's very peculiar. We can't rule out that he could be infected with the Grim, a minion of the Shadowling. We need to know where he is.'

The captain grinned, that dark glint in his eye again as he stood up. 'Well, we have some good news for you, then.'

They followed him down into the depths of the ship, where moisture seemed to have leaked into the walls. There was a constant dripping, the dark corridors groaning eerily. It was here that they found the brig, with four cells in total. Metal bars hummed with ward magic, spells that would stop anyone inside from performing instrumentation.

Each cell had chains attached to the shiplap walls, but only one set of them was attached to a prisoner.

'Here he is,' the captain announced, gleeful. 'We caught him in a dinghy heading away from the ship before we got you all.'

Jonas's eyes went wide, and Buttonbug jumped down from his shoulder. 'Oh my god.'

There, chained to a wall, on a creaking cot, his clothes and hair utterly filthy, was Prince Teddy.

12

Stowaways

'Finally, some civilized company,' the prince drawled. With a dark bruise on his jaw, his lips could only twitch in an approximation of his usual smirk. Jonas couldn't help but be at least a little impressed by his consistency.

'Oh, for heaven's sake,' Lorelei moaned, smacking Captain Kane on his shoulder. 'You can't keep Beatrice's son in a cage, you buffoon.'

He seemed genuinely surprised by her outburst, as if he'd thought she would be impressed instead. His golden parrot squawked on his shoulder, which Lorelei levelled with an intimidating look.

'Easy, sunshine,' the captain cooed, and it almost seemed like he was speaking to Lorelei. 'We found this boy dozing in a dinghy sailing away from the *Tidebinder*. Mighty suspicious, if you ask me.'

'You found me passed out!' the prince retorted, gritting his teeth as if he'd been going round in circles.

'*Tomay-to*, tomato.'

'Enough,' Magnus interrupted, fire in his voice that made Buttonbug's fur bristle. 'Theodore, what precisely happened?'

The prince sighed. 'Well, one moment I was tied up in

the apothecary, and the next I was being taken aboard by a bunch of bumbling pirates.'

Magnus and Lorelei glanced at each other.

Lorelei asked, 'Who tied you up?'

Heat burned through Jonas's cheeks, and he thanked the Twelve Spells that at least Astrid was still in their cabin and not here to witness this.

Prince Teddy was just about to open his mouth, sure to say something that would have Jonas wanting to throw himself overboard, when Gwen – blessed, wonderful Gwen – stepped forward.

'We want to speak to the prince alone,' she announced, with a surprising amount of authority to her tone. 'Just Jonas and me. If he *is* infected with the Grim, perhaps I can hear it, but I need peace and quiet.' Then she leaned over to Jonas to whisper, 'We're even now, for you taking my side in this whole reading-the-book thing.'

The captain blinked. 'You're going to interrogate him . . . without us?' He looked put out, as if Gwen had just suggested taking away his favourite toy.

Lorelei elbowed him in the ribs. *An odd relationship these two have indeed*, Jonas thought.

'Yes, of course,' Lorelei said. 'We'll be on hand if you need us.'

Magnus offered an encouraging shoulder-squeeze to Gwen as they left, but something about the droll smile playing over his lips told Jonas he had a good idea of who had tied the prince up. And how utterly mortifying was that?

Once they were gone, Prince Teddy leaned back against the wall, so casually you'd almost believe he'd chosen to be chained up.

'Can you really do that?' he asked, raising an eyebrow. 'Hear if a person has sided with the Shadowling?'

Gwen snorted. 'Heck, no,' she hissed, after making sure no one was listening. 'I couldn't even tell that Sister Seraphina was so riddled with the Grim she was barely human.'

'Well, in your defence, neither could any of us.'

Jonas watched the exchange with growing discomfort. Someone had tampered with the runes, and he needed to find out who. But he also needed to get Gwen to speak to Astrid so she could explain what had happened with the spell. Astrid had refused to tell Jonas until Gwen was awake, so it had to be now. They needed to sort this whole thing out so they could get on with saving the world.

Which meant he had to question the prince on his own.

'Gwen,' he said, sighing. 'You should speak to Astrid. I know you want to. I can deal with this.'

Hesitating, Gwen was clearly conflicted.

'Trouble in paradise?' Prince Teddy said, unhelpfully, as he stood and came over to crouch by the bars where Buttonbug had settled, his fingers scratching at her fur.

'Quiet, you,' Gwen spat, and yet the prince's words seemed to spark something in her. 'What Astrid did . . .' Gwen gulped, unsure. 'Jonas, I begged her not to use that spell. We can't let her try to cast it again. Ever.'

Genuine fear had crept into Gwen's voice, the words shaky.

'Maybe you can talk some sense into her,' Jonas offered. 'If anyone can persuade her, it's you.'

Gwen sighed but her fists clenched, a fresh wave of determination washing over her.

'Fine. But come find us when you finish here,' she instructed.

With Gwen marching off up the stairs to the cabins again, Jonas was left alone, with the prince. Fantastic.

'Well, that's one way of getting me alone,' the prince said, sighing as he stood again and returned to the dirty cot. He looked up at Jonas through his lashes, a captivating glint in his eye. 'So, what's going on with your sister?'

'I wish I knew,' Jonas said softly. Then, shaking his head, he trudged up to the bars. 'But more importantly, what the hell happened to you?'

The prince shrugged. 'I wish I knew,' he repeated back.

The constant dripping through the wood was the only sound to pierce the awkward silence – Jonas growing increasingly annoyed, and the prince not seeming to care. Jonas scooped up Buttonbug, and, in that moment, he became suddenly aware of how cold it actually was down there. They were far north of Scotland now, deep into the Norwegian Sea. In this part of the ship, the icy waters bled cold into the very walls.

Trapped in the cell, the prince looked almost tragic – a rare, beautiful animal caught in a cage.

'Here,' Jonas said, handing him his own cloak.

Prince Teddy took it without a word. For just a second, their fingers touched.

Jonas pulled back like he'd been burned.

'I didn't do it, you know,' the prince said, looking stung at his reaction. 'I didn't break the runes, or call the mermaids.' There was a sadness in his voice that unmoored Jonas's frustration with him. 'There were people on that ship I've known since I was a boy. I would never, ever do something like that.'

This, at least, seemed honest to Jonas.

The prince sighed. 'And I know she seemed scary, but Isobel Thorn was a really good friend of my mothers.'

The name went through Jonas like a bolt of lightning, the memory so gruesome he'd nearly suppressed it.

'The Black Savonnettes,' he spluttered, the words getting ahead of him. 'They're weapons, right? What do they do? How do we use them?'

Reaching into his trouser pocket, Jonas found it – the Black Savonnette Lieutenant Thorn had given them before she died. It sat heavy in his hand, an alive thing, its oily sheen making it look almost like it was wriggling. Running down his shoulder, Buttonbug sniffed at it with her little cat nose, her soft dark fur and feathery antennae stiffening in reaction to the Bloom.

The lieutenant had risked everything to find them, clutching on to life until this object was in their hands. She must have wanted them to use it.

'Oh, er, I don't know,' Prince Teddy confessed. 'My mothers called them a *"last resort"*, whatever that means. Only the most trusted soldiers were given them.'

Jonas pondered the information, staring at the object like it might start speaking. Or moving.

'Listen, I've heard them talking about the plan,' Teddy said, interrupting his thoughts and coming to stand closer, a crumb of his usual bravado returning. It seemed more forced than usual. 'I'm going to prove I'm innocent. I'm willing to send a letter by peregrine falcon to Mother stating that we are all well and still heading to the Borealis Sanctum. I can make it sound as if it was all a total coincidence that we bumped into a Rogue pirate ship, and I can broker some sort of peace. If, that is, they deliver me safely.'

The words hung in the air, and although the prince wouldn't dare to admit it, Jonas could see he was frightened.

The Rogue pirates clearly despised the Order. He was deep in enemy territory.

Jonas was tempted to lord it over him, to make him squirm. But somehow, after all that Jonas had witnessed – the ship going down, Astrid nearly using a Cursed Melody – he didn't much feel like teasing anyone.

'I won't let them hurt you,' he said, leaning into the bars.

A breath, and Teddy leaned in too, his face softening, only for a moment. Gratitude. And something else, a flicker in those starry eyes, something sweet that put a fist round Jonas's heart and squeezed.

And then Teddy smiled, a rebellious little curl of his lips. The mask was back on. 'So, you trust me?' he asked.

Jonas sighed. 'I'm trying.'

He left the prince there while he headed back to the deck. He needed to find Astrid. He wanted to feel their bond and know she understood every weird and confusing thought in his head. But he also needed to give her time with Gwen. Jonas conjured the image of her on the sinking boat, that twisted spell spilling from her lips. It had been terrifying. Astrid could not have known the way it felt under his own skin as she had sung that song. Whispers of malice, darkness trying to dig deep into her blood. Delicious, addictive, *evil* power that wanted nothing more than to use her voice to lay the world to waste.

Magnus had been right. Whatever magic lay in that book, they needed to leave it well alone. Astrid needed to leave it alone, and Jonas feared for the first time in his life that he might not be the right person to get through to her.

This was Gwen's task.

Outside, the sea was calm, but the air was cold, and Jonas was starting to regret leaving his cloak with the prince.

Buttonbug curled tighter round his shoulders, the two seeking each other's warmth. The crew of the *Sea Reaper* seemed immune to the freezing temperature, their writhing tattoos on full display as they hauled and shouted and went about their work.

One of the crew – a broad-shouldered woman with a scar down her cheek – spat on the floor, before stamping her foot and singing a spell to help another crew member haul a net of fish. They emptied them haphazardly over the wooden deck and began killing and gutting them right then and there. Jonas watched with gory fascination as they threw the guts back into the water, hands bloody. Gulls circled above, waiting to feast on the detritus.

This crew was certainly different from the crew of the *Tidebinder*.

Jonas thought he would find such things gross or cruel, but there was a sort of poetry in the way they handled the fish. A rhythm to the work that matched the beat of the waves.

'Want to join us, little changeling boy?'

Jonas lifted his nose at one of the jerking dead fish as the pirate passed him a sharp knife. He supposed he had time to learn a new skill.

'Why do you call us that? *"Changelings"*?'

She laughed, knotted hair falling over her face. She pushed it back, smearing blood on her forehead.

'You've got the air about you,' she said.

The other pirate, an olive-toned man with wooden piercings through his nose, murmured in agreement.

'Inhuman.'

Jonas watched as they put the knife through each fish, pulling out the insides in one go. It was disgusting, yet oddly therapeutic. He tried his hand at it, finding that the knife glided through the dead creatures smoothly. He pinched a mass of guts and fed it to Buttonbug, who lapped it up greedily.

'You won't hear this from the Order, but humans and fae once lived together,' the scarred woman said. 'Elves, fairies, centaurs, sirens, magical creatures with their own societies. They were the first to be extinguished when the Red Bloods decided magical things were too dangerous. Then they came for the witches.'

Jonas pondered this as he gutted another fish. They had learned about witch trials in school. Now he understood that it was no coincidence that Lady Jane Grey had established the Order in secret only ten years after the practice of the craft became a capital crime. She'd saved the last remaining dregs of the Bloom Blooded world and died for it.

'If the Order wants to bring back magic, why not the fae too?'

'They can't, or they won't. Too complicated. They like the magic they can study and maintain. They want to keep the peace they have with the Red Bloods.' She spat on the floor again.

'Bullshit, we say,' a man nearby chimed in, voice gruff. 'It's time for magic to come back into the open, for the Red Bloods to know about it, and for the chaos of the old ways to return.'

It was a dangerous thought. The Order of Pendragon protected Red Bloods from monsters and magical things without them even knowing. Even though it sounded as if Red Bloods had nearly wiped them out once upon a time.

Throwing a chunk of guts into the sea, Jonas couldn't help but think of the Shadowling. He'd told them that he wanted to end humanity. He saw people as a plague on the earth, both Bloom Bloods and Red Bloods. Where did that hatred come from? What had happened in the past to bring about all these terrible divides and animosity?

'Maybe it's only a matter of time until magical things cannot be contained any more,' Jonas said, staring out at the sea.

And it was then, with this thought in his head, that something flew out of the water and on to the deck. Grey fur and slobbering mouth, it came darting at him, knocking him right over into the pile of dead fish. Buttonbug went flapping into the air, hissing.

'What in the –'

The thing licked him across the face. It smelled like sweat and salt water.

Jonas sat up so he could see the beast. And there he was. Tongue lolling to the side, that red-headed boy Eddie's otter-dog, Biscuit.

The pirate lady cackled, turning to call to the rest of the crew. 'Looks like we got ourselves a stowaway.'

13

Who Are They?

Astrid lay on the floor of the cabin, hammocks swinging above her. An empty plate of food sat beside her; a strange, pointy-eared pirate had brought it to her. There was an empty feeling at her chest where her pendant usually sat. She'd given it up, in the hopes of helping Gwen. Everything she did was to help Gwen. Magnus had to understand that.

If he could forgive Lorelei for summoning the pirates, he could forgive Astrid. They were both trying to solve a problem.

The Bloom was still bubbling under her skin from nearly casting the spell. A sensation like sucking poison, like her body wanted the rot out, but the rot was fighting back.

It was fascinating, and terrible.

It made her blood boil. Fury. Destruction. The spell begged to be completed. To use her body as a tool for desolation. A dangerous thing indeed, but necessary. She was sure of that, because of what she had learned.

It sat on the tip of her tongue, as though waiting. She thought about the melody of it, how it had lit up in her body, familiar from a memory.

The question was, whose memory was it?

Someone – or *someones* – were trying to communicate with them from the past. People who'd fought the Shadowling before, who'd used the spells in *The Cursed Melodies*. That's what Gwen was hearing. Someone from the past. That's who was guiding her to the sword.

Knowing this, finally understanding it, made singing the spell worth it. Magnus had been so upset, the same fear and anger parents experience when their children foolishly put themselves in danger. But she was alive and well. No one had been harmed.

How could she explain it to them? She'd learned so much from nearly using just one spell from the book; what else was there to discover? It felt like all the answers were just out of reach. If she could just hear that voice again . . .

She'd do anything to find the truth. For Gwen.

The door opened. Astrid sat up.

Gwen. Perfect and furious Gwen. Astrid wanted nothing more than to grab her, to hold her close, to smell that sweet bonfire scent she carried with her. But the rot of the Cursed Melody still blistered under Astrid's skin. Her fingers still itched to cause chaos.

Astrid pushed the feeling down, calming herself. 'I've been waiting for you,' she said, crossing her legs. 'Close the door.'

Gwen did as instructed, coming to stand over her. The room was filled with animal skins and woven blankets. Astrid held one out for Gwen to wrap round her shoulders. It was getting cold.

Gwen snatched it from her hand. 'I'm still mad at you,' she grumbled. 'But I need you.'

The confession made Astrid's pulse quicken. 'Where's my brother?' she asked, swallowing. She had expected them to come together.

'He's with Prince Teddy.'

Astrid certainly hadn't been expecting that.

Gwen shook her head. 'Long story, but Teddy's being held captive on the ship.'

That was explanation enough for Astrid. She was sure Jonas would handle it.

Astrid watched Gwen as she wrapped the blanket round her shoulders. She was nervous, chewing at her bottom lip, still refusing to sit down. Astrid knew she'd upset her – hell, she'd upset everyone, including her brother. She didn't regret it, but she needed to put it right.

'What I did, Gwen . . . Everything I do is to keep you safe.'

Gwen sighed, shaking her head, then it all came out at once. 'I know that, but *you can't*. You must believe me. There's something wrong with that book, with the spells inside it. It did something to my body when I cast it. I don't want to find out what would happen to you if you did the same.'

Astrid nodded. 'I know,' she said calmly. 'I felt it . . . feel it.'

Gwen paused, giving Astrid a wary look. 'You did?'

Astrid nodded again. 'It's still there, in my body. Remnants of the Bloom. It wants me to cause harm, and it's very compelling,' she confessed, aware of the horror building in Gwen's face.

Astrid's fingers twitched again, like the residual Bloom wanted her to hit or scratch. But her mind won.

'You're shaking,' Gwen said, her concern rising.

'I'm OK,' Astrid tried to reassure her. 'I've got it under control.'

Gwen shook her head, furious. 'You must never, ever attempt to sing it again. I know you're strong-willed, but not even you can handle this thing. Whatever magic is in *The Cursed Melodies* – it was locked away for a reason, and I won't let you experiment on yourself to find out why.'

Astrid couldn't help but chuckle, earning a scowl from Gwen.

'And yet . . . the spell – that's not really why you're here, is it?' Astrid said, glancing up at the girl whose thick brows were furrowed in determination. There was an air between them, electric. They were on the precipice of something; they both felt it. 'Tell me, Gwen, what is going on in your head? What did you feel when the ship fell into the water?'

Gwen crossed her arms over her chest, protective and indignant.

'You know already, don't you?' she huffed, her nose scrunching up in that way Astrid found so delightful. 'You've noticed it . . . something in me: it's changing, or waking up.' Gwen rubbed her forehead, her expression pained like she had a headache. 'My mind is confused. I feel like . . . like there are other people inside my head. It's like I finally got rid of the Shadowling lurking in my mind, and now there's something else.'

'The spell,' Astrid said, and Gwen glanced at her. 'It revealed something to me.'

Sighing, Gwen gave in.

'I don't condone any of this, but . . . urgh. What? What did you learn?'

Astrid grabbed Gwen's wrist, pulling her down to her level. The dark Bloom still under her skin was quiet, for now.

'Come here.' Astrid held out both hands for her to take. Gwen conceded, her skin warm to the touch. Gwen was always warm, like she had a fire burning inside her. The two sat opposite each other with their legs crossed, like a prayer circle. Astrid took a deep breath; Gwen did the same. Their heartbeats fell in sync with each other. It felt like they were about to perform a spell. Perhaps they were, in a way.

'Using that melody, it was like I knew it already,' Astrid explained. 'Or more like someone else had known it. Someone who was trying to communicate with me. Someone who had wielded the sword you're going to use to kill the Shadowling.' Astrid's eyes flicked up to Gwen's, holding her gaze.

Gwen's eyes widened. She didn't say a word; she didn't need to. Confused, she shook her head, pulling her hands out of Astrid's. 'But how is that possible?' she practically groaned.

Astrid shrugged: she wasn't sure herself. There was still so much she was hungry to understand.

'I think history is repeating itself. Or perhaps it's trying to fix itself,' Astrid suggested. 'And, well . . . it's using you to do it.'

At this, Gwen huffed, falling back against the floor until she was staring up at the ceiling of the cabin, her hair splayed out like ink.

Astrid came to join her, the two side by side.

'OK,' Gwen said, determined. 'So, someone in the past used the sword to defeat the Shadowling and now they're guiding me to do the same thing. So, we just need to find out who they were, and what they did. If the Shadowling was locked away once, then we can do it again, right?'

'We'll find out who they are,' Astrid assured her.

Gwen's eyes lit up. 'The temple under the castle at Windsor was full of relics from the past that seemed to be linked to the Shadowling. They're taking me to a temple at Runefjord, too. There will be something there to give us a clue. I'm sure of it.'

A smile spread over Gwen's face as she propped herself up on one elbow. It was a true, beaming thing that filled Astrid's heart until she thought it might burst. 'Astrid, I think we can do this. We might actually be able to defeat him.'

Astrid edged a little closer, taking in the delicate curve of Gwen's nose, her thick, heavy lashes. She was so beautiful, so fierce. 'I think we've only just scratched the surface of all the amazing things you're going to do, Gwen.'

Astrid leaned in more. She wasn't even sure what she planned to do. Kiss her? Hold her? She was simply overwhelmed by the desire to be close to Gwen. She wanted it more than she'd ever wanted anything. Almost as if she were being compelled by forces greater than her. Which had her thinking . . .

'Gwen . . .' Astrid began, her eyes locked on Gwen's lips. 'Do you ever feel like the past wants more from us than just to defeat the Shadowling?'

'What?' Gwen gasped, a small sound. A revelation.

Astrid didn't need to answer: they both knew.

'I think . . .' Gwen swallowed, wetting her lips. She wanted this too – Astrid was sure of it. She felt that same pull. 'I don't know . . .'

The door crashed open, a great clattering sound.

Gwen quickly moved away. For Astrid, it was like having a piece of her heart violently pulled out.

'Urgh, Queen's mercy, get down!' Jonas shouted. He wasn't alone. Flapping around his head was Buttonbug, fur flying. And following behind him, jumping up like an excited pup, was Biscuit. 'Someone get this damned beast to leave me alone!'

Astrid cut her eyes at Gwen, but Gwen refused to look at her. She could see Gwen's chest heaving, her breath ragged, but the moment was gone.

There was an aching hole inside Astrid that she now knew could only be filled by one thing. It seemed, though, that right then she would have to make friends with the pain.

'A stowaway?' Astrid said instead, turning to face her brother and the beastie. Her voice was calm, measured, even as her heart felt squeezed. 'What a clever thing, to follow us here.'

'Ummm, what is that?' Gwen asked, backing away slightly. Likely from the smell of the poor thing.

Jonas pushed the otter-dog down, patting his tilted head. Biscuit's tongue lolled to the side.

'This was one of the younger crewmen's pets, Biscuit,' Jonas explained to Gwen. 'He . . . well, he's alone now.'

Astrid saw as well as felt the guilt on Jonas's face. Eddie Clam had been a sweet boy. He hadn't deserved to go down with the ship. No one had.

'He must miss his master terribly,' Astrid lamented, rubbing under Biscuit's chin.

At this, Gwen's fists balled at her sides, a look of fierce resolve overtaking her.

'Don't worry, boy,' she said, leaning down to pat the creature. 'I'll make the Shadowling pay for everything he's done. We're getting close now.'

Astrid glanced at her brother, and he too looked back at her. There was a question poised in his expression. One about Gwen, about their conversation.

'So, what amazing discoveries has performing an evil spell blessed you with, dearest sister?'

She held his gaze, that identical glacial blue. Did he feel it too? Did he hear them? The voices of the past? Were they all just pieces on a chessboard that had been set up thousands of years ago?

'Well, first of all, I didn't actually cast the spell.'

'Semantics,' Jonas said, rolling his eyes. 'Just tell me what you found.'

'That this has all happened before,' she told him, the words heavy. 'And this time, the people it happened to in the past are trying to achieve a different outcome.'

'Oh?' Jonas looked at Gwen, then back at his sister, then at Gwen again. His eyes went wide. '. . . Oh.' Astrid felt the realization spark inside him like a seed sprouting into the light. 'And this is good? We can trust these . . . *voices?*' he said, his words distant as he processed their entire lives with new understanding.

Gwen nodded vigorously.

'Yes, it's really good. I think, with their knowledge, whoever *they* are, we truly have a chance of defeating the Shadowling. I'll see if I can find a way to communicate with them at the temple in Runefjord. Maybe they can even tell me what I need to do with the sword once we find it.'

'Quite,' Astrid hummed, thinking to herself that reading the book had, in fact, been beneficial to them all, and worth the risk. 'And you, dearest brother – what of the prince?'

Jonas sighed, coming over to pet Biscuit again. 'I fear he might be innocent.'

Astrid tutted. 'Oh dear.'

Gwen, on the other hand, was clearly confused. 'Wait, isn't that a good thing?' she asked.

Jonas stepped away to stare out of the porthole at the wide expanse of frosty blue. 'It would be, yes . . .' he said. 'Except, if Prince Theodore is innocent, then who destroyed the runes?'

14

The Dance at Runefjord

To the Esteemed Magister Ragnar of the Order of Pendragon's Arctic Sector.

I hope this letter finds you well, though the circumstances of its writing are less than pleasant. I write to assure you that I, and the members of the Faymore Cluster, are in good health, despite the exceptional tragedy we have experienced. The ship was subjected to a deadly attack by a pod of Grim-possessed mermaids. Although the crew fought valiantly, none but myself and the Faymore Cluster survived. The Tidebinder and her shipmen have regrettably been lost to the seas. It was only by sheer good fortune that we were charitably rescued by a ship of Rogue pirates who have offered us passage to the Borealis Sanctum and have assured my and the Faymores' safe return to the Order.

The course remains as planned, and I have full confidence that we will arrive as expected. However, it would be wise for all parties involved to avoid any unnecessary actions that might complicate matters. While my well-being is not in question, interference at this juncture could lead to . . . complications that none of us desire. I trust you will understand the delicacy of the situation.

Rest assured, the Order's patience and discretion will be appreciated.

Sanguis Noster, Officium Nostrum.

Prince Theodore Doria of the Western European Faction of the Order of Pendragon

The *Sea Reaper* arrived in port at the Rogue settlement of Runefjord three days later. Hidden between two crumbling statues carved into the mountains, the air shimmered and heaved as the boat passed through. Children ran up the gangway to greet them, chubby-cheeked and smothered in fur-lined ponchos. They waved excitedly at the new arrivals.

So deep into winter, the sun was already low by late afternoon. Snow-tipped mountains once home to Vikings and fairies cradled the fjords, their jagged forms like sleeping giants. Far in the distance, on one of the hills, an ancient melody of Bloom groaned like tired bones and echoed its way down to the village – the old temple that Lorelei wanted to take Gwen to.

Gwen stepped off the ship with newfound determination. Tomorrow she would visit the temple, and the twins would fix the Savonnette. Victory felt within her grasp, with all the missing answers just over the horizon. They were going to do it. They would locate the sword and discover how the Shadowling had been defeated in the past, and Gwen could finally obtain justice for all the people he had hurt.

'How many places are there like this?' Gwen asked Lorelei. She didn't need to emphasize what she meant: magical settlements where the Order had no control.

'Rogues have settlements like this all over the globe. We . . . I mean *they* sail between them, a life of land and sea.'

'I'll take land, thank you,' Jonas said. And with that, the twins were off, flushed with relief as they ran to the grass beyond the pebbly shore, leaving Gwen and the rest of their Cluster behind on the gangway. Buttonbug flapped around them in excitement, while Biscuit ran in circles; they were growing quite the menagerie.

Jonas's nose and fingers were turning red at the tips from the cold, as were Astrid's, but they were in bliss, curling their fingers into the earth. Gwen could only imagine how hard it must have been for them being stuck at sea.

And then Astrid laughed, the sound gripping Gwen's heart.

She remembered what it was like to be so close to Astrid, to feel her breath against her cheek. She'd wanted it. For Astrid to lean in, to kiss her.

They hadn't spoken of it since.

Astrid, as if she had some sixth sense for Gwen's emotions, suddenly turned to look right at her.

Heat burned through Gwen's cheeks, and she half feared the snow would start melting at her feet. The past was going to help them – great. Amazing. But Astrid was right: it seemed the past also wanted something else from them. Something that made Gwen's breath catch in her throat.

'Is everything all right, Gwen?'

Gwen glanced up at Magnus as they walked to the grass. He was dressed in black furs so thick he could almost have been mistaken for a bear from a distance. His face had that concerned look, the one that always made Gwen squirm.

'Nothing! I mean, yes, I'm fine,' Gwen said, stumbling over her words.

They all convened on the grass, waiting for the captain. There was someone missing from the disembarkation. Jonas was the one to ask about him.

'Umm, what's to happen to the prince?' he asked.

'Some of the crew are staying on the ship,' the captain told him. 'They'll watch him.'

Jonas stared back at the ship, like he was almost thinking of staying too.

'Ahoy!' a boy called from up ahead. He was perhaps not much older than Gwen and the twins, and he was tall, with a sharp, pale face and shadows under his eyes that almost looked like bruises. He might have seemed creepy – spectral, even – if not for his wide grin and the way the children jumped around him adoringly.

'Shay, my lad,' the captain greeted him, coming to ruffle his long dark hair. 'How is the feast coming along?'

Other pirates strolled past, too, greeting him warmly.

'As planned. Is this them? The ones from your letter?' He gave Gwen and the twins a once-over while the little kids hid behind him, suddenly shy in front of strangers.

The captain winked. 'These three here are going to save the world from the magical plague, and this here –' he paused to clap Lorelei on the shoulder, proud – 'is the greatest woman you'll ever meet.'

Shay grinned wider, until something caught his eye and all the joy dropped from his face. His eyes were on Magnus – or rather, his Savonnette.

It seemed the Order was not welcome here.

Magnus quickly cleared his throat, wary of the sudden shift. 'Perhaps we should all head inside out of the cold, hmm?'

'Quite,' Lorelei said. She seemed almost bashful. 'And Dorian, what's this about a feast?'

'It's a celebration tonight, my dear,' the captain said. 'We can save the hard work for tomorrow.'

'Celebration?' Astrid questioned. 'Whatever for?'

'You, of course, little changeling,' Captain Kane chuckled, clapping her on the back so hard she stumbled forward. 'We're celebrating you three.'

A celebration in Runefjord was not, as it turned out, a small affair. Gwen and the twins were ushered to the inn where they would be staying and given appropriate clothes for the occasion. Lorelei was in Gwen's room with her, helping with her dress and jewellery. The rooms were simple, wooden beams and beds with little handcrafted oak ornaments lining the shelves that jostled every time the floor shook from the party downstairs.

'Pirates, honestly,' Lorelei muttered as she pulled the dress tighter. 'Any excuse to drink themselves silly.'

Gwen looked at her own reflection in the tall wood-framed mirror and gasped. Her hair had been braided in twists and plaits, and the emerald fabric of her dress flowed down and pooled at her ankles. Round her neck were cords adorned with bone charms and runes.

She looked like some ancient thing. A deity from another time. The very thing they all saw her as. A force that would stop an ancient evil.

'I look . . .'

'You look powerful,' Lorelei told her.

Downstairs in the tavern the music and mayhem were growing in volume. The floor shook again.

The music made Gwen's heart race, a wild beat. She could do this, she told herself again. She would find a way to defeat the Shadowling.

She followed Lorelei down into the tavern, where the full extent of the chaos revealed itself.

A stone hearth was spitting stories built from Fire. Tankards of frothing liquid flew through the air. People danced and stomped their feet while fiddles and flutes played. Spells were used haphazardly, fizzing and whistling. They saw pirates from the ship in a whole new light, dancing and singing with the people of Runefjord.

Amidst all the bedlam, Gwen's eyes locked on to Magnus and the twins. The sight of them made her pulse quicken.

The twins, too, had not escaped being dressed up like dolls in the Runefjord style. Draped in crimson fabric, their white-gold hair was braided into intricate plaits. Twisted steel ornamented their heads, a pattern of thorns and roses that looked almost like horns when they turned their heads. Like they were creatures from the woods.

Nervous suddenly, and utterly furious with herself for it, Gwen marched towards them, doing her best not to start sweating under Astrid's stare.

'Gwendolyn, don't you look lovely,' Jonas said.

A mug came careening towards them. Magnus sighed, whistling a lightning-quick tune that had it dropping to the floor.

'Sorry!' someone shouted.

'I really wish they'd stop doing that,' Magnus moaned, at which Lorelei patted him on the shoulder sympathetically.

Swallowing, Gwen turned to Astrid to find she was still staring at her.

'You look beautiful, Gwen,' she said, and the sincerity of it pulled the air right out of Gwen's lungs. Queen's mercy, Gwen wanted to shake herself. She had to wonder, was Astrid even thinking about the near-kiss? Was she waiting for Gwen to say something? Before she even knew what she was doing, words began to spill out.

'Astrid, I wondered if –'

She was, unfortunately, immediately cut off when Captain Kane came barrelling through and jumped up on a table.

'All right, you rascals!' he hollered over the crowd, and they cheered back. 'Tonight is a glorious night.' Someone handed him a tankard of mead that he held up, victorious. 'Our Lady Viper has returned, and she brings with her a cure for the rot.' He winked over his shoulder at Lorelei, who looked like she wanted to melt into the wall. 'These young scallywags are from the Order of Pendragon ...' Everyone jeered and spat while Dorian Kane hushed them. 'Quiet, quiet. They're welcome here at Runefjord and on my ship. They're our guests, and they're the ones who are going to end the darkness infecting the magical world, the Grim, and bring about a new order of Bloom.' Everyone was enraptured by his words, his low, steady voice charming the whole tavern, but Gwen went rigid. 'These three here are a sign that the old ways of magic are finally going to return.'

An explosive energy consumed the room, everyone responding with a full-throated roar. It took a second for Gwen to realize ... they were all cheering for them.

'Now, let's celebrate!'

While the music picked up again, Gwen and the twins stood thunderstruck as the pirates and people of Runefjord ruffled their hair and patted their backs.

'You're smiling,' Astrid said, her voice like honey.

Gwen blinked at her, then laughed. 'Yeah, I guess I am.'

Another spell went whizzing through the air, exploding in red and green.

'Lorelei, my dear,' Captain Dorian said, holding a hand out. 'Won't you dance with me, for old times' sake?'

Lorelei huffed, but even she was not immune to the captain's charms. He pulled her in with a twirl, and the two were off, joining the rest of the tavern in a dance Gwen had never seen before that involved lots of clapping and stomping.

Sighing, Magnus put his drink down at the bar. 'If you'll excuse me, my young Pledges, I'm going to go send a message to my husband. Truthfully, watching everyone dance together is making me miss him terribly.' Seeming to remember himself, he put his pleasant smile back on. 'But you three enjoy yourselves. You've got a busy day tomorrow.'

And then it was just Astrid and Jonas with Gwen.

The air was suddenly thick, Gwen staring at Astrid, Astrid staring back with those icy-blue eyes. There were a million words caught in Gwen's throat, and for some reason all she could think about was reaching over and touching those horn-like accessories on Astrid's head. Or better yet, they could dance?

They spoke at once.

'Astrid, I –'

'Gwen, maybe you –'

'Mother Mary!' Jonas interrupted both of them. 'What the hell is going on with you two?'

Gwen scowled at him, opening her mouth to speak again, when she was once more interrupted.

'So, you lot are the ones going to end the magical plague?'

Gwen jumped; the boy seeming to appear out of thin air. It was him, the sunken-eyed, dark-haired boy – Shay. He was dressed in a deep-blue outfit, almost black, his lashes so heavy and dark it almost looked like he was wearing make-up.

'Rumour is, it's a dragon causing it.'

Gwen put her hands on her hips and said with newfound confidence, 'Yes – I'm going to kill him.'

The boy smiled. One of his teeth stuck out a little sharper than the others, like a fang.

'I'd like to see that. I'll be joining the crew. Maybe I'll get a chance to. And you two –' he turned to face the twins – 'what's your role in all this?'

The twins regarded him, as though in a stand-off, trying to decide if he was trustworthy. He watched them with intense scrutiny, like there was no party, no music, no one else in the world at all. The very same way the twins looked at Gwen.

'We're going to serve her,' Jonas said at last. Gwen expected Shay to be shocked or confused by the response, only his smile seemed to widen.

'And how does one join this exclusive service, say, if one wanted to help make sure they succeeded?'

'They don't,' Astrid and Jonas said as one.

Shay shrugged, not giving in. 'And what if one had a personal vendetta that would compel one to join?'

'Join the club,' Astrid said, unimpressed.

At this, the boy laughed, a spluttering, airy sound that almost turned into a cough.

'Well, this club doesn't seem to be taking new members. But OK, I get it. I'll back down . . . for now,' he added with a wink, laughter still tickling his words. 'But can you three do me a favour?' he asked, his voice suddenly sharper. 'When you finally end him, make sure it sticks this time.'

Now it was Gwen's turn to smile. 'Oh, don't worry,' she said, thinking once again of all the people who had been hurt by the Shadowling. Of everything he'd done to the magical world. 'I'll make sure he's dead.'

15

Friends with the Shadows

Gwen was still fast asleep in her room when the twins woke up. Before grabbing their cloaks and boots, they tiptoed in to see her. Astrid leaned over her where she was sleeping, her hair like black satin over the dusty pillow. Breathing deeply, she looked peaceful. Today, she was going to find something important: Astrid was sure of it. And the twins, in turn, were going to fix the Savonnette for her. It felt good – *right*, even – to be doing things for her. Serving Gwen on her journey to victory.

The sun had not yet risen and all was quiet downstairs in the tavern, the dregs of the party still staining the floor and walls. After the innkeeper had dished them up porridge and tea, Jonas asked Astrid, 'You kissed her, didn't you?'

Astrid sipped her drink. 'I tried.'

Jonas looked thoughtful, staring down at his bowl. There was a distinct aura of disquiet about him, like he wanted to say more.

'There's something different about her,' he said, then glanced up. 'Us too.'

Astrid nodded. 'I think the past is catching up with us.'

Taking a bite of his breakfast, Jonas sighed.

'Well, can it run a little slower, please?'

Chuckling, Astrid held out her hand for him to take. He placed his palm in hers, warm and familiar.

'Whatever these people from the past want from us, you're still Jonas and I'm still Astrid and you're still my brother. The other piece of my soul.'

'I just . . .' Jonas hesitated, the prickles of confrontation running along both of their skin. 'You have to promise me you won't try and do anything so completely cracked as summoning a Cursed Melody again.' His eyes narrowed, and Astrid already knew what he was going to say. 'I felt what it did to you. It's still there, isn't it? Remnants of that spell trying to drag you under?'

Astrid squeezed his hand, staying calm. 'If I hadn't tried to cast it, then we wouldn't have figured out that –'

Jonas cut her off. 'Astrid, you must promise me. Don't you remember what Magnus said about Quin Larkspur? Using that kind of magic is dangerous. It could –'

'Umm, hi.' They both startled, staring up at the intruder. 'Sorry to interrupt . . . whatever's going on here.' It was the strange boy, Shay, his shaggy black hair loose around his grey eyes. After last night, Astrid still hadn't made up her mind about him. They couldn't trust anyone.

'I'm supposed to be taking you both to the blacksmith.'

Astrid pulled her hand away from Jonas's. 'Lead the way,' she said.

Outside, Astrid closed her eyes, listening to the steady melodies of the earth. Here it was a soft sound, wetted by the snow, but the place was still ripe with Bloom. It was like being back inside an Enchanted Quarter, except this cold, magical land was limitless. There were no wards here.

When she opened her eyes again, Shay was staring at her. He smiled when he caught her eye. She did not smile back.

Most of Runefjord was fast asleep after the festivities. There were just the screams and giggles of a few children speeding their sledges down the mountain, and only a few of the huts had smoke at the chimneys – the bakery and, a little further up the mountain, the blacksmith's.

Shay stopped at the baker's and reappeared with a handful of pastries.

'*Kanelboller*,' he told them, taking a bite of his own and holding the still-steaming buns out to both twins. 'Alba, the baker – she charms the dough with spells to wake you up.'

The buns smelled like cinnamon and had a hum of music like early morning birdsong.

'Have you lived here your whole life?' Jonas asked him.

He smiled. 'Not yet,' he said, winking, then gestured for them to follow.

'He's funny,' Jonas mused when Shay was a little further away.

'Is he?' Astrid said bluntly. She would not be easily charmed.

The blacksmith's was a round stone hut with a flaming hot forge at its centre. Metal sizzled in a barrel of water, steam bleeding into the air. Thick with heat and smoke, the room was sweltering, and they took off their cloaks.

'Morning, Shay. What can I do for ya?'

The blacksmith was an old man with leathery skin that was almost impossible to see under his heavy salt-white beard and eyebrows.

'Morning, Reiner,' Shay said, chucking him another bun. 'Dorian Kane brought some guests with him. They have an old Savonnette that needs fixing.'

'Savonnette?' Reiner eyed them warily, wiping his hands on his thick cowhide apron. 'That's Order paraphernalia.'

'Not this one,' Astrid said. She handed him Rupert's old relic and both their shards.

The twins watched as he took the pieces to his workbench, placing them amongst an array of intricate tools and spell ingredients. Pulling out a magnifying glass, he hummed Fire to light the relic clearly.

He gasped, astonished.

'This is pure arcanium,' he marvelled. 'A very rare material, this one. Old as the gods themselves.' He spoke with a kind of reverence, almost religious. 'I've never seen it in such a quantity as this.'

'Can you fix it?' Astrid asked frankly.

'Aye, it'll take me an hour or two, but I can fix it.' He was already picking out his fine-work tools. 'Should have the Savonnette in full working order by the afternoon.'

'And what'll it cost?'

Reiner grabbed an apron, throwing it at Jonas. 'About a day's work. You can help me sort these minerals, and you two –' he pointed to Astrid and Shay – 'you can fetch me more purple frostwort. There should be some a little further up the mountain in the woods. You can take my baskets.'

Jonas muttered under his breath: 'Wonderful.'

'I'll find you later,' Astrid said, offering her condolences.

Walking in silence, Shay led Astrid up the grassy trail to the lip of the woods, where the clouds hung low and the air shimmered. The trees creaked as they entered the woods, their shadows bleeding over them. Inside were the whispers of Bloom, and the distant cackles and whistles of strange creatures.

'There's usually some frostwort around the bushes,' Shay called over. 'It's purple with little –'

'I know where it is,' Astrid said coolly.

Leaning into the earth, each plant and root greeted her, an abundant land of strange and magical flora. The purple frostwort was not far.

'This way.' Astrid walked a little further into the woods, the light turning murky through the spruce trees. The ground was mossy and wet and alive. She jumped over roots, and down into a ditch, and there, growing in swathes, was the elegant purple flower.

Shay didn't say a word as Astrid leaned down, placed her palm to the earth, and began to whisper thanks for what she was about to take. It felt cruel to ask such a thing, and yet it had to be done. Fortunately, the earth replied, humming its approval, and Astrid began to cut at the stems.

She was vaguely aware of Shay watching her where she knelt deep in the wet ground, until he too joined her in the harvest.

It was simple, relaxing work, the kind that reminded Astrid of being back at Faymore Manor collecting ingredients for Elijah. She wondered how Gwen was getting on in her day. By now, she'd probably be at the temple . . .

Lost in her thoughts, Astrid almost forgot Shay was there at all, until he suddenly spoke.

'Did they tell you about these woods?'

Astrid hesitated, then shook her head.

'You'll love this, I think,' Shay said presumptively. 'The people here believe that many of these trees are fairies. That when magic had to go into hiding, they turned their bodies into bark, and their arms into branches, and their fingers into leaves.'

Shay had been right, and Astrid found herself leaning towards him ever so slightly, eager to hear more.

'People like Dorian think that one day, when magic is restored to the way it was, the forests will wake up again, and fairies will walk amongst us.'

'Interesting,' Astrid said honestly.

And then Shay ruined it by completely crossing the line of acceptable conversation.

'That girl – the one who's going to save the world? You like her.'

Astrid froze. The earth too seemed to still, awaiting her answer like a nosy relative. It was a loaded question, and yet the answer came tumbling out of her with no holds barred.

'I do not *like* Gwen,' Astrid began, her Bloom fizzing in her throat. 'I am devoted to her, body and soul. I would find her in every lifetime and pledge every beat of my heart to her success. She is the earth's answer to evil and the very reason for my existence.'

Shay blinked at her. 'So, yes?'

Dazed from her own confession, Astrid huffed, turning back to the herbs.

'And what of it?' she muttered.

Surprising her, Shay didn't laugh, or goad, or comment on her strange choice of words. In fact, from the contemplative look upon his face, it seemed he understood.

'I can see it, in you *and* your brother. It's almost pious.' He spoke calmly, methodical in his harvest. 'You'd do anything for her. Sometimes the people we love don't understand the extreme measures we'd go to for them. The things we'd do to keep them safe.' He cut one of the flowers out of the ground. 'Even when it's for their own good.'

It appeared Shay had heard quite a bit of her and Jonas's conversation at breakfast.

'No, they don't,' Astrid said. She watched him now, intrigued. He was gentle with the plants, good with the knife. And clearly attentive. Now Astrid had to wonder, who exactly was this boy? 'What are you doing here, in Runefjord? Where's your family?'

He shrugged, smiling, still focused on the plants.

'Don't have one,' he told her. 'I don't know where I come from. I spend half my life here, and half of it on the ocean.'

Astrid's eyes narrowed. 'Is that so?'

Now his eyes met hers, glacial blue on mist grey. 'Seems like maybe you and your brother know a little something about that yourselves.'

'We . . .' Astrid began, but suddenly found the words a little tricky to speak. 'We grew up in the Red Blooded world. We knew nothing of Bloom.'

Shay, who Astrid now realized was quite a clever boy, understood immediately.

'What did they do with you?' he asked.

Astrid winced, the dark memories coming back to her, and with them, the tiny flecks of that new, corrupted Bloom hissed inside her. Willing her to hit and bite and destroy.

She swallowed the urges down and said simply: 'They locked us away.'

Flicking his fingers, Shay fisted the knife and slammed it down hard into the mossy earth.

'Dreadful,' he said with feeling. 'I've always felt myself a bit of an outcast. The wild Rogue boy with no family.' He tilted his head, considering, his hair falling over his shoulder. 'And my Bloom, I suppose . . . it's a little different from everyone else's.'

Astrid took the bait. 'How so?'

He grinned at her, his sharp tooth flashing. 'I'll show you mine if you show me yours.'

Astrid chuckled. 'Well, all right, then.'

There in the woods, after being on the ship for so long, it wasn't just easy for Astrid to call upon the earth, it was a pleasure. The Bloom pulsed and crackled under her skin, melodies as old as time reaching out to her. Astrid hummed with it, soothing the burn in her throat. The earth answered.

At her feet, the grass bloomed wild, spreading out in a wave of abundant green. The branches of the nearest trees extended to meet her, twisting round her wrists and waist. They lifted her high, then threw her, only for another to catch her. Then again, and again – she was almost flying.

This was power intensified, from the land, or something else – she couldn't be sure. She felt giddy with it, her magic electric inside her. Her vision glowed green at the edges.

When she landed, Shay let out a whistle, impressed.

'Your turn,' Astrid said, pulling a leaf from her hair.

Shay took a step towards the nearest tree. Astrid thought he might put his hands on the bark, but he leaned down and placed them in the thick shadow the tree left. Like sinking into water, the darkness melted over his skin. He raised it up and up, the shadows extending . . . and then he vanished.

'What the –'

Astrid ran forward, only for him to reappear, this time by another tree.

He laughed, the sound confusingly distant. Like leaves shaking in a gust, the sound moved. Shay disappeared, then reappeared again. This time right next to her.

Astrid nearly stumbled back, only for Shay to grab her wrist. He pulled her up to standing, then reached out and plucked another leaf from her hair. The move was so fluid, so quick. Like a shadow.

'The shadows and I – you could say we're friends,' he told her, gleeful.

Astrid snatched her hand back but couldn't help smiling. 'I feel the same about the earth. That was amazing.'

'Really? You seem like someone who's not easily amazed.'

'I'm not,' she confessed, then she looked at their baskets, which were almost full. It was getting late. She'd let time get away from her with Shay, and she needed to stay focused. 'Perhaps we should head back to the . . .'

Astrid froze mid-sentence. Her heart pounded painfully. The earth screamed.

Without another word she dropped her basket and ran full pelt to the blacksmith's, leaving Shay behind. Jonas met her halfway, running up the path, frantic.

'Astrid!' he shouted across the green, his face pale as he gasped for breath. She didn't need to answer. They both knew.

In the distance, there was a *boom*, so loud it sent birds screeching from the woods. Then, a great crescendo of twisted melodies.

It was coming from the temple.

It was coming for Gwen.

16

Old Kings

Gwen woke up ready. The twins had left to fix the Savonnette, and it was time for her to do her part. They'd explained to Magnus and Lorelei about their theory that people from the past were trying to communicate with Gwen. That they might be able to tell her how to use the sword and defeat the Shadowling. It truly felt like hope. Real hope. That they might really win.

Last time Gwen had been to a temple of old magic, it had been under Windsor. She'd been unprepared, knowing nothing of the Shadowling or her part in his conquest. Now she knew one thing with total clarity: she had to stop him.

'Ah, Gwen!' Magnus beamed at her when she came down to the tavern. 'Are you ready?' he asked, tying a cloak round her shoulders. It was thick and warm, and smelled like a bonfire.

'I have to be,' she told him, scrunching her nose up.

Magnus chuckled, the sound strangely melancholic. 'You know, sometimes you really look like her.'

Gwen's heart lurched. There was no need to ask who. She knew he meant her mother.

'All righty, scallywags. Time for an adventure!' Dorian Kane declared from the inn's double doors. Gwen could peep at Lorelei beyond, prepping their mounts – four gorgeous shire horses. The sight of them had Gwen missing her own horse, Willow.

Gwen thought of Astrid last night, so perfect and beautiful in that crimson dress. She'd wanted to reach out to her, dance with her, kiss her, and yet something always seemed to get in the way.

And now she simply needed to save the world and get them all back home to Faymore Manor where they'd never have to worry about evil or the past again.

Then Gwen could figure out once and for all what she wanted to do with Astrid.

Gwen clenched her fists. 'Let's go.'

The temple was high up the mountain, where the snow was thicker. As they approached, a warren of blue-furred jackalopes hopped away, a reminder that this place was wild with Bloom.

They tied up the horses nearby, clambering over the grass and rocks until they were standing at the entry. Reclaimed by nature over the centuries, the runes etched into the giant stone pillars flanking the entrance were buried by moss and vines, as though the plants were trying to keep the temple's secrets.

A breeze blew from inside. Gwen was sure she heard it whisper her name.

'Now,' Dorian Kane began, loading a pack with potions for Magnus and Gwen, 'this temple is as old as magic, and we've never been able to get past the first door. That means –'

'No one knows what's actually in there,' Gwen finished for him.

'Right.' He winked at her, clearly enthralled by the idea.

'Let's just hope whatever's in there can tell me what I'm supposed to do with the Shadowling,' Gwen muttered to herself.

'We'll wait out here, Gwendolyn,' Lorelei said, kissing Gwen on the crown of her head. 'Magnus will take care of you in there, but if there's any sign of trouble . . .'

Magnus nodded at Lorelei, a silent exchange.

'I'll take care of her.'

Setting off with confident strides, Magnus lit silver flames to guide them. 'Stay close to me, Gwen, dear.'

That, at least, provided Gwen with some comfort. With each step, the scent of wet soil and the hum of old magic grew around them.

She reminded herself that Magnus had likely done this all before, with Elijah and Rupert and her mother, back when he was a Rapscallion. They would have traipsed through tombs linked to Ancient Magic, stumbled across relics and ruins. Adventure and mischief of the highest order.

Eventually the light at the entrance completely disappeared. They were on their own, heading deeper into the mountain.

Here, the Bloom began to speak to her.

The whispers made her uneasy. Her instinct was to block out the strange sensation and turn back round. *Astrid wouldn't quit*, she told herself. Astrid would be running her fingers along every leaf and vine, leaning into the power with reckless abandon until she'd uncovered every secret of the past.

And suddenly, before she could stop herself, a question tumbled from Gwen's lips.

'When you met Elijah, how did you know you were in love with him?'

Magnus smiled fondly at the memory, and for the first time ever, Gwen thought she might actually understand that smile.

'Well, Rupert and I, we . . . well, we had a lot of partners when we were younger,' he said, chuckling to himself. 'Poor Elijah was so patient. Truth is, when he first told me how he felt, I didn't reciprocate. Or at least I didn't let myself. I was afraid that I'd hurt him.'

'Why?' Gwen asked. It was nice to have this distraction, something to take her mind off how far they had already walked, and the growing whispers.

'There was a lot going on in our lives. I didn't want to drag him into my family's problems. But then, one day, a girl on exchange from Easter Island Academy asked him to the Winter Solstice. I saw him there, dancing with this pretty thing, and I knew then that I couldn't bear to see him with anyone else.'

Gwen nearly balked at his honesty, imagining a young Magnus and all the trouble he must have got into with the other Rapscallions . . . with Gwen's own mother.

'Luckily, Elijah is a very generous and forgiving person,' Magnus went on, that warm smile returning. 'We've been together ever since.'

The silver flames abruptly stilled, the two of them coming to a stop. There was nothing but solid stone in front of them. They should have reached some kind of door here, but this was just a giant slab of dirt-caked rock. Beneath the centuries of moss and roots, Gwen saw there were etchings – spiral patterns, like the ones on the Savonnette.

A whisper. Voices Gwen knew, just like in her dreams. Gwen's vision split, memories leaking into the edges. Temples from the past, where terrible things had happened.

She had to do this; she had to listen and lean in. She needed to know.

'There's something here,' Gwen said. 'Something that's only for me.'

Gwen took a deep breath, and Magnus simply stood silent. Waiting.

She reached out her hand and placed her palm on the cold stone.

The cave rumbled. The rocks hissed. The vines snaked away.

'Remember, Gwen, you can turn back at any time,' Magnus told her, putting a reassuring hand on her shoulder. 'We'll do whatever you think is right.'

Gwen smiled up at Magnus. Her teacher. The man who'd practically raised her. Just having him there, knowing he would be happy to let her turn back at any moment – that was enough to give her the confidence to continue forward.

Tuning in to the Bloom at her core and through her fingers, she saw herself as a beacon of light. She concentrated on that feeling, like she had when she'd faced the Shadowling. Her Bloom sang triumphantly under her skin. She could do this. As long as she focused on the light, the shining centre of her magic, she had the power.

Her muscles tensed and she pushed against the stone.

The stone moved. And it kept moving, scraping along the floor, and the ancient door of solid stone, heavy as a mountain, was opened by a single girl.

Still huffing from the exertion, Gwen's mouth fell open at the sight before them. 'Whoa,' she breathed, staring up.

On the other side there was an entire pantheon.

As if welcoming them, green moss-light spread like fire, catching on lanterns, and, further up still, the depths of the immense temple. It was a circular cavern, like the temple she'd been in before, with a similar array of giant statues peering down at them. They looked like deities, there to judge her worth.

She wondered how many of these temples there were around the world, buried for centuries, waiting for the return of . . . well, what exactly, she didn't know. This one was unique in that its ceiling was so high she could not see it at all. The walls twisted, extending far up to the top of the mountain, with curiously hollowed-out tunnels, as if the whole structure were an instrument.

'Hello?' Gwen called.

The word echoed up and up the spiral walls, the sound twirling through the hollows and back down. The sensation was eerie, like a thousand voices calling back. Like the temple itself was talking to them.

'Perhaps we should speak quietly,' Magnus said, his voice as low as possible.

Gwen nodded. There was a sweet scent to the air, as the feet of every statue were overwhelmed by large, flourishing sprays of shiny flowers.

'Silver pansies,' Gwen whispered. Like in the book, and in her dreams.

She took a step back, her shoe grazing a groove in the floor. When she looked down, she nearly jumped out of her skin.

'Argh!' Gwen screamed, the sound echoing back at her, the temple screaming with her. Because in the stone, there was a dragon.

Blinking, Gwen's brain quickly made sense of what she was seeing. The entire central section of the floor was made of a curled-up creature with the face of a dragon. Not an image of a dragon, but the actual thing, embedded in a transparent rock-like material. The thing was huge, and Gwen had to wonder how terrifying it would be to see it unfurled.

Magnus rushed over, eyeing the floor with equal wariness.

'A lindworm – it appears petrified,' he mused, though he didn't sound too concerned. 'Perhaps it got stuck down here.'

Shuddering, Gwen backed away from it as much as she could: its face was far too similar to that of the Shadowling. She twirled on the spot, taking in the great expanse, the statues, the carvings and altars. There had to be *something* here, a way to communicate with the past.

'What am I supposed to be looking for?' Gwen muttered, just loud enough for Magnus to hear.

'Hmm, well, what do you feel when you use that strength of yours?' he asked, donning his scholar hat. 'How do you summon it like you did just now to open the door?'

Gwen poked at one of the pansies with her toe, trying to sort her thoughts. Above her, a mountainous statue of a woman holding a bow and arrow glared into the distance.

'I don't know. Sometimes I can't,' she explained. 'When we fought the Shadowling before, I lost the ability: it's like the shadows snuffed out the light. I lost my hold on it. When it works, it's sort of like a ball of warmth in my chest. But also when I'm angry, too: it's almost a quick burst of energy.'

Magnus came to stand beside her to stare up at the statue. 'And what do you get angry about?'

'I get angry when I'm worried about everyone,' Gwen said, the words coming easily. 'Or about the world, about our Cluster and my sister, and Jonas, and Astrid.'

Magnus smiled down at her, though his eyes were heavy. 'It's quite a burden you carry, Gwen.'

Suddenly uncomfortable with the attention, Gwen took a turn around the space. Every step echoed off the stone, like she was some giant thing stomping about and not just a small girl. She stopped at one statue, staring up at the stone man, his cape covered in lichen. There was a mural behind him, etched into the wall.

'I saw some of these people, in the temple under Windsor,' Gwen said, glancing around. An odd sensation came over her as she spoke, the scent of the pansies filling her nose. So familiar, a memory that wasn't hers.

'Our old rulers of magic,' Magnus told her. 'It's believed they were the bridge between Bloom Bloods and the fae, the earth and the celestial. When we studied Ancient Magic, we found relics that suggested they would pass their knowledge down to each new ruler, but these tomes, if they ever existed, are long lost.'

'Who's this one?' Gwen asked, her eyes locking on the carved face above her.

'That's likely Arthur, who the Order of Pendragon is named after. Many relics of Ancient Magic seem tied to him.' Magnus rubbed his chin thoughtfully. 'We've lost most information about the old kings, but we know he was the last before the magical dark age.'

Slipping past, Gwen went round to the back of the statue where the etchings were hidden. Only, it was not the etchings that had her jaw falling open. She had found another statue.

Attached to the back of Arthur, the two carved from the same stone, was another man. He was hooded, his face obscured. And he was holding a sword.

A sword Gwen knew.

'Who's this?' Gwen asked, suddenly feeling light-headed.

Coming to join her, Magnus scrutinized the stone. 'You know, I'm not sure. It could be one of Arthur's knights, or perhaps – yes, it could be Merlin.'

Blood rushed in Gwen's ears. Whispers at her neck. This was it. The sensation was stifling. A hundred voices speaking at once. She could feel it and hear it just like she did with the book – a frantic crescendo. There was something here. The past trying to speak to her.

'Merlin was part of his council,' Magnus went on, oblivious to the riot happening in Gwen's head. 'Some scholars believe all the great magical rulers had a fae consort.'

Gwen choked. 'Merlin was fae?'

'It's only a theory – Gwen, are you all right?'

No, she wasn't. Her legs had gone wobbly. Reaching out her hand, Gwen floated her fingers above the sword. At the hilt with a silver pansy.

She felt her mind cleave, her limbs tremble.

She knew exactly whose memories kept bleeding into her own.

'This is the sword I have to find.'

Arthur had wielded that sword in a battle that was not yet finished. One that was still being fought a thousand years later. By Gwen.

'It's them,' Gwen breathed. 'They're the voices I'm hearing. The same voices in *The Cursed Melodies*. The ones in my dreams . . . They're coming.'

She needed to tell Astrid this. Now.

'Gwen, who's coming?' Magnus asked, but Gwen could no longer hear him.

She couldn't hear anything but the voices in her head, every whisper of the past like they were right beside her. They were screaming for attention, desperate to warn her of something. She was so close. Whatever had happened in the past with the Shadowling, she was so close to understanding . . .

Gwen.

You must see.

Look what he did to us.

'What?' Gwen shouted, the words roaring back down around her through the hollows. 'What happened? How do I defeat him?'

Eyes out of focus, Gwen stumbled. There was a hissing at the nape of her neck, and Gwen was vaguely aware of Magnus calling her name.

It was all so loud and bright. The past was too much to take in.

The sword.

Look.

Touch it and see.

'Argh,' Gwen groaned, covering her ears. In a fit of desperation, she reached out and placed her palm on the statue's sword.

And then all was quiet.

The quiet of death.

'Gwendolyn!' Magnus shouted, rushing to her side. He grabbed her round the waist, hauling her backwards.

Gwen's vision cleared, and she saw what she had done. The rot came first, black bleeding from the statue's eyes and mouth. Then the sword fell, crashing to the ground and shattering with a near-deafening boom. The howling, discordant sound came next, like the shriek of a dragon awakened.

The Grim.

It was here, somehow. This room was infected, and by touching the sword, Gwen had woken it up.

Under her feet, the floor began to move.

'No, oh no!' Gwen's eyes went wide.

Unfurling beneath them, the lindworm was waking up. They jumped to the side just as its tail uncurled, smacking into the side of the temple. Rocks fell, statues split. The whole place was starting to crumble.

'Up, now, Gwen, quickly! We have to run!' Magnus grabbed her and ushered her through the tunnel in the mountain as he hummed the spells of Fire and Wind at their backs.

There was an earth-shattering crack, the entire mountain rumbling and shaking and nearly knocking them off their feet.

'Don't look back, Gwen!' Magnus ordered.

But she did. She did look back. A serpent's face. Teeth like a hundred knives. Eyes like an abyss.

Evil had its eyes on them, and if they didn't make it out of the mountain, they were going to be eaten alive.

17

Extreme Measures

Astrid had never run so fast or hard in her life. Her legs burned, the earth screaming at her to go faster. At her side, keeping perfect pace, Jonas was just as frantic, the two of them pushing the limits of their bodies. They darted over snowy rocks and frozen streams, singing to the earth to clear their path.

They had to save Gwen.

But there was one more person, behind them, running with equal conviction. Shay.

'Stop!' Astrid shouted. The ground rumbled as snow and rocks came crashing towards them from further up the mountain. They were getting close.

Together, the twins pulled up roots, pushing the rocks away and continuing on. Ahead was the temple mouth, the stone pillars ready to collapse if not for Lorelei and Dorian using every ounce of their Bloom to hold them up.

Without a word, the twins skidded in, calling to the earth to help them hold up the entrance. Vines and roots lunged from the ground, holding the stones in place with tremendous effort.

'Lorelei!' Astrid shouted. 'Where's Gwen?'

'What's happening?' Jonas added over the noise. The ground was groaning.

'They're still in there!' Lorelei wheezed.

The hum of Push and Bind and Pull still twinkled in the air from the weight of their spells. It wouldn't be enough.

'Something's coming,' Shay said, his voice low. 'We need to move.'

'What?' The twins spoke in unison, sweat building on their brows.

Shay didn't wait to explain; he grabbed them and pulled them back. The entrance grumbled, near ready to collapse. Then they heard it: a monstrous shriek, followed by two voices echoing down the tunnel.

'Run, you fools!'

Shay pulled the twins further back just as Magnus and Gwen came barrelling out of the cave mouth. They were not alone.

Falling back in horror and awe, Astrid watched as the entrance in the mountain all but exploded. Rocks and snow flew through the air, the sound like a thunderclap. From the chaos arose a monster of legend, the size of a god. A giant lindworm.

'Holy mother of earth,' Jonas breathed.

With its scales coated in dust, it looked half made of stone. From it, an unbearable, discordant clang of Bloom rang out.

'Gwen!' Astrid shouted, launching herself into the air.

The beast righted itself, tail pummelling the ground. The earth shook. Then it turned its sights on Gwen.

She was panting in the snow, her hair loose from the exertion, a waterfall of black round her shoulders. She looked so tiny, this little ferocious thing turning to face a giant beast. The monster shrieked, lunging towards her, teeth bared. For a moment Gwen looked as if she were debating whether to punch it or run, but at the last second she dived out of the way, sending the creature crashing into the ground. Magnus rushed in, pulling out his ocarina. He played a spell of Wind and Chaos and Ice and, in one fell swoop, conjured a snowstorm to contain the beast. The monster hissed and spat, writhing around. It gave the twins just enough time to grab Gwen and duck under a rocky ledge.

'Are you hurt?' Astrid cried over the noise, gripping Gwen's shoulders.

Gwen shook her head, her eyes wide. It wasn't just fear: there was that fire. Wild and determined. She'd learned something in that temple.

'We have to stop it before it gets to the village!' Gwen shouted, then her nose scrunched up. 'I think . . . I think it's a message!'

'What?' Jonas's face contorted, and Astrid was equally confused.

'The lindworm!' Gwen rubbed her face in her hands, like she was trying to make sense of her own thoughts. 'I touched the statue of the sword and then . . . urgh, I can't explain it. But I think they – the statues – they woke it up to show me something. The temple is infected with the Grim and, somehow, it's a message.'

'Wonderful,' Jonas said, rolling his eyes. 'How very helpful of them.'

Astrid peeked over the ledge to watch the lindworm. The thing lifted its head up over the blizzard, the size of it nearly unfathomable. Lorelei and Dorian were at Magnus's side, bolstering the spells to keep the snow flurry going.

'There's no simple spell that can stop that thing.'

Gwen and Jonas startled at Shay's voice, the boy appearing to materialize from nowhere. Astrid knew now, though, that this was his power: like the twins and Gwen, his Bloom was unique.

'Extreme measures.' Astrid spoke calmly, despite the chaos around them. Shay's fog-grey eyes locked on to hers and darkened.

Astrid licked her lips, her tainted Bloom burning in her throat.

'No.' Gwen's voice cut through. 'Whatever you're thinking, no. We can use my strength and the earth, maybe we can –'

The lindworm did not wait for her to finish.

A bloodcurdling screech arose from it as its face, lined with rot-dripping teeth, came clear of the blizzard, its tail swinging dangerously close to Magnus, Lorelei and Dorian, who jumped out of the way just in time. The beast was heading straight for the teens.

'Time's up!' Astrid said, pulling Gwen and Jonas to standing.

There was no way they could run fast enough: they needed something else. Something like what the Runefjord kids had been using to get down the mountain. In a snap decision, the twins nodded at one another. Jonas hummed the snow into ice beneath them, making a disc.

'Smart,' Shay said, using a quick spell to melt his feet into the ice to keep him in place.

There was a shout behind them, Magnus screaming at them to run. The ground shook, the serpent crashing towards them as the mountain trembled.

Gwen looked about. 'What are you – Argh!'

'Hold tight,' Astrid instructed, pulling the girl close.

The lindworm charged.

Thank the Twelve Spells they weren't at sea any more.

Astrid reached out to the earth, and the ground gave way beneath them.

For a split second they were free-falling. All four of them on their makeshift ice sledge, plummeting down where the ground had given way. Behind them, the lindworm's breath ghosted hot at their backs, rot spitting.

They landed with a thud, the beast just missing them. Then they were off, the world a blur, riding an avalanche down. Gwen screamed. Jonas made a noise somewhere between a laugh and a shriek. The lindworm kept coming.

In another time or universe, when they didn't have giant serpent jaws gnashing at their hair, perhaps it would have been fun to go careening down a mountain at ungodly speeds. Right now, though, the mountain was rumbling behind them, with snow and rocks cascading. If they made one wrong move, missed one turn, the giant worm would swallow them whole.

They just had to make it down to the –

'The village!' Gwen cried, gripping on to Astrid for dear life. 'We can't lead it to the village!'

Jonas bellowed, just as the worm screeched again. 'She's right: we need to lead it away!'

He tried to turn the sledge, but Astrid held it in place. They skidded over a ledge, free-falling again for an exhilarating moment.

'The only thing I care about is getting Gwen away from it!' Astrid shouted back, resolute. 'There are enough distractions in the village to give us time to figure out how to kill it.'

Even careening down the mountain with a deadly worm at their backs, Astrid felt the nauseous waves of shock from her brother.

'No, Astrid,' Gwen growled, authoritarian. Like a command. 'You must care about them too. It can't just be me.'

Astrid chewed her lip. The worm was gaining on them, the giant thing sure to crash down into the village of Runefjord and wreak havoc.

'Then we'll need another distraction,' Shay announced, his voice cool. 'Astrid?' He said her name like a proposition.

Astrid knew without a shadow of a doubt that Gwen would be furious with her. But she needed to keep her safe, no matter what, and if Gwen wouldn't let her use the village as a distraction, she'd have to use herself.

'Jonas, get Gwen to safety,' Astrid said, nodding to her brother.

Then she and Shay jumped off the sledge.

'Astrid!' Gwen screamed.

Jonas, now understanding, held Gwen in place, stopping her from jumping off too.

The lindworm roared, a terrible warbling sound that rattled the mountain. Momentarily floating, Astrid hummed Fire, just enough to get the monster's attention on her. It worked: the beast started hissing, its sights moving away from the sledge so Gwen and Jonas could continue down the mountain to safety.

Astrid rolled along the ground, frantically righting herself. She called to the roots beneath her, wrapping them round her ankles, holding her in place before she could slip. Her fingers trembled from the cold, but her Bloom thrummed warm under her skin.

The monster twisted on the spot, grey scales wriggling. With every movement, it shook the ground, its body pulling up trees and knocking over giant rocks that tumbled downhill.

Shay ran to her side.

'We have to kill it,' he said, a chill to the words, as cold as the snow beneath him. 'Do you know anything that could kill something like this?'

Astrid swallowed. 'Yeah – I know a spell that can kill it.'

The earth screamed at her, willing her not to do what she was planning, yet her pulse was strangely calm, the remnants of the dark Bloom feeling settled, like it was holding its breath. The spell was a patient thing, and it knew it had already won.

She would cast it, and face the consequences later.

In the split second they had as the beast squirmed to face them, Shay gave her that curious look, a spark in his mist-coloured eyes.

Astrid parted her lips. Her body remembered the spell like her tongue remembered the taste of honey. A sweet craving. The Bloom burned in her throat, desperate to be soothed.

She took a deep breath and sang the Cursed Melody.

The music scorched through her blood, sizzling under her skin. Just as it had before, the magic was light and warm as the sun. But like the sun, it burned a pure, destructive fire. This time, she would follow it through. She was going to stay with the melody, trace the rot along the edges, persevere through the gnarled, twisted parts of it. This time, she was going to complete the spell.

Astrid could feel it like the sun in her palms and decay at her feet. Burning rot. Such a curious sensation. The spell, upon closer inspection, felt changed somehow, like the past remembered it differently. Either way, the power was unfathomable, an entire army in one person. The kind of power Gwen held deep inside her.

Next to her, Shay's eyes widened – in horror or awe, it was hard to tell.

The lindworm screeched, the elongated face of twisting scales flying towards them. Astrid stared down the layers of teeth. Gwen had said it was a message, some kind of warning from the past, and now Astrid was going to kill it.

Beneath them, a ring of power was spreading, and everything in its path burned. The plants died and Astrid had to ignore their cries.

She held out her hand, unleashing the magic.

A whisper and a scream. The music that flooded into the air tore through the mountain, and where it went, the land was scorched. The lindworm went up in a blaze of white. Writhing, it screamed as it burned, a dreadful sound.

Shay and Astrid watched, hearts pounding, as the once flourishing earth and pure-white snow turned to ash. Total desolation in a single song.

This was the power of a Cursed Melody.

When she stopped the music, Astrid could feel the grimy residue of the spell staining her Bloom like a dissonant note. When she glanced down at her hands, her fingernails were blackened at the edges. Fascinating and terrible.

She felt the urge to cough, to get it out of her, and yet the magic persisted, promising power, fury. Destruction of all her enemies.

'What have you done?' A ragged voice came from behind them.

Astrid turned slowly, panting. The spell had taken every ounce of energy from her.

Face drawn and pale, his pupils reflecting the fire, Magnus was watching the scene in horror.

'What have you done?' he repeated, the words now bolstered with anger. He marched towards them, and Astrid mentally prepared herself for the barrage. She'd known very well how this move would be received. Magnus would likely never forgive her, but she'd had to do it. She had to protect Gwen, no matter what.

Surprising her, Shay stepped in front.

'It was my fault,' he lied smoothly. 'I got myself in danger. She had no choice.'

'Oh, she most certainly had a choice,' Magnus insisted, shaking his head.

'Magnus.' Another voice – Dorian. He was rushing to his side down the mountain. 'They saved the village!'

'Queen's mercy!' Lorelei declared, clutching her chest as she took in the desolated ground and the giant smoking carcass of the worm.

The earth was destroyed, acres upon acres of land scorched of all life. There was no screaming flora, no plant left to sing its fury. All Bloom had been burned from the ground. Life snuffed out.

'I've never seen such destruction.'

'And it would be worse if these two hadn't stopped that thing,' Dorian continued. 'We owe them thanks, not shock and interrogation.' At this, the pirate captain sauntered forward, clapping them both on the shoulder.

But Magnus didn't even glance at Shay or the captain – his eyes were firmly on Astrid, his gaze so piercing she felt a chill. Astrid did not look away. She was ready for him to shout at her, to scream his disappointment and his desire to be done with her. That's what the adults in her life had usually done.

Only, the anger suddenly drained from his face, and he looked naught but pitiful.

This was somehow far worse, and, at last, Astrid had to look away.

'I think it's time we got back on the boat,' Magnus said. He turned his back to her.

In the aftermath of the spell, the feverish feeling beneath her skin, Astrid could still hear the earth far in the distance where she hadn't devastated the land. She couldn't tune it out, even as it hissed at her. And there, growing, practically *grinning*, was the evil Bloom now firmly planted in her blood.

Behind her, the worm still burned.

'Hey,' Shay whispered at her ear. His breath was cold. 'It's OK. I'm sorry. I should have stopped you –'

It happened before Astrid could hold back. Her hand shot out, fingers flexing. Her body wanted to cause harm, the Bloom still hungry for chaos. She was aiming for his throat. Shay moved out of the way in time, eyes widening.

'Sorry, I . . . sorry,' Astrid faltered, grabbing her hand like it was a dangerous weapon.

'You're OK. You've got this,' Shay said, soothing. 'Just take a deep breath . . .'

'Astrid.' A fierce voice cut him off, one that made Astrid's heart lurch.

Astrid turned to see her. Gwen. Her face was sickly with shock. She was staring at Astrid's blackened hands. She'd seen it. She'd seen Astrid reach for Shay. She'd seen the evil that was taking root inside her.

'Gwen, I –'

But there was no chance to finish, because the cheering began. The people of the village, the pirates – they all came rushing to the scene. A wave of jubilation while the mountainside burned. Celebrating the destruction Astrid had unleashed.

Under her skin, the dark coils of Bloom rejoiced.

18

Good and Evil

The world was a blur. A frenzy of burning and cheering, where nothing made sense. Gwen thought she was about to be sick. Astrid's fingers. Her *hands*. Stained with evil. She couldn't look at her. They were all being jostled about by the Rogues. She couldn't think. Why was everyone cheering for this?

'Gwen, I had to!' Astrid shouted over the crowd. Her voice was warped, something un-Astrid-like about it. The spell still caught in her throat. 'It was the only way. I can't lose you. I lo–'

'No!' Gwen shouted the word, not sure who she was even talking to.

Her mind split, another memory.

A similar image: trusted friends, their hands and eyes blackened by terrible magic.

She knew whose memories they were now. Arthur's. The old kings'. They were speaking to her.

Look at what it does, the voices hissed in her ear.

Hatred. Vengeance.

Gwen blinked, and she was back.

Horror. Desolation. The lindworm was but a smoking husk, and all around it the earth was barren, like a great black scar against the mountain. The residual hum of the melody was rotten, like the Grim. Gwen took in the awful and utter destruction. And worst of all, what it had done to Astrid.

'Gwen, please –'

'Don't talk to me!' Gwen shouted back. 'I can't look at you right now. I need to think.'

'Astrid, how could you?'

She heard Jonas raise his voice at his sister; the two were suddenly locked in a stand-off. Lorelei had to pull them apart.

'Enough!' Magnus's voice cut through the celebrations, his cloak coming to wrap round Gwen. 'We must get back to the boat. Now.'

'I need to be alone,' Gwen said in a hushed voice to Magnus. He nodded, not questioning her further.

While the land burned behind them, Gwen and the rest of the Faymore Cluster were escorted back on to the boat. Gwen would not speak to Astrid. She would not speak to anyone as she headed straight for her cabin. She was furious and confused. But she knew what she had to do, how to fill the gaps of missing information.

She needed to speak to the book of Cursed Melodies.

The room was cold, and silent but for the creaking of the ship and Gwen's own spinning thoughts.

They'd set sail just before dinner, after Magnus and Lorelei had collected the Savonnette, and yet Gwen had hardly moved from the cramped little cot in her cabin, with her arms crossed over her chest. Simmering with fury, her body felt hot. In response to her frustration, the book of Cursed Melodies hummed. The voices of the past were trying to reach her.

The old kings.

'What are you trying to tell me?' Gwen growled. She couldn't calm her anger. 'And why on earth are your voices trapped in this mercy-damned book?'

She'd wanted to tell Astrid what she'd found in the temple. Who precisely from the past she believed was guiding them. Now the whole thing made her feel sick.

The scene played over and over, how the whole village had acted like Astrid had saved them all.

With the Savonnette fixed it was only a matter of time until she found the sword. Until they were all cheering for her like they'd been cheering for Astrid. And that was precisely what Gwen was suddenly so unsure about.

Why, if the old kings had been leading her to the sword, had it crumbled in her hand?

And why had it unleashed the lindworm?

Outside her cabin, she could hear the pirates, even rowdier now after dinner. They retold the tale to each other, as though Astrid had committed some legendary feat. It was all backwards.

'Is that what it will be like?' Gwen wondered out loud. 'When I kill the Shadowling?'

There was no reply. She could never hear the voices when she needed them.

Gwen had felt so close to the past in that temple – all those kings. Arthur and Merlin. She was sure now: they were the ones guiding her. She remembered how it had felt when she'd touched the statue. The rotten horror of it. What kind of messed-up message could the past possibly be trying to give her? The Order wanted to control and study magic, while the Rogues wanted to set it free, consequences be damned. So what did the past want?

And what did Gwen want?

Only that morning it had seemed so simple. Gwen had been letting her fury guide her. The path had been clear. She would find the sword and kill the evil dragon that had caused so much harm.

The book of Cursed Melodies still sat on the bedside table. It had no eyes, and yet Gwen felt its presence like it was watching her. The book and the past – they were linked, cut from the same cursed cloth. How could something so evil, that had caused so much harm, also be guiding her? It had brought the Shadowling back into the world; it had set the Grim into Bloom Blooded society; and now it had charmed Astrid, putting dark melodies into her very blood.

'Urgh,' Gwen groaned again, punching the pillow. Feathers flew from the side.

She could not help but feel it was somehow her fault. If only she hadn't given in to the book, if she'd never agreed to read it, then Astrid would never have heard the damned spell in the first place.

'Why did you make me sing it?' Gwen hissed at the silent book.

There was nothing but the hush of the sea in response. Out on the ocean again, Gwen might have felt the biting cold if not for the anger warming her body. What she did feel, though, was hunger. Her stomach rumbled, annoyed. And then, a knock at her door.

'You did not come for dinner,' Lorelei said by way of greeting. She was wrapped up in a fur cloak, and in her hand was a tray of bread, cheese and meat that she placed on the table.

Gwen could have kissed her.

'I didn't want to see her,' Gwen said, as she dug in greedily. With each bite and swallow, her eyes stung, her throat going scratchy. Damn it, she was about to cry.

'It's all right, Gwen,' Lorelei soothed.

'No, it's not.' Gwen swallowed another bite hard, wetness spilling down her cheeks. She didn't even have the strength to be embarrassed. 'I'm so confused. Sometimes it feels like the book and the past – they're trying to guide me; and sometimes it feels evil, like the Shadowling. It doesn't make sense. How can it be evil and good at the same time? What does it mean?' Gwen rubbed at her eyes with her sleeve aggressively, trying to stop the tears. She didn't even know who she was talking to any more; it was all just spilling out. 'I'm starting to feel like this whole mission, this whole plan to get the sword . . . it's all wrong. Something about it doesn't feel right.' She hiccupped a sob. 'And Astrid, how could she . . .'

Sitting beside her on the bed, Lorelei rubbed Gwen's back, the action reminding her of when she was little, when she'd scraped her knee or broken a toy. Through the blur of tears, she could see Lorelei had this look on her face like she was going to say something she really didn't want to.

'Gwen, I think it's time I told you how I came to be in the Faymore Cluster as Magnus's research partner.'

'What?'

Blinking at this unexpected turn in the conversation, Gwen nearly let the food drop out of her mouth. Lorelei's origin story was a mystery Gwen had thought she'd never uncover, one even Thomas didn't seem to know. Gwen continued to eat in silence, scared that if she spoke, Lorelei might change her mind. Then Lorelei stood up and walked to the porthole, like she was telling her story to the sea.

'My father and his sister were Rogues from far across the ocean, while my mother had given up the sea and settled at Runefjord. I spent half my life at sea, and half my life running wild with my brother and cousins around the isles. We grew up believing that the Order was bad, that magic was meant to be wild, that the world needed to get back to the old, ancient ways.' Lorelei paused, her breath hitching. 'And then, one day, the Grim came for my family.'

Gwen remembered what it was like, the first time she'd faced the Grim: the confusion, the fear. A thing so rotten and wrong that it had shattered her understanding of Bloom. She wondered what it must have been like for Lorelei the first time she was faced with it, having no idea what it was.

Lorelei turned to her, face half silver in the moonlight.

'Only baby Thomas and I survived.'

The words pierced Gwen's heart, fresh tears spilling over that she couldn't have stopped even if she'd tried.

'I took him away in the night, and even though it went against everything I believed in, I went to the only people I could think of who might know something about the horror I'd seen.'

Gwen swallowed. 'You went to the Magisters.'

'That I did,' Lorelei said, nodding. There was no regret on her face. 'Magister Beatrice herself told me they knew who'd caused it. The Faymore Cluster.'

'I'm sorry.'

'That's not your burden, my dear,' Lorelei insisted. Now she came back to the cot, clutching Gwen's hand. 'She made me a deal. I could join the Faymore Cluster in secretly researching the Grim, to learn how to stop it. But she made me swear not to mention Rogues to Thomas or anyone, that I was to allow the Order to raise him, to send him to

Fountains Abbey, and I had to commit myself to the duties of the Order of Pendragon.'

Gwen couldn't imagine anything worse. Having to work directly alongside the people responsible for what had happened to her family. And worse still, having to strike a deal with the very figurehead of everything you believed was wrong with magical society.

Gwen could hardly find the words, so she settled on the simplest:

'That must have been hard for you. Working with the Faymores.'

A small laugh escaped Lorelei.

'Oh, yes, I thought so too, but then I met Magnus and Elijah and Rupert, and your mother and father and little Jan.' Something warm and fond settled over Lorelei's usually stern face. 'Even though I was an outsider, they welcomed me into their Cluster, and I swore I would do everything to help. I realized that this evil thing they'd unleashed – it didn't make them evil people. Do you understand?'

Gwen felt her heart heavy in her chest as she took in the information. There was urgency in Lorelei's eyes.

'Life is not so clear-cut, Gwendolyn. Sometimes the best people can do bad things.' Lorelei squeezed her hand, an imperative to her words. 'And sometimes the best of intentions can have terrible consequences.'

Gwen knew exactly who she was talking about. Astrid. But her intentions didn't make what she'd done any better, did they?

'I'm sure the people I left behind were hurt by what I did, but it was the right thing in the end.'

With that, Lorelei stood up, dusting her hands off as if she'd just engaged in some messy work. Gwen supposed she'd feel the same way if she'd had to lay her heart out like that.

And then something in Lorelei's words snagged at Gwen's memories.

'Oh my god,' she gasped. 'It's you! You're the one Dorian was talking about! He said the Shadowling stole his wife and her family from him . . . You . . . no way . . .'

Lorelei looked suddenly as if she might combust on the spot. 'That's between me and the sea. You hear me, Gwendolyn?' she said, pointing her finger.

Gwen suppressed a smile. 'My lips are sealed.'

'Good lass.' Lorelei nodded. 'Now, will you be all right if I leave you?'

'Yes. I have a lot to think about.'

Once Lorelei was gone, Gwen lay back in her cot. The story repeated behind her eyelids, everything Lorelei had sacrificed to find and end the Shadowling. How must it feel for her, to know that Gwen was the one chosen to do it? The pressure was insurmountable. Lorelei, Magnus, her sister and everyone in their Cluster – everyone in the whole Bloom Blooded world, for that matter, Order and Rogue – they were doing everything to protect Gwen.

All so she could kill the Shadowling.

What would they do if they knew she was suddenly having doubts about the plan?

But then there were the twins. Why did they fight for her? They, more than anyone, had sworn to keep her safe, but thinking of Astrid, it wasn't about duty, or about what Gwen was going to do. For the twins it was something else. And for Astrid it was because . . . Gwen swallowed, her heart thudding at the thought she wouldn't finish.

Sometimes it felt as though Astrid didn't care about the Shadowling, or the world at all. She only cared about Gwen.

There was another knock at the door.

Wiping her face on her sleeve, Gwen reluctantly went to open the door. She had a feeling she knew exactly who it was going to be, and she wasn't sure she was ready to talk to her yet.

'Hi,' the person on the other side said.

'Oh.' Gwen took a step back. It was not who she'd expected at all.

19

Rupert and Quin

Hunched over, Astrid focused on her breathing. In, out, in, out. Nausea had set in after the spell, her body trying to reject the dark Bloom it had left behind. She wasn't suffering alone. On the other side of the table in the now near-empty mess hall, Shay patted her back.

'Mercy, I wouldn't have let you cast it if I'd known it would do *this*,' he said, mustering a laugh.

'You couldn't have stopped me anyway,' Astrid said honestly.

She'd thought she knew the consequences when she cast the spell, but now she could really feel it. It was clear now: the more you used *The Cursed Melodies*, the more its evil got inside you.

It didn't help being back on the ship. Some crew had stayed behind in Runefjord, and others had joined, including Shay, yet the atmosphere was the same. The dank air, the swaying, the jeering and shouting. Once again, Astrid was severed from nature, and now from Jonas too. He was refusing to speak to her.

'You know you mustn't ever cast it yourself?' Astrid said, her voice clear despite the sickness under her skin. 'I shouldn't have let you hear it.'

Shay gave a nod, his face as serious as death.

'You can trust me,' he said, a lock of hair falling over those eyes. They were so cold, so unreadable. The exact opposite of Gwen's.

'It's fascinating, though, isn't it?' He stared down at her hands. Her fingers were still blackened at the tips, veins of black and dark purple extending out like an infection. 'I've never known spells that leave such marks on the body.'

A fresh wave of nausea overtook Astrid, her own Bloom fighting back against the call for destruction. All she knew was that despite the unpleasant aftermath, her body somehow craved it. Her throat burned to sing the song again. Her fingers itched to spread chaos.

And yet, she didn't regret it.

She'd done what she'd needed to do. She'd saved Gwen. She would turn the whole world to ash if it meant keeping her safe.

'I'm sorry for trying to, umm ... throttle you earlier,' Astrid said earnestly.

'It's OK. You have it under control now,' he reassured her.

But Astrid wasn't sure she did. The feeling of the dark Bloom was searing her insides, trying to take over. She needed to quell it. Now. She needed to keep herself together for Gwen.

There was only one person who could help her with this.

'I'm going to find my brother. Will you be OK?'

Shay gave a thumbs-up. 'Do whatever you need to.'

Determined to fix this, Astrid marched down the swaying corridors of the ship. She was not going to let the Cursed Melody win.

Dorian's pirates were strewn about the ship, singing and merry-making. There'd been more celebrations, drinking and feasting after the village had been miraculously saved by Astrid. Because of what she'd done. What she'd sacrificed.

When she opened the door to their cabin, Jonas was sitting on his bunk reading a book. The sight was so reminiscent of their time at the group home that it made Astrid pause. He didn't look up.

Buttonbug was sitting on his lap, and when she saw Astrid, the little menace hissed, her dark fur standing up.

'Well, that's a bad sign,' Jonas muttered, petting Buttonbug to calm her.

'Jonas, we need to talk,' Astrid said, shutting the door behind her.

'You're right.' He closed his book, then threw it at her. 'How could you be so stupid?'

Astrid batted the book away just before it hit her. 'I saved us.'

'Oh, really?'

Excited by the shouting, Biscuit jumped up at Jonas from under the bunk, long tongue lapping at his neck.

'Calm down, Biscuit,' Jonas scolded, then turned back to Astrid. 'We could have thought of something else. You were just gagging to use that spell, weren't you?'

Astrid didn't answer, and that was answer enough.

Biscuit made an odd, wet barking sound, his claws scratching at Jonas's jacket as he jumped up again.

'Queen's mercy, would you calm down, Biscuit, please!' Jonas snapped, only to let out a sigh and pet the poor otter-dog's head. 'Sorry, boy, I know. Here.' Jonas pulled some dried fish from a pouch in his pocket, which Buttonbug immediately decided she had to get involved in, too.

He let out a world-weary breath as he soothed their little menagerie with the Calm melody. Astrid leaned into the music, finding she too needed comforting.

'Astrid, I just . . . I can feel what it's doing to you. And not only that, you performed the spell in front of Shay. You taught *him* a Cursed Melody. It's too dangerous to spread.'

'He's like us, Jonas,' Astrid told him. 'We can trust him.'

Jonas stared at her, the prickles of confusion running over their skin.

'His Bloom is different, and he doesn't know where he came from,' she added.

At this, Jonas rolled his eyes dramatically. 'Oh, yes, OK then, by all means teach this boy every evil spell you can get your hands on!'

'Jonas, please.' The words were like a weight on her tongue. The dark Bloom still in her blood hissed, and she swallowed another wave of nausea. 'I don't regret it. I saved you and Gwen. But more than that, my scientific brain needed to know. And, well . . .' Astrid took a calming breath. 'I wanted to. My body wanted to cast it. If I can harness more power to help Gwen, I'll do it. I'll always choose her. You know that, but, Jonas . . . damn it. I think I've bitten off more than I can chew.' Jonas made a hissing sound through his teeth. 'I'm not here to apologize; I'm here because I need you to monitor me.' Jonas cocked an eyebrow. Astrid could feel the waves of curiosity from him even through his anger. 'You're right: the spell has done something to me, and I need you to study it and keep me in check.'

There was nothing more Astrid could say. She could only hope Jonas felt the sincerity of it.

'You need to get a hold of yourself,' Jonas said, grabbing her by the shoulders. The contact felt like finally being able to breathe again.

'I know.'

Jonas squeezed her.

'Good,' he said, then shrugged, humour entering his voice, forced as it was. 'I suppose there is always the possibility there's another universe where you didn't use the spell and we're all dead.' He turned contemplative, looking off into the distance. 'It was rather incredible, even if I can literally feel the remnants of evil it's left under your skin.'

Smiling, Astrid held his cheeks in her palms, relishing the familiar feel of him. Her soul whole again.

'Truce?' she offered.

Jonas huffed, his eyes going soft. 'You'll really do anything for her, won't you? Even destroy yourself?'

For a second the dark Bloom under Astrid's skin went quiet.

Once again she said nothing. This time she felt the stab of pain in her brother's chest, but he quickly covered it up with a smirk.

'You know, it's not really me you need to speak to. If you really want a truce, next you have to speak to Magnus, and then . . . Gwen.'

Astrid cursed. She knew it was inevitable, of course, but that didn't mean it would be pleasant.

'Yeah, this is going to be extremely painful. For *you*, that is – I can't wait to see you grovel.' Jonas chuckled to himself demonically, pulling Astrid out of the cabin, then paused.

'Is he really like us – Shay?'

Now Astrid laughed, tapping her nose. 'In more ways than I've yet to solve.'

They found Magnus on deck, his cape rippling in the sea breeze. While the crew members of the *Sea Reaper* sang songs and drank under the moonlight, he stood out. A solemn figure.

Ushering Astrid towards him, Jonas prompted, 'Go on.'

'All right, all right,' she hissed, stumbling forward.

'Magnus . . . I –'

As if he had eyes in the back of his head, Magnus held up a finger.

'Shh,' he told them. 'Come here, you two.'

Confused, the twins exchanged a glance then stepped forward. Out there, the fresh, cold scent of the sea was formidable, the air chapping their cheeks. Despite the wind and the noise, Magnus stood stoic, concentrating. He was staring at something in the near distance. So, the twins looked that way too. They heard it first: a strange and haunting call, almost like a whistle. For a moment they couldn't see anything at all. Nothing but the endless, profound black of the midnight ocean. Then there was a flash, a ripple, a shimmer. Off the side of the boat, flitting in and out of the moonlight under the waves, was a whole pod of mermaids.

Astrid's Bloom fizzed in her palms, her heart racing, and with it a hiss of that new Bloom, itching to sink its claws into something.

'It's OK now,' Magnus said, holding up a hand. 'These ones appear harmless. They're only curious to find a magical thing so close to the surface.'

Calming her pulse, Astrid took another step forward, both twins leaning over to get a better look. Glowing white eyes winked in and out of sight. Without the rot of the Grim, they were mesmerizing. They glided through the water, sleek as a ribbon dance, their skin shining like the inside of an oyster.

'They'll see nothing but iron ships and Red Bloods on their cruises,' Magnus said. 'Magical creatures of the sea have the good sense to hide from Red Bloods. It must be fascinating for them to find Bloom in such a strange vessel.'

One mermaid darted briefly out of the water, sharp teeth flashing, the spikes on its tail a deadly weapon.

'I thought Lorelei said mermaids were dangerous, even without the Grim,' Astrid said, reminding herself to stay calm.

'Oh yes, they can be, if handled incorrectly,' Magnus agreed, then turned sombre again. 'As with all magic.'

Astrid felt it there, that hum of Bloom. Like calling to like. These mermaids were wild and fierce. They had magic like the twins'. How terrible that so many of them had had to die in the tragedy of the *Tidebinder*.

'They're beautiful,' Astrid breathed.

'Indeed. Dangerous things can be deceptive.' There was a taut silence before Magnus turned to face her at last. 'Will you show me your hands, Astrid?'

Suddenly ashamed, she didn't want him to see the blackened marks. Her hands moved behind her back, like she could hide her sin.

'Magnus, I'm sorry. I had to protect Gwen.'

'You know,' Magnus interrupted, 'something I didn't tell you about our old friend Quin is that he somehow managed to learn a spell from *The Cursed Melodies*.'

Jonas sucked in a breath at her side. Such a thing seemed impossible.

'We don't know how. Perhaps it was all the time he spent whispering to it. Maybe it finally whispered back.'

The idea sent a chill through Astrid, thinking of Gwen, of her strange connection to the book. Did it whisper to her too?

'It was the very last thing he did before we lost him. He was protecting Rupert on one of our missions to hunt down the Grim. He sang a melody we'd never heard before.

Magic that had been lost. It was a song that shone warm like sunlight, but laid waste to the land. A rotten thing, cursed.' Astrid knew exactly what he was going to say next, and yet it still shocked her. 'The very same spell you sang today.'

Horrified, Jonas stared at his sister. 'What exactly happened to him?' he asked Magnus.

'We saw his hands turn black, and his eyes turn to fog,' Magnus said severely. 'The curse of the Grim grew from the inside out.'

'The Grim? No . . .' Panicking, Astrid stared down at her hands, at the black stains like powdered coal in the beds of her fingernails. They were fading, but not fast enough.

'Do you understand how serious this is, Astrid?' Magnus implored, grabbing her hands to inspect them.

Shaking her head, Astrid said, 'But that doesn't make any sense. The book is Gwen's. What do the Shadowling and the spells in that book have to do with each other?'

Jonas nodded. 'That's right. The book has information on how to destroy him, so why would it also be on his side? How do you know the spell caused the Grim?'

'We know nothing,' Magnus said, the words hard and frightening. Astrid had never seen their mentor like this. His hair and cape undulated black around him, his red-tinted eyes darker, like he was remembering something dreadful.

'The only thing we do know is that you two and Gwen are the last hope we have.' The words sank down like a lead weight. 'We must do everything we can to protect you and guide you. But it is all of our individual responsibility to make sure we are always fighting for good, and with love. Quin thought he was acting out of love, but the dark parts of us are good at playing tricks. We must always exercise the good in us – do you understand?'

Astrid thought of the spell, the way it stuck to her like syrup. Like she wanted to lick it off her skin to get another taste. And she also thought of Gwen, how everything Astrid did, every dark thought she had, was for her. Gwen was the good she needed to protect. Even thinking of her seemed to calm the remnants of the spell in her blood.

'I understand,' Astrid said at last. 'Thank you, Magnus.'

Without another word, she turned, walking fast across the deck. Jonas fell in step with her.

'There's something I need to do on my own,' Astrid told him.

She felt that spark of recognition. Of total understanding.

'Yes,' he said. 'Me too.'

They parted in the corridor, Astrid heading to Gwen's room, and Jonas heading to the cells below.

20

We're All Doomed

Before venturing down to the ship's cells, Jonas made a stop at the kitchens. Passed out over a barrel of honey mead, the pirate Silverfang was snoring in the corner. Too much celebration. Jonas sidestepped him, rifling through the chaos of the storecupboard. He needed to find a gift, or more: a peace offering.

'Aha.' Jonas grinned. This would certainly do.

Down in the bowels of the ship, the air was frigid, the stink of salted fish seeping into the wood from the store beneath. As Jonas strolled down the corridor of cells, the metal bars hummed their subduing melodies, his own Bloom feeling stifled in their presence.

And there, in the last cell, wrapped in furs, with a plate of bread and meat, was Prince Teddy. He looked up from his book, the one Jonas had given him. His hair had grown a little, a curl setting in at the ends, his Mediterranean side coming loose. It made him softer, his edges smoothed.

'We'll reach the Borealis Sanctum in the next three days,' Jonas told him. 'You'll be free to go.'

The prince cocked an eyebrow. 'Is that why you're here? To tell me things I already know?'

Jonas suppressed a laugh. Perhaps it was because Teddy was still behind bars, but suddenly he found the prince's commitment to being a pest rather enjoyable. Maybe he always had. Maybe he didn't want to think too hard about that.

'I brought you something.' He showed the prince a slice of chocolate cake on a cloth napkin, the icing practically sparkling in the dank underbelly of the boat.

The prince put a hand to his chest. 'How very kind.'

Though he jested, he got up and reached between the bars for the cloth, fingers delicately removing segments of the cake, which he brought to his lips. Jonas had never seen someone eat with their hands so gracefully.

'Listen, I'm, well . . . I regret that I can't get you out of here sooner,' he confessed. The truth tasted good on his tongue, so he kept going. 'It's becoming clear to me that you didn't do anything wrong, and if I hadn't left you there in the apothecary, things might have gone very differently.'

The prince slowed, licking frosting off his fingers. His eyes flicked up to Jonas, rich brown like the cake in his hands.

'Careful – that almost sounded like an apology,' he purred. Then he swallowed, his mask slipping ever so slightly. 'Did you find any clues to who did it?'

Jonas considered him. They had no information at all. Every logical part of his brain knew that the evidence pointed to the prince. He'd vanished from the *Tidebinder*; he'd been found escaping as they were all attacked. Yet here Jonas was, giving him chocolate cake.

'We've found nothing at all. Actually, we've been a little preoccupied.'

He explained all that had happened, and the prince chewed over this new information, his face very still in contemplation.

'What about the Black Savonnette? Did you find out what kind of spell it performs?'

'A mystery still.' Jonas patted the pocket it was in, the fabric still a little moist from where Biscuit had licked at it.

'So then, if you have no new information, and no new suspects, what makes you trust me now?'

Jonas sighed. The twins had always struggled with *good*. They had always been told as children that they were *bad*, that they were difficult and unruly. Now, as fate would have it, they were caught in a battle that relied on their goodness, and that meant recognizing it, and protecting it.

'The truth is, Theodore –' the prince's breath visibly hitched at the use of his name – 'as irritating as I find you, I do not believe you capable of great evil. I have seen evil; I have heard its melodies, and felt its magic. But you – you're self-absorbed, arrogant, a thorn in my side, and yet I know that if we're going to beat evil – true evil – then we will need you on our side.'

The prince went quiet, placing the napkin and cake down on the little table, then he wiped his hands on a cloth in the corner where a bucket of water sat stagnant. Finally, he turned to Jonas and pleaded.

'Would you please, please let me kiss you?'

Jonas blinked, taking a small step back.

'Excuse me?'

'Mercy, do you have any idea how attractive that speech was?' the prince implored, coming right up to the bars so Jonas could see the gold flecks in his eyes. 'You're the most endlessly fascinating and irresistible person I've ever met.'

Jonas shrugged, the compliment rolling off him. 'Well, I suppose that is what I came down here for.'

Now it was the prince's turn to be confused. 'Huh?'

Rolling his eyes, Jonas stepped up to the bars, the two of them mere inches from each other, their breath mingling between them. The prince smelled like chocolate icing. Without any other warning, Jonas reached up and pulled him down by the collar of his shirt. Prince Teddy let out a tiny gasp that was swallowed by Jonas's lips.

Recovering from the initial surprise, the prince melted into the kiss, his experience guiding the two of them. He was a natural, the feel of him warm and inviting. It was the kind of kiss Jonas had read about in books and hardly believed to be true. The kind of kiss that could make you fall in love.

And as quickly as it had begun, it stopped. Prince Teddy leaned back, panting, the air now hot around them. Jonas felt his cheeks flush and was fascinated to find himself a little dazed.

'Any traces of evil?' the prince asked, his mouth curling up at the corner.

Jonas put a finger to his chin, pretending to think.

'Perhaps I'll have to check again.'

'Hi,' the lilting voice said.

Shay.

Gwen took a step back, embarrassed. 'Oh, sorry . . . I thought you were someone else.' She sniffed, rubbing at her face again to try to hide the swelling from her earlier crying. 'What do you want?'

Gwen hadn't meant for it to sound so pointed. Her mind was still reeling.

Shay stood slightly awkwardly in the corridor, staring down at her. 'I just want to apologize,' he said quickly, doing a very good job at pretending not to notice the state she was in. 'I should have told Astrid not to cast that spell. If I'd known you didn't want her to, I would have reminded her as much.' He gave a small smile, that sharp tooth flashing. 'I don't want us getting off on the wrong foot. I want you to be able to trust me, like Astrid does.'

Gwen let out a shuddering breath. She couldn't blame the boy, not really. Though it stung to know Astrid trusted him so much – so much so that she'd performed the Cursed Melody in front of him.

'You couldn't have stopped her anyway,' Gwen said gravely.

Shay nodded, a small smile on his lips. 'That's funny – she said the very same thing.'

Despite everything, Gwen laughed. Of course Astrid had said that. Gwen knew it. Astrid knew it. Astrid would damn herself and the whole world for Gwen, and no one could stop her.

'She's a force all of her own,' Shay said thoughtfully.

Gwen couldn't disagree.

'Speaking of, please don't tell her I came here. She is quite protective of you.'

Gwen nearly laughed again. *Protective* was an understatement.

'I just want you to know that I'll keep an eye on her in the future,' he added warmly. It should have been the end of the conversation, and yet he lingered. The sound of the boat creaking was the only thing between them as he still stared down at Gwen expectantly.

Gwen sighed. 'Look, if you're trying to get me to agree to let you help us kill the Shadowling, it's not going to work.'

Now it was his turn to laugh, a soft, airy sound. 'It was worth a shot, wasn't it?'

Swallowing, Gwen felt the humour die in the room. She was reminded once again of what everyone was expecting her to do. The whole world wanted her to wield this sword and end evil forever.

'Why do you want to be involved in his demise so badly anyway?' Gwen asked. The question hung in the air between them. Too personal.

Shay's eyes darkened and so too did his voice. 'He needs to be killed, Gwen.'

Gwen nearly gasped. For a split second it felt as if he could read her mind. As if his stormy eyes were drilling into her head, all her thoughts and doubts about killing the Shadowling laid bare.

Gwen scrunched up her nose, looking at the floor.

'I know,' she said, though she wasn't sure she did. She quickly changed the subject, something to convince him she was still committed to the mission. Something to convince herself. 'Listen, I don't know what the Shadowling has done to you personally, but I hope you do get to see it when he dies. If it means so much to you.'

'When you kill him,' Shay prompted, waiting for Gwen to look at him again.

'Yes,' Gwen confirmed.

'OK,' Shay said, satisfied. 'I'll leave you alone now.'

He left quietly, his footsteps silent on the floorboards.

After he was gone, Gwen felt her breathing speed up. They'd be at the Borealis Sanctum in the next few days and they'd all expect her to figure out the map and find the sword – this thing the Shadowling was so determined for them not to get their hands on. And then what?

She'd kill him. Was that what had happened in the past? Was that what Arthur Pendragon had done?

What if it was wrong? But how could she tell them all? They wouldn't want to hear it. There was no one she could speak to – no, there was one person. The person who'd burn the world down for her.

Gwen rose and went to the door, her heart racing. She pulled it open . . . and there she was. Astrid.

Hand raised to the door like she was about to knock, her fingers were blackened like she'd dipped them in soot, and her face was pale, more so than usual. There was a slight sheen to her skin, like she might be sick. Her hair hung loose round her shoulders, a little damp from the sea breeze. It was the first time Gwen had seen her truly dishevelled. And yet, she was still the most beautiful person Gwen had ever seen.

Opening her mouth to speak, Gwen found no words would come. And then, before she even registered what she was doing, she dived into Astrid, wrapped her arms round her body, and squeezed. Her heart panged at the contact of nuzzling her face into her chest. She felt as well as heard the shock of breath from Astrid.

'I need you,' Gwen demanded.

'Gwen, I – it's OK.' Astrid's hand came down over Gwen's head, patting her hair softly as she led her back into the room, shutting the door behind them.

Settling down on to the bed, the two girls sat side by side. Astrid's darkened fingers curled over the bedspread.

'I know who the voices belong to,' Gwen said, surprising both Astrid and herself.

'You do?' Astrid's eyes widened.

'They're the old kings. I think – no, I'm sure – Arthur Pendragon was the one who fought the Shadowling. It's his sword we're looking for.' Gwen was aware her voice was cracking as she spoke, but she couldn't help it. Speaking of King Arthur set dread into her stomach.

The steady sound of Astrid's breath filled the room, her icy eyes calculating, thinking a million thoughts.

'Well, are you going to say anything?' Gwen huffed.

'Truthfully, I came here thinking you'd be furious with me,' Astrid confessed. 'I wasn't prepared for this . . . discovery. Or for you to sound so upset about it.'

'I *am* furious,' Gwen said, standing up abruptly. 'Queen's mercy, Astrid,' she groaned, walking to the porthole. 'When we arrived in Runefjord, I was so sure we were on the right track. Victory felt within my grasp. But after the sword crumbled in the temple, after what you did, and the voices in my head . . . I'm so confused. I don't know if I can do what everyone wants of me.'

And there it was, the truth. Because Gwen knew Astrid was the only person in the whole world whom she could tell this to. Who would be on her side no matter what.

Her eyes darted down to Astrid's blackened fingers again. She couldn't bear it. Knowing that Astrid would so willingly sacrifice herself.

'OK,' Astrid said, her voice calm, and Gwen knew she understood completely. 'It's all right, Gwen. For now, the mission is the same. We're trying to find a way of stopping the Shadowling. Whether that be using a sword or something else, we'll find it. And you'll stop him, I'm sure of it. You'll find the answer to defeating him and I will be here no matter what your choices are.'

A tear escaped Gwen's glistening eyes, salty and warm down her cheek. Everything Astrid said was exactly what she needed to hear, and it made one thing crystal clear to her. 'I can't lose you, Astrid,' she said, her voice fragile. 'You have to promise you'll never leave me.'

It felt petulant, like Gwen were a child demanding things that were out of anyone's control, and yet Astrid didn't hesitate. She leaned forward to grab Gwen by the shoulders before she could back away.

Gwen stared her down, scrunching her nose to stop more tears from spilling over.

'I might do terrible things for you, Gwen. I might destroy myself and level mountains. But you won't lose me. I can promise you that.'

'How can you be so sure?' Gwen asked, her voice cracking again.

'Listen to me. Magnus told me he'd heard the spell I sang, that he saw it infect someone with the Grim. But it didn't do that to me.' Gwen shuddered, her eyes wide with horror at the possibility. 'I can feel it under my skin, trying to coax me, but I can simply bat it away. And the only reason I can think this way is because of you. What I feel for you, the strength of it, your unstoppable goodness – I need it. You are the thing that keeps the light in. You won't lose me.'

Astrid leaned over her, eyes firm and sure.

'I believe in you. Whatever you decide to do, no matter what the Order, or the Rogues, or the whole world wants. I will fight only for you.'

'Astrid . . . I –'

'You have to see it, Gwen. You are the good in the world. You shine with it. You are love and light and hope in human form, and you don't even know.'

'How can you be so sure that I can save us? That I can save *you*?'

Astrid took one more half-step forward, taking Gwen in with that reverent fascination.

'Because I'm in love with you.'

Gwen's heart thudded; time seemed to slow. She felt as if she were staring up at Astrid for an eternity, like the moment had been cast in stone. Somewhere, in the crevasses of her mind, she was sure: this had happened before.

Astrid leaned down, her breath ghosting over Gwen's lips.

'I'm in love with you, Gwendolyn Chatterjee. I don't care if fate brought us together, or what plans the past has for us. I love you, and it's more powerful than any Cursed Melody.'

Entirely undone by the words, Gwen breathed in slowly. She could smell her, her skin's lingering earthen scent. She could feel it, too – something between them. The past but a whisper away. If she just went up on her tiptoes. Just got a little closer. Maybe the past would come to greet them as their lips met.

'May I?' Astrid asked.

Gwen lifted her chin, ready to say yes.

There was a knock at the door. Again.

'God damn it,' Gwen hissed. 'Why has everyone decided to use my cabin as a drop-in?'

Flustered, she stomped over to the door, throwing it open.

'What?' she groused. It was Captain Kane, an amused smirk spreading over his lips at Gwen's attitude.

'Interrupting something, am I?'

Gwen scowled up at him. Behind her, Astrid gave him a look that promised a slow death if he didn't get on with it.

'Sorry, sorry,' he said, holding his hands up for mercy.

Gwen could smell rum on his breath and clothes. Had Lorelei really been married to this man? It seemed impossible.

'I've good news, lassies. The winds have been kind to us, so we should make it to the sanctum sooner than expected.'

Gwen's body went stiff. That meant she was getting ever closer to finding the sword. Yet, one glance at Astrid and she stood up straighter.

She could do this.

'And,' the captain added, grinning, 'some of us will be joining you. We want to make a peace offering to the Order, to help in the fight.'

'Good,' Astrid said over Gwen's shoulder. 'We need all the people we can get. Who's coming?'

The captain nodded, pleased with her response. 'Just two of us,' he said, something devious entering his eyes as he stared at Gwen. 'We don't want to overwhelm the Order, so it'll only be me and Shay. We give them their prince back, unharmed, and in exchange, they let us watch when you kill the Shadowling.'

21

The Borealis Sanctum

Ragnar Frostbjorn, Magister of the Arctic Sector of the esteemed Order of Pendragon, was sitting in his office at the top of the ice tower. There had been another mermaid attack, on the west side of the archipelago. Their research bastion was being hit harder by the Grim than any other faction in the world.

It was utterly infuriating.

A girl, Magister Beatrice had told them – a small one at that – was meant to fix this problem. She and a pair of twins who could wield magic the likes of which had not been seen in centuries.

As he sipped his fireweed tea, he thought to himself that if this Rogue pirate ship didn't arrive soon with these miraculous Pledges, he wasn't sure how long their facilities would last. Their medical bay was already at its limit.

A whistle blew, a cold, clear sound. Down at the dock, voices rose, shouts and excitement.

An unknown ship was passing through the fog barrier.

Standing on the bow of the *Sea Reaper*, Astrid peered up at the great expanse of the Borealis Sanctum – a frozen fortress with towers reaching up into the sky. The entire thing was made of ice, charmed never to melt. Above, the light was turning pink, the entire snowscape blushing like a rose. And beneath the snow, nature hummed, a strange new land of songs Astrid had never heard. The land here twinkled, the Bloom as delicate and profound as the patterns on a snowflake.

Gwen shuddered as the ship approached, and not from the cold.

'He's passed over here,' Gwen whispered, her breath visible in the air. 'I can feel his shadow.'

Astrid watched the girl, her hair blowing in the icy wind, the determined set of her brow – even now, when Astrid knew she'd been having doubts. After the other night, it was clear that Gwen needed her. For now, all that mattered was working out how Gwen was going to defeat the Shadowling, and Astrid would do the dirty work. No matter how it stained her hands.

'Look at you all,' Lorelei said, hand on her heart as she took in Gwen and the twins. 'We made it here in one piece, despite everything.'

Magnus, back in his black furs, was smiling down at them. Astrid felt a little awkward under his eyes, until he patted her on the shoulder gently. 'You must keep taking care of each other. I fear the hard part is about to start.'

'Of course, Magnus,' Astrid promised. 'I won't let you down.'

Something melancholic entered his eyes as she spoke, and he gazed at them like they were the most precious things in the world. Astrid never wanted to disappoint him again.

'Christ, is this really necessary?' Jonas cried, pointing at the charmed chains round Teddy's wrists as they brought him out to the gangway.

Captain Kane held one end of the chain in his hand, his entire crew following behind him. Although they were formidable, standing with their weapons and weathered armour, Astrid noticed the light glinting off unshed tears as they prepared to bid the Faymore group farewell. Silverfang's lower lip visibly trembled as he spoke his goodbyes to Lorelei.

'We need them to know we mean business,' the captain said, jangling the chain in his hand, then, to the prince: 'You understand, right?'

Prince Teddy simply shrugged.

'Perhaps if someone else were carrying the chain.' He pretended to look around. 'Jonas, perhaps?'

Jonas narrowed his eyes only to smile, something fond passing between the two of them.

Gwen balked at the exchange, while Astrid simply chuckled.

A lot could change in a night.

The crew of the *Sea Reaper* delivered their dramatic goodbyes, and the twins found themselves jostled and ruffled.

'Good luck, little changelings!' Silverfang called.

Shay had moved away from the rest of the pirates to get a better view of the sanctum, staring up at it intensely. He caught Astrid's eye, a similar determination in his misty irises. He was on a mission, like Gwen.

After a week amongst Rogues, Gwen found being welcomed back into the Order's fold to be stifling. They were greeted off the boat by Custodians in furs and robes, each identically dressed with their Savonnettes proudly displayed. At the front of the welcome procession was a silver-haired man with a sharp silver beard. He had a regal air, and a stern look upon his long, wrinkled face. Trailing behind him, a white robe hovered above the snow, its seams lined with charms to keep it from getting wet.

'*Sanguis Noster*,' he said in greeting.

It was, of course, at this moment that Biscuit decided to run full pelt towards him.

'Down!' the man commanded, his voice booming across the snow.

Biscuit, to the surprise of everyone, stopped dead in his tracks, and sat prettily. Following the otter-dog's example, the Faymore Cluster bowed.

'What are you doing?' the man asked, his voice suddenly devoid of any commanding aura. 'Oh, you're bowing,' he said, surprised. 'Well, stop it.'

Confused, they all stood straight again to find the man had entirely dropped his regal front. He shrugged off his robe irritably, throwing it at one of the Custodians as he began muttering about formalities and nonsense. The Custodians around him seemed both world-weary and entirely accepting.

'Magister Ragnar, it's an honour to meet you,' Magnus said, introducing himself. 'I'm Magnus Faymore.'

'You're all early,' the man said, cutting Magnus off with a scowl. 'Magister Beatrice won't arrive until tomorrow.'

'Our apologies.'

'What? No, that's wonderful news!' The Magister chuckled, an odd trilling sound. 'And where are they?' His gaze landed on the twins. 'You two. I was told to make sure you don't get up to any mischief. Will you?'

The twins only shrugged.

'Right. And you?' Now he turned to Gwen. 'You're going to stop this Grim that's causing so many problems in our research? You're going to kill the Shadowling.'

Gwen could not hide her fleeting hesitation from Astrid or Jonas, but she swallowed it down before anyone else could notice.

'Yes, Magister. I'm here to find a way to stop him.' She spoke the words like she was manifesting.

Astrid smiled, encouraging her.

'We believe there's a weapon here, something that I can use to defeat him. If we can find it.'

The Magister sighed in relief, clutching his chest like a fainting lady.

'Oh good, thank the heavens. Let's get inside, then.' For a split second a modicum of his earlier frightening aura appeared, his eyes darkening as he muttered, 'The sooner that nuisance dragon is dead, the better.'

Turning on his heel, he snapped his fingers, commanding them all to follow him to the sanctum. Except, there was one giant elephant left unaccounted for.

'Er, wait, Magister, aren't you forgetting something?' Lorelei called, catching up with him. 'Did you not see they have the prince in chains?'

The Magister turned violently, looking utterly bewildered.

'Who?' he grumbled, then finally seemed to notice Captain Kane and Shay and Prince Teddy. 'Oh yes,' he laughed. 'Bea's boy. Well, OK. What do they want – treasure? Gold?'

Caught entirely off guard, the captain stepped forward, mustering as much bravado as he could in the odd circumstances. 'We want to help fight the Shadowling.'

Magister Ragnar laughed. A single honking sound. 'Why in the Twelve Spells would you want to do that?'

The captain's mouth opened and closed. He looked like he might be about to start laughing, but then he stepped forward with his hand on his chest in a valiant pose.

'Because he destroyed an entire ship of your people,' he declared.

The Magister winced, a darkness settling over him that reminded Astrid of the vengeful spark she often held on behalf of Gwen.

Captain Kane went on. 'Because he's evil incarnate. Because he's destroying the balance of magic, and he might be the thing that dooms us all.' He glanced at Lorelei, eyes softening. 'And because he hurt the woman I love.'

While Lorelei looked as if the snow might start melting at her feet, the Magister pondered the speech, that unusual darkness still casting shadows over his face. Then, as if placing a mask back on, he smiled, clapping his hands.

'OK, then. Very well. Just two of you, is it?' They nodded. 'We should be able to make room.' He laughed again, that goose-like honk, as he nudged the prince with his elbow. 'I must say, I'm rather relieved. I was dreading having to tell your mother that you were being held for ransom by pirates. An utterly frightening thought.'

'Wait.' The prince froze, confused. 'You did tell my mother about my letter, right? You told her what happened to the *Tidebinder*?'

Magister Frostbjorn let out another cackle that turned into a cough.

'Good heavens, no. Do you think I'm a fool? She'd have burned the oceans down looking for you, and our mission to the stop the Shadowling would have got delayed. Can't have that, can we?'

Without another word, he snapped his fingers again and marched off. The procession of Custodians behind him followed contritely.

'Oh my god,' Gwen said, eyes wide. 'He's totally mad.'

The prince blinked in shock. 'He didn't tell Mother.'

'We'd better keep an eye on him,' Shay said.

Astrid nodded. 'Yes. He's unpredictable.'

'Our ship was destroyed, I was kidnapped by pirates, and he didn't even tell Mother.'

Jonas tutted, helping the prince out of the wrist chains. 'Well, we'll just have to tell her ourselves.'

They were escorted into the sanctum. Unlike Fountains Abbey, the only other Order academy they'd ever been to, the Borealis Sanctum did not have a village like Fountains Vale surrounding it. It became clear to Astrid quite quickly that this was not a place for Pledges or families. The research here was dangerous and unpredictable, every labyrinthine inch of the interior as cold and deliberate as its ice and marble walls.

Their belongings were taken to the Custodians' Quarters along with Biscuit and Buttonbug. Their Cluster (plus two) were escorted past cavernous libraries and potion stores, each suffused with a melodic hum from crystalline lanterns floating along the arched ceilings. The walls shimmered faintly, like they might be wet to the touch. Sometimes it almost felt like they were underwater.

First they stopped at a large hall. The door was open, and even before they peered inside, Astrid could hear the gentle music of the Calm and Heal spells. They stepped through to find it filled with beds, each containing an injured member of the Order. Some were sleeping, with charmed bandages wrapped round eyes and limbs. Others were awake, staring at them, wide-eyed. Astrid knew that look; you could never escape it. These people had come face-to-face with the Grim.

'Dear god,' Prince Teddy muttered.

At Astrid's side, Gwen's fists balled, her breathing heavy. Her eyes flashed gold.

'So, it's true,' Lorelei said. 'Grim-infected magical creatures have been attacking your researchers.'

The Magister hummed in acknowledgement. 'Yes, until the Shadowling set his sights on our sanctum, we had perhaps a few magic-related injuries a year? Usually an over-eager student getting too close to a devil-toothed squid or the like. But now we have had to repurpose our largest music hall for casualties caused by the Grim. Diving expeditions have stopped entirely.'

Satisfied they'd seen enough, Magister Ragnar escorted them back out. Next, he took them down a corridor to the back of the sanctum.

'Here we are,' he announced.

They stopped at a pair of ice doors so thick that the room on the other side was nothing but a watercolour blur. Then Magister Ragnar hummed, and the doors flew open with a crystalline twinkling.

'Welcome to our Great Celestial Hall.'

The hall was a sprawling atrium at the heart of the sanctum. Custodians in fur hats and cloaks filled the long tables, busy with papers and quills. Above them was an ever-shifting star map, its constellations rearranging themselves in accordance with the real night sky.

Captain Kane whistled. 'We could do with a map like that for the ship.'

By now every Custodian had noticed their arrival, each peering up from their work.

The Magister clapped his hands. 'Everyone, get out!'

As if this were a common occurrence, all the Custodian scholars immediately began collecting their things. Robed researchers bustled out, bowing as they passed. Only two people stayed put, dressed in the familiar purple trim of Ambassadors.

'This is Ambassador Lunaris –' she was an older woman, short, with dark leathery skin and chunky grey streaks in her hair – 'and Ambassador Spike.' He was a younger man with thick braids and a scar across his lip.

The Magister gestured for the visitors to take a seat at the long mahogany table, the chairs pulling themselves out for their guests.

The Ambassadors bowed their heads, their gazes locked on Gwen in a way that was both curious and derisive. It made Astrid want to poke them in the eyes.

Easy, she reminded herself. The dark marks on her fingers tingled.

The Magister took his seat at the head of the table. 'Now, we've been told that the reason the Shadowling is paying so much attention to our faction is because there is likely something here he does not want us to find.'

Magnus spoke for the Cluster. 'That's the conclusion we have come to, yes.'

'Magister Beatrice also informed us that you would know what this *thing* is by the time you arrived here. If not, we were to imprison you all for treason.'

The prince spluttered, choking on his own shock. Apparently he had not been party to that part of the conversation.

'So, tell us,' Ambassador Lunaris began. 'What is it you've found that's going to stop the Shadowling?'

Magnus gestured for Gwen to speak, giving her the floor. Watching her, Astrid noticed how she determinedly didn't retreat into herself. She sat up tall, heroic. Like a king at his own court.

'We're looking for a sword. The same one we believe Arthur Pendragon used to stop the Shadowling hundreds of years ago.' She spoke frankly, not even a quiver on her lips. 'And we have this.' She gestured to Jonas, and he pulled an object from the inner pocket of his coat, placing it down with a metallic *thud*. 'It's the Savonnette that originally contained him.'

Ambassador Spike raised an eyebrow at the object.

'All we know – or at least, what we *believe* – is that there is a weapon that can stop him, and this Savonnette can lead us to it.'

The Magister licked his lips. 'How?'

The spell broken, Gwen dropped her gaze to stare at her hands. She was wavering again, unsure of herself, but Astrid sat firm at her side.

'Umm, we don't know,' she said.

'So, how did you figure this all out?'

'From dream-walking, Magister.'

'That's old magic,' Magister Ragnar said, surprised. He sat back in his chair, tensing his fingers as he hummed to himself. Then he clapped his hands. 'Very well. If dream-walking got you this much information, perhaps it can give you more. Ambassadors Lunaris and Spike, you will help me set up the Scrying Pond to trigger a fugue state in our Pledge here.' He stood up, his chair screeching on the marble floor. 'Come, everyone.' His eyes locked on Gwen, he licked his lips again. 'We're going to send our little hero here into her own dreams.'

22

Scrying

'No.' Astrid spoke the word like a weapon at the Magister's throat.

'Astrid, it's fine,' Gwen insisted, tugging at her sleeve.

Jonas shook his head, scowling at the pond. 'Astrid's right. No way.'

The Scrying Pond, they had discovered, was a circular pond under the sanctum. And by *pond*, the Order really meant a five-hundred-metre-deep pool. In other words, a watery black abyss.

'I think it looks quite relaxing,' the prince declared, earning an eye-roll from Jonas.

The water was almost entirely motionless but for the ripples of light coming from the sconces on the wall: green flames caged in ice.

'You don't have to do anything you don't want to do,' Magnus reminded her gently.

Gwen stared down at the pool. It was a perfect mirror. Of all the things she'd seen and fought, a creepy well of black water was child's play, surely?

'What do I have to do?'

'You simply have to get inside, and we'll close the ice sheet over you,' Ambassador Lunaris explained patiently.

'We'll leave enough space above you that you'll still be able to breathe while you float.'

'No,' the twins repeated.

Rounding on them, Gwen huffed, 'Either I'm doing this with you in the room, or I'm kicking you out. Choose one.'

Chuckling, Captain Kane nudged Shay. 'She's feisty, this one. Can tell she was half raised by our Lorelei.'

Locked in a battle of wills against Astrid and Jonas, Gwen stared them down. Astrid had that look about her, the one Gwen now understood as a dark side, a part that allowed Astrid to do unspeakable things to keep Gwen safe. The part of her Gwen needed to keep in the light.

Finally Astrid sighed. 'If for a second you sense something is wrong, we're getting you out of there, even if I have to destroy this entire room.'

Gwen smiled. 'Fine by me.'

'Wonderful,' the Magister announced. 'Let's begin.'

Given some privacy, Gwen changed into a simple white tunic. When she was done, she was surprised to find that upon dipping her toe in the water, it was almost like she was touching nothing at all.

'The water is charmed to match your body temperature perfectly. It should feel totally comfortable, to enable you to really lose track of yourself.'

Taking in the words of the Magister, Gwen lowered herself fully into the pool. The sensation was utterly bizarre. Somehow, she was buoyant, like stepping into air. Floating in nothing. The water, she realized, smelled like lilies, the flower of death.

'Now we will close the ice lid, and you must shut your eyes and drift,' Ambassador Lunaris explained. 'We will activate the spells from out here to send you into a state of calm. Simply knock on the lid when you are done.'

Taking a deep breath, Gwen gave them a thumbs-up. She felt entirely weightless. Above her, the Ambassadors pulled out strange, skinny flutes, playing to the ice until it covered her and the pool entirely. The last thing she saw as her view was cut off was Astrid's piercing blue eyes.

Now, floating in a sea of black, Gwen blinked out the world, and waited. All was silent, any sound stolen by the charmed ice lid of the pond. She was vaguely aware of her body relaxing, her muscles untensing, her mind going still. Time seemed to slip through her fingers like the water surrounding her limbs. Perhaps she was there for hours. Days. It was impossible to tell, and suddenly she didn't care.

You must find it.

The voice came to her like her own thought. Distant and near all at once.

Gwen opened her eyes. There was nothing but golden light. She walked through it, searching for something. In the corners of the world, shadows moved, watching her. They were always there, following her through time.

You must see what he did to us.

To all of us.

The sword – she was looking for the sword. She kept walking, her body light on its feet.

Follow the spirals.

The gold began to shift, a kaleidoscope. Spirals on spirals, emerging from the sea. Twirling islands cresting out of the water. At their centre, emerging from the deep, a sharp, glowing thing. The sword. It hissed as it emerged. The blade was consumed by shadows.

You are so close.

Do not make the same mistakes.

Gwen wanted to talk back to the voices, but she knew she couldn't. She knew they weren't really there. Only an echo of something long ago.

Gwendolyn. The past spoke her name, clear and righteous, and told her the message she had come to hear:

You must not kill the Shadowling.

Astrid was the first to rush forward when Gwen knocked on the ice lid. Without waiting for permission, she and Jonas hummed to the ice, pulling it back.

'Gwen!' Astrid called down; only, Gwen was not there. Her body was, but her eyes, though open, were steeped in gold.

'Gwen?' Jonas tried.

She didn't answer. Instead, as if pulled by invisible strings, her body began to lift out of the pool. The twins moved out of the way, holding out their arms to prevent anyone from stepping forward to intervene.

'What in the Twelve Spells is happening?' the prince breathed.

Then Gwen gasped.

She landed on the ground. Her eyes cleared.

'I know where the sword is!' She choked the words, doubling over. Astrid ran to her side, holding her up as she came back to herself.

'What happened?' Astrid prompted, helping her to sit down.

'The archipelago. The middle glacier – at the centre, there's a spiral, just like we suspected. The sword is there. In the ice.' She huffed between each word, as if she were drawing them out of the air itself. 'But the Savonnette isn't just a map. It'll awaken when it's near.'

Lorelei ran forward, draping her in her cloak.

'Gwen, that's incredible!' Magnus said, eyes wide. 'You've done it.'

But Astrid and Jonas could feel that something was wrong. Gwen shrugged Astrid off, shaking her head.

'What's wrong, Gwen?' Astrid asked, her voice low.

Looking around as if confused, Gwen rubbed at her arms. The whites of her eyes glowed in the green flames, frenzied. Something had frightened her.

'I can't do it.' She spoke the words distantly, then louder, panicked like a cornered animal. 'There's something wrong. I don't know what. I don't even understand it.' She grabbed Astrid's hand, beseeching her. 'I can't get the sword.'

'What?' the Magister spluttered. 'Yes, you bloody well can!'

'What are you talking about?' the captain demanded. 'Isn't that why we're here – so you can get the sword and kill the Shadowling?'

'You must get the sword. That is your purpose here,' Ambassador Spike added unhelpfully.

Shay held up his hand. 'Quiet!' he demanded, the force of his voice shocking even Astrid. 'Let her speak.'

Panting, Gwen righted herself. Standing there in her drenched white tunic, her hair dripping down her shoulders, she looked like something mythical. A holy thing.

'Listen, everyone.' She spoke carefully. 'The past is trying to communicate with me. It's trying to tell me that this sword – there's something wrong with it.' She took a deep breath, squinting her eyes as if she had a headache. 'We shouldn't get it or use it until we know exactly what happened before.'

A taut silence filled the domed space, the Magister tensing his hand irritably.

Magnus cleared his throat, coming to her side. 'Perhaps Gwen is right. Magister Beatrice will be here tomorrow morning. We can at least wait until she arrives to explain the situation to her, can't we?'

The silence seemed to grow tenfold as everyone waited for Magister Ragnar's decree. He did not look pleased.

'We cannot hold off any longer. We need that sword, and we need the Shadowling dead.' He spoke with finality, all his earlier frightening aura returned. 'Except . . .' he added with a sigh, 'travelling out to the centre of the islands could prove dangerous right now without proper back-up.'

Gwen looked up, hopeful for a long delay.

'Then it's decided. We shall wait for Magister Beatrice's arrival tomorrow and then set a course to collect the sword.'

'But –'

The Magister turned on his heel. 'Let's escort our guests to their quarters for the night.'

The prince's mouth fell open, but he quickly recovered from his surprise, offering the Faymore Cluster an apologetic look. It seemed even he couldn't do anything to solve this.

For a second Gwen looked like she was debating whether to bash a hole in the wall and make a run for it. Astrid put a soothing hand on her arm.

'I'll fix this,' Astrid said.

They were taken to their sleeping quarters, with Custodians perched nearby should they *need anything in the night*. The real purpose was clear to everyone: to make sure none of them attempted to leave.

'Astrid! Jonas!' Gwen whispered to them before they were separated. 'I can't get that sword.'

In the twins' room, Astrid paced back and forth like a caged animal. The space was opulent with crystal, ice and marble, their beds overflowing with crisp white sheets and piled high with pillows and furs. Yet, once more, the Order had them feeling like they were trapped.

Astrid took a seat by the fire burning in a pit in the middle of the room. The flames were pink and blossom-scented, giving off a gentle hum of Bloom.

'We need that sword,' she said, glancing up at Jonas.

He tensed where he was seated on his bed. 'She said no.'

'She said *she* can't get the sword. She didn't say *we* couldn't.'

'Astrid.' Jonas said her name in warning. 'You can't keep taking on these extra levels of responsibility. You don't have to throw yourself head first into danger. I mean . . .' He sighed, shaking his head. 'Look at your hands. How stained do they need to get before it's too late?'

His words hung heavy in the air, his concern seeping into her like blood into cloth.

'What happened with you two?' Jonas asked.

Astrid came and sat with him on the bed. 'I told her the truth.'

'That being?'

'That I'm willing to get my hands dirty for her.' Jonas frowned, but she cut him off before he could speak. 'That I believe evil cannot truly take me if I'm fighting for her.'

Scoffing, Jonas looked like he didn't know whether to laugh or cry. 'You can't be serious? Astrid?'

In the blue-and-pink light of their sanctum dorm room, their hair was like silver. For the first time in a long time, Astrid felt the strength of how different they were from other people. The frightening angelic teenagers that strangers saw when they first encountered her and Jonas.

'We're different, Jonas.'

'Yes, obviously. But, Astrid, no one is immune to the Grim. I'm supposed to keep you in check, remember? We're here to serve Gwen and find out where we come from, and I cannot do either of those things if you – what? Become some evil witch?'

'That's not going to happen,' Astrid insisted. She could feel Jonas's anger rising like the sting of a nettle against her skin. 'Jonas, listen to me. The only reason I'm telling you this is because I need you to trust me. Whatever happens, you have to believe that I'm going to be OK. What we . . . what I feel for Gwen – it's stronger than the Shadowling. I know it, and I'll do whatever it takes to get Gwen the answers she needs to save the world.'

For a moment Astrid could feel him turning, the soft cushion of trust, his soul knowing hers. And then it snapped.

'Whatever you're planning, I want no part in it.' Jonas spoke with finality. 'I'm going to sleep, and you should too. We can figure out a plan with Gwen tomorrow when you're thinking like a normal person again.'

'Jonas –'

'We're not getting the sword.'

Before Astrid could say anything else, Jonas pouted and curled himself up in the bed.

'Goodnight.'

There was nothing more to say.

Astrid awoke with a start, a shadow looming over her.

'Shh . . .' The figure held a finger to their lips.

Shay.

Pulling the cover back, Astrid sat up. The moon was still high, silver light flooding through the window. It couldn't have been long past the witching hour.

'What are you doing here?' she asked.

On the other side of the room, Jonas groaned in his sleep, rolling over. Biscuit made a yipping sound while he dreamed, cuddling up closer to him and Buttonbug.

Shay and Astrid both went silent, waiting to see if her twin would awaken. When they were sure Jonas had stilled, Shay smiled, his face half obscured in the shadows.

'I know a way out of here. Come on,' Shay said, holding his hand out.

'Where are we going?' Astrid asked.

He grinned at her, his fang flashing like a knife. Then he lifted his hand, and there, dangling on its chain, was the white-gold Savonnette.

'We're going to get that sword.'

23

They're All Dead

The words repeated themselves in Gwen's head as she slept.

You must not kill the Shadowling.

It went against everything that was expected of her. Everything she'd been preparing herself for. So, if she wasn't meant to kill him, what the hell was she meant to do?

She'd placed the book of Cursed Melodies on the side table. Not because she wanted it close, she told herself, but because she naively hoped it might give her more answers as she slept. It didn't. All she felt from it was an ominous sense of expectation. Like everyone else, it wanted something from her.

Gwen awoke to a clear, bright whistling. Rubbing her eyes, she got out of bed. The floor cold beneath her feet, she moved to the arched window of the dorm.

Outside, the world glowed orange with the sunrise. The snow beamed. People were calling, preparations being made. Glancing up, she saw a dark mass emerging from the fog barrier north of the harbour – the bow of a ship. Magister Beatrice had arrived.

Throwing on her boots and furs, Gwen ran down, shouting as she passed the Custodians on guard: 'Magister Beatrice is here.'

She had to speak to the queen immediately. Panting, she nearly ran straight into Prince Theodore.

'Gwen!' he said, equally out of breath. 'My mother's here. We should speak to her about the *Tidebinder* and the sword before –'

'Way ahead of you,' she huffed.

He nodded, the two taking off together, boots squeaking on the marble.

Outside, Gwen was somehow not surprised to find that Magnus had beaten them to it. He stood patiently in his black furs as they lowered the gangway to the ship. Surrounding him were Custodians in their identical black robes, and, of course, Magister Ragnar. He glanced at Gwen disapprovingly as she approached.

'I hope a good night's sleep has got you thinking clearly again,' he said, smiling.

She ignored him. Her eyes were on the boat.

A figure appeared, hard to see at first in the streams of dawn light. One thing was clear: it was not Magister Beatrice. But it was someone Gwen knew very well.

'Jan?'

Gwen had to assume she was delirious with stress, because there was absolutely no way her sister was somehow in the Arctic. And it wasn't just her: coming up behind her, also in the identical black capes and Savonnettes of Order Custodians, were Thomas and Elijah.

'Gwenny!' Jan shouted across the dock when she spotted her.

Dazed, Gwen could do little but stand there trying to process what she was seeing. Jan ran down the gangway, wrapping her arms round Gwen as the rest of the crew disembarked in precise lines. Only Jan, Thomas and Elijah had broken rank.

'I've missed you so much!' Jan said, squeezing her tight before holding her at arm's length. 'Look at you! It's not even been two weeks, but I feel like you've grown.'

Thomas came up next to her, one eyebrow raised in that cocky way of his. 'Still in one piece, then?'

Gwen gaped. 'What are you all doing here?'

Jan smiled, stepping back to proudly display her new uniform. Up close, it was a little different from the usual Order capes and slacks. It was tighter-fitting, and the cape had a collar that framed her neck. The kind of thing that had Gwen thinking of an army regiment.

'We're joining the mission,' Jan said, still beaming. 'We're part of Magister Beatrice's special task force.'

Gwen frowned, her brain struggling to keep up with the information.

'What? No . . . And Elijah, why?'

He marched forward at his name, rubbing his thumb affectionately over Gwen's cheek. 'Gwen, dear, I do hope you've been keeping warm.' He turned his sights on Magnus, who, after recovering from his own shock, practically had hearts in his eyes. 'Magnus, my love, was the journey pleasant?'

'Not at all, my darling,' he replied. 'But it'll be much better now you're here . . . Why are you here, exactly?'

Elijah looked confused then, like Magnus was speaking nonsense. 'I'm not very well going to let you all save the world without me,' he said, crossing his arms indignantly. 'We started this mess, and it's only appropriate we finish it.'

There was a shift in the crowd, with all the Custodians suddenly standing rigid. Jan and Thomas fell in line with them – their regiment.

Gwen turned to see her. This was not like the shack in Scotland; this was not an impromptu meeting over tea. This was Magister Beatrice in all her commanding glory.

Even from a distance, Gwen could hear the hum of Bloom from the queen's white fur robes, spells of Fire and Bind woven into the fabric. These weren't just protective: this was a magic that could, if woven differently, be explosive.

She stepped down from the gangway, dark coils of hair pouring over her shoulders. With harsh eyes, she analysed the scene before her. She was about to address them when a voice spoke:

'Mother!'

The harshness melted like the snow at her feet. Grabbing her dress, she rushed forward, entirely disregarding Magister Ragnar as he stood nearby.

'Darling, let me look at you!' she cooed, checking Teddy over. The prince, though he tried to seem bashful, was clearly relieved to be in the hands of one of his mothers again.

Gwen wanted to think it childish, or the prince pampered. But instead she wondered whether she would react the same, if she had a mother to run to.

'Was the journey good? Are you well?' Magister Beatrice asked, her eyes turning serious again. 'Did they find what the Shadowling is looking for?'

'Yes, Mother, but there's something we need to discuss –'

Teddy couldn't get another word out before Magister Beatrice interrupted:

'Where are Captain Bellamy and Lieutenant Thorn?'

As soon as she asked the question, her gaze settled on a point behind him, where Lorelei and Captain Kane were coming down to the dock.

Her face contorted. Furious. Gwen thought for one dreadful moment that she was about to unleash a barrage of spells. She could practically hear the Bloom burning in the queen's throat.

Prince Teddy, sensing it too, tried to stop her.

'Mother, let me explain. A lot has happened.'

'You!' she hissed, putting her son behind her. 'What did you do? We had a deal, Lorelei.'

Now Thomas stepped forward, breaking rank.

'Cousin?' he asked, confused. 'What's going on?'

But it was not Lorelei who answered. Captain Dorian Kane marched proudly to meet the Magister head-on.

'Your Majesty, she saved the Faymore Cluster from certain death on your ridiculous palace of a ship with your pampered crew, and then we safely escorted them and your son here free of charge,' he declared, matching the Magister fire for fire. 'I believe the words you're looking for are *thank you*.'

Lorelei swore under her breath. 'Dorian, watch your tongue.'

But Magister Beatrice was no longer listening. Her fire had turned to a simmer. Gwen recognized that look.

She spoke slowly, her gaze distant. 'What happened to my crew?'

Teddy, for all the disagreeable encounters they'd had with him in the past, showed his true colours then. His face broke, real pain coming through. What had happened on the *Tidebinder* had hurt him deeply, and it was only in front of his mother that he really, finally, let it show.

'Mother, they're all gone,' he said, a quiver in his voice. 'Someone destroyed the runes and summoned a fog and somehow called an entire fleet of Grim-possessed mermaids.

If Lorelei hadn't sent out a signal to Captain Kane and his crew, we'd all be dead.'

Magister Beatrice took a slow breath.

'Who did this?'

Gwen swallowed. She wished she had the answer. 'We don't know.'

Magister Beatrice's eyes widened, the whites near glowing. Freshly furious, she turned her gaze on Gwen, and the mission.

'Have you at least found what it is we're looking for?'

Now was her chance: Gwen could explain. Surely, after all this, Magister Beatrice would see reason. Would trust her that the sword could not be used.

'Yes, she has. And she won't bloody get it.'

Gwen went rigid as Magister Ragnar beat her to it, his voice nearly shrill.

Around them, the neat lines of Custodians began to fidget, hushed whispers passing between them.

'Excuse me?' Magister Beatrice said. 'What on earth is going on?'

Both Magisters' eyes were boring into her, fire and ice. They had reconvened in the Great Celestial Hall, a Magister at each end of the table.

'It's not that I don't want to. The old kings are telling me that there's something wrong with it. I'm sure of it. That's why they wanted me to touch the sword in the temple, to see it crumble,' Gwen explained for what felt like the hundredth time. She wished she'd woken up the twins before starting this whole thing. Their presence beside her was bolstering and soothing, like two guard dogs. Now, under everyone's intense stares and whispering, she could scarcely tell what was nerves and what was her temper rising. 'I don't want to attempt to get the sword until I know exactly what happened in the past.'

Gwen's eyes flickered to Jan where she sat next to Magnus. There was an air of authority to her, a coldness Gwen was not used to from her usually honey-sweet sister. How had this happened?

'And how do you expect to find this information?' Jan asked.

Gwen swallowed. 'I don't know.'

The Magisters scowled.

'We don't have time for this,' Ragnar Frostbjorn complained, slamming his hand on the table. 'We'll get a fleet ready tonight and get the sword, then we will devise a plan to find this damnable dragon and have the girl kill him.'

Gwen's vision flashed gold. 'No.' There was a rumble of Bloom in her voice, her fingers tingling. 'You must listen to me. There is something wrong with the sword. With this whole plan, I'm sure of it. I can't – shouldn't – no, *won't* kill him.'

Magister Beatrice stared at her, dainty fingers tapping on the table. It was a stand-off, each of them holding back the full extent of her frustration. Gwen could not and would not let mistakes be made again on her behalf.

'Umm . . . what's that noise?' Thomas asked.

Gwen blinked, surprised by the interruption.

Everyone paused, going quiet to listen. Gwen heard it immediately, a distant shouting. Panic and upheaval.

'That's Jonas,' Gwen breathed, heart thudding.

Rapid footsteps stomped outside, followed by desperate banging at the ice doors until Magister Ragnar whistled them open.

And there he was, gasping for breath.

Without a word, Prince Teddy ran to Jonas's side, helping him to a chair. In all their lives, Gwen had never seen Jonas so panicked. His face was pallid, green-tinged like he might be sick. The look of someone who had seen their worst nightmare come true.

'She's gone!' he huffed.

Magnus stood up immediately, his chair falling back and crashing on to the floor. 'Where?' he demanded.

Confused, Gwen looked around, not yet comprehending the gravity of the situation.

'They took the Savonnette,' Jonas wheezed. 'Astrid and Shay. They've gone to get the sword.'

And in that moment Gwen felt her entire heart rip in two.

24
Handsome Devils

Rainbow colours flashed across Jonas's eyes. He felt dizzy with panic.

Astrid was gone.

His entire life, they'd always been mere moments from each other. Now he felt her absence as an acute pain. It hurt, unbearably, and he had no way to make sense of it.

In his peripheral vision, he was vaguely aware of the rest of his Cluster, of Magister Beatrice, and of Teddy holding him. He leaned in, grasping for a modicum of comfort.

'What wonderful news,' Magister Ragnar declared, clapping his hands. 'I do so love when young people take some initiative.' He honked a laugh, and Jonas wanted to throttle him. 'It seems our problems are solved. Your sister will bring back the sword, and we can continue our plans.'

Bloom tingled in Jonas's fingers, his throat hot with it. Just one wave of his hands, a little hum, and he could have Magister Ragnar begging for mercy.

'Easy, Jonas,' Magnus muttered in warning. Then he asked calmly and clearly, 'How long ago did they leave?'

'I don't know. Probably not long after we went to sleep.' Jonas gasped a breath, his voice hitching. 'I've never . . . we've never been apart . . . I –'

Prince Teddy rubbed his shoulders soothingly. 'It's OK, we'll find her.'

'She couldn't . . . she wouldn't . . .' Gwen's fists balled at her sides, a fire igniting in her eyes. 'We need to leave now. We have to go get her.'

Meeting Gwen's eyes, Jonas nodded his agreement. No matter what, he knew he could trust Gwen to understand.

Slapping his hands on the table, Magister Ragnar stood, outrage in his eyes. He opened his mouth to speak, but there was suddenly a thick, wet slapping sound in the room. One Jonas knew very well.

Bumbling into the room, Biscuit began barking desperately. A Custodian tried to grab him, but he slipped through, barrelling towards Jonas.

'Down, boy,' Jonas said. 'Come on, Biscuit, it's OK. Calm down.'

The otter-dog kept jumping up. His barks turned more aggressive.

'Who let the Dobhar-chú in here?' Magister Ragnar tutted.

'He's just overexcited from all the commotion,' Jonas said, trying to soothe the pup. Somehow having Biscuit to comfort made him feel slightly better. Like he was soothing himself.

A voice spoke up from the other side of the room.

'He's not excited; he wants something.' It was Thomas. 'Look, he's licking at your coat!'

'What –'

Jonas's heart thudded. Time seemed to slow down.

The Black Savonnette.

He nearly slapped himself. As quickly as he could, he retrieved it from his inner pocket, shining obsidian in his hand. It had always seemed alive, but now more so than ever.

The moment he held it out Biscuit barked, trotting backwards and pawing at the floor.

'Where on earth did you get that?' Magister Beatrice asked, pulling up her dress to march towards him.

'Lieutenant Thorn gave it to us . . . before she . . .'

Jonas couldn't finish the sentence before she snatched it out of his hand, holding it up to the light. Barking even more, Biscuit jumped up at Magister Beatrice. Calm as snowfall, she placed her hand on the otter-dog's head, soothing him.

'We thought it was a weapon,' Jonas said.

'A weapon?' the Magister replied, her eyes wide.

'You called it "*a last resort*",' Gwen reminded her.

'Yes, it's a last resort. A special Savonnette issued to only the most trusted and respected Custodians of the Order.' Her voice went a shade darker. 'This Savonnette does not just hold magical creatures, but Bloom Bloods too.'

As though the words had created a vacuum, the whole room went deathly silent. Everyone was too shocked to speak. The very idea – it was unfathomable, and Jonas had to wonder, who had they been intending to use them on?

'That's why they had them,' he said, with dawning understanding. 'In case they needed to use them on us, if we wouldn't cooperate.'

Outraged, Teddy bristled. 'Mother, is this true?'

She only waved her hand dismissively.

'That's neither here nor there. What matters is who, exactly, is in here . . .'

Without another word, she placed the Savonnette on the table. The ritual was different from the one Jonas had seen before – and surprisingly simple. Magister Beatrice retrieved an ornate pipe from her sleeve, playing a melody that was both quick and complex. Music crafted with surgical precision. On the table, the Savonnette lifted into the air, spinning wildly as she played. The music came to an abrupt stop, the Savonnette suspended above the table. Its lid clicked open, and everyone covered their ears as the room was startled by a great pop, the air pressure shifting.

And out sprang a boy. Red hair, freckles and a disarming air of innocence.

It was Eddie Clam.

'What . . .' he mumbled, shading his eyes from the light. He was dressed in the exact same uniform he'd been wearing the night the *Tidebinder* was attacked. 'Where . . .'

At last reunited with his master, Biscuit barked and bolted, running around and jumping up with unbridled joy. He barrelled the poor boy over, diving on to his chest and licking his face.

Eddie giggled, ruffling Biscuit's hair, then gradually sat up.

He stared at them all, blinking in confusion, until his eyes widened, shock and horror creeping in.

'We're under attack!' he shouted, utterly panicked. 'Someone broke the runes!' Then he blinked again, taking in all the faces. Absorbing the fact that he was most definitely not on a ship. And that he was face-to-face with not one, but two Magisters.

'Holy smokes . . .' he breathed.

'Eddie,' Jonas said, putting a soothing lilt into his voice. 'We need you to stay calm, OK?'

He looked like a cornered animal, his gaze darting about. But he nodded, swallowing his confusion.

Stepping forward, Teddy – much to Jonas's admiration – took charge of the situation.

'Eddie, the *Tidebinder* was attacked. Isobel Thorn put you inside a Savonnette to protect you.' He spoke clearly but softly, easing Eddie into the news. 'We've just got you out, and we need you to tell us: did you see who destroyed the runes?'

Eddie trembled, holding Biscuit close.

'Yes, I did.'

Magister Beatrice let out a breath, her gaze severe.

'Tell us. Now,' she said. 'Who amongst the crew of my ship betrayed me?'

Shrinking under her stare, Eddie looked terrified. If he'd been a rabbit, Jonas imagined he'd have been burrowing a hole in the ground right about now.

'There wasn't . . .' he said, his voice shaking. 'It wasn't anyone I recognized.'

Teddy glanced at Jonas, the two trying to make sense of it.

'A stranger on board? What about Biscuit?' Teddy asked. 'Surely he would have sniffed out someone new?'

'No, it was utterly weird,' Eddie said, shaking his head. 'Biscuit didn't react to him at all. It was like he wasn't really there.' Jonas's ears pricked up, a cold dread setting in as Eddie continued to speak. 'He had black hair and dark circles under his eyes, and he seemed to just disappear into the shadows . . .'

Jonas gasped. 'That's Shay.'

He looked at Gwen, both their eyes wide.

'What? No!' Captain Kane almost tripped over his words. He looked utterly lost. 'I've known Shay since he was a boy. It's not possible. How?'

'I'm sorry, Dorian,' Lorelei said, though her expression lacked any remorse. 'We have to stop him.'

In front of Jonas, Gwen began to sway, gripping her forehead like she was in pain.

'The sword!' Gwen hissed, her eyes blazing with fear. 'In the temple at Runefjord, when I touched the statue, the whole place turned rotten with the Grim. That's what it was trying to tell me. That's what Shay is going to do – don't you see?' She turned to Magnus, desperate. 'He's going to get Astrid to seize the sword. And when she does, whatever's wrong with it will be wrong with her too.'

'We have to leave. Now!' Magnus declared. 'Come on.'

Magister Beatrice rounded on her Custodians. 'Take Captain Kane to the cells bellow. We can't risk his involvement. And prepare my ship – I want it battle-ready. Today, the Shadowling is making his move.'

'Then we will make our counter-move!' Magister Ragnar said, almost gleefully.

Reluctantly, Lorelei let go of the pirate captain with a single kiss, and he did not resist; he was too shocked. But he also understood the importance of locking people up out of precaution.

Jumping to, Jan and Thomas began organizing themselves as Magnus, Lorelei and Elijah ushered Gwen and Jonas out of the room.

'I'll join Thomas and Jan,' Elijah told Magnus. 'You take Jonas and Gwen.'

'We still have time,' Magnus said, though his face was anxious. 'We must have faith in her, OK? We have to trust her.'

The words put dread in Jonas's stomach, heavy as lead. He couldn't feel Astrid at all, just a hole in his soul, like she'd been torn out.

Beside him, while everyone rushed around, Gwen was staring up. Her eyes were focused on the ceiling, sweat forming on her brow.

'Jonas, I feel like something terrible is about to happen. Here – now.'

The words were but a whisper, just between the two of them, as the world sped up around them.

Jonas listened, leaning in. It was faint, a low hum one might almost miss, but there nonetheless, and growing: a note of discord bleeding into the twinkling Bloom of the sanctum.

'Everyone, stop!' Gwen shouted, her eyes flashing gold. Her command carried like a war cry, stopping everyone in their tracks. 'If the Shadowling knows the sword is cursed with the Grim, then why would he want to warn me away from it?'

Jonas felt sick to his stomach, the truth now clear in front of him. How completely and royally they had messed up. Magnus and Elijah seemed to understand too, their eyes darting around.

'He didn't want to scare us away,' Jonas breathed.

'No,' Gwen said. 'He was trying to lure us all here.'

It was the last thing she was able to say before the roof of the Great Celestial Hall exploded in fire.

25

Sword in the Stone

Moving through the shadows, Shay had taken Astrid to a boathouse down a path at the back of the sanctum. Outside, the swirling colours of the aurora made purple and green ribbons in the sky, yet the night was still, and the ice crunched softly beneath their boots. The rowing boats had magic propellers, but they agreed the melodies would be too loud. Instead, Shay used the oars, just the two of them rowing out into the enchanted waters and away from the safety of the Borealis Sanctum.

The water was eerily calm. Astrid could see them: things moving beneath the surface, eyes glowing. The spray or splash of a whale in the distance. A tail breaching the surface. A unique place, the whole area was alive with creatures both magical and not. A rare sort of harmony, reminiscent of the old ways that the Rogues talked about.

'It's beautiful here,' Astrid said, her eyes on the horizon.

Shay hummed in agreement, staring up at the kaleidoscope of colours above. His skin seemed to reflect it, shimmering with an opalescent sheen. Like this, so tranquil and determined, it would be easy to be charmed by him.

Up ahead was the central glacier. A mammoth island of ice, it towered over the sea, frozen walls rising up and cresting on both sides like the outstretched wings of a great celestial being.

Tying the boat up, they disembarked, Astrid holding out the Savonnette like a dowsing rod to locate the sword.

'Look!' Shay said, excited. They'd been walking for no more than a few minutes into the centre of the glacier when the Savonnette began to glow. It was that same golden glow Astrid recognized from the flashes in Gwen's eyes. It was her power, that shining thing at the centre of Gwen's Bloom, here, in Astrid's palm.

Except, where was the sword?

'Spirals,' Astrid pondered aloud. 'Why would there be spirals in the ice?'

It was utterly cold, and Astrid could no longer feel the tip of her nose. When Shay replied, she could see his breath in the air.

'The spell,' he said. 'The one you performed on the mountain. It left spiral marks in the earth.'

Astrid paused, remembering. A song that scorched – the same song that the book had made Gwen perform when it was showing her the sword. Of course! It seemed so simple.

Astrid sighed. 'It seems I'll have to sing it again.'

She stared down at the now-fading black round her fingernails. She supposed it didn't matter anyway. What mattered was Gwen, and Astrid was willing to sacrifice herself for that cause.

'Hold this,' she said, relinquishing the Savonnette into Shay's palm.

Her tongue grew wet at the prospect of performing that dark-tainted magic again, desperate for a taste of the sound. The earth, meanwhile, screamed at her. Even in this distant land, a world she hardly knew, it understood the consequences. The sound was pleading, desperate.

So, she drowned it out with her own voice.

At only the first note, she felt soothed. A discomfort she'd grown to tolerate was mollified. The burn of Bloom in her throat was doused in the icy-cool feel of the melody.

She knew the patterns now, the way the music would twist at the edges. How it would bleed shadows, a darkness seeping into the otherwise golden light of the glorious spell. She felt it too, cold over her skin, the ink of evil crawling across her fingers.

And suddenly, it was no longer just the Savonnette that was glowing. Like light breaking through a crack to breach the dark, it spread across the ice. Spirals of light awakened at their feet. And the light burned.

Searing hot, the ground melted, the ice giving way. As the spell came to a close, Astrid had a split second to remember that she, of course, could not swim, before there was suddenly not enough ice left underneath them. There was a harsh *crack*, and then they were falling.

Except, they didn't land in the water beneath. There was no cold-shock or drowning panic. Where the ice had melted, they were, miraculously, pulled down and down, as though in a vacuum, sucked down through the ocean far beneath the waves.

Astrid screamed; she couldn't help it, both elated and terrified. Grabbing on to her protectively, Shay held tight as they plummeted. When Astrid could not fathom going any deeper, they stopped abruptly. Like someone had pulled a parachute cord on their backs, they floated gently down to the sand.

'Well, wasn't that thrilling?' Astrid laughed, righting herself.

Shay helped her to standing, both of them glancing around.

There was sand and stone at their feet, and they were deep underwater, but they were in a dome that dampened the scent and sounds of the sea. The edges looked like glass – except they rippled. Outside the dome, frightening things passed by them, the forms of giant creatures flashing in sudden bursts of bioluminescent light.

'We're in an air bubble,' Shay said, sounding amazed.

But Astrid's sights had already moved away from the edges of their miraculous enclosure, for there, in the centre, was the sword.

Hilt pointing upward, the blade was trapped in stone. Someone, somehow, long, long ago, had placed the sword here, and here it had spent an eternity waiting for the one who would wield it against evil once more.

It was waiting for Gwen.

Approaching carefully, Astrid took in the fine details, the way the metal sang sharply, the delicate engraving of a pansy at the hilt. It hummed and pulsed with golden light, like a heartbeat, growing and fading.

'Remarkable.' Astrid was awestruck, the blade singing to her, begging her to touch it. 'I can feel the power.'

'This is it,' Shay breathed, reverent. 'This is the weapon that can kill him.'

They were both mesmerized, their faces illuminated gold.

'Take it,' Shay insisted. 'Use it.'

Astrid's fingers hovered over the hilt, the strength emanating from it utterly tantalizing.

Then she pulled back her hand and laughed.

'It's insulting, really, how naive you think I am.'

Shay blinked at her, confused. 'What?'

Still chuckling, Astrid pondered how the events must look to everyone else. Astrid falling for evil. Astrid being lured into a trap. She hadn't been able to tell anyone what she knew, because Shay had been watching. A shadow on the wall. She'd known the moment he'd shown his powers that she had to get friendlier with him, to find out who he *really* was.

Sometimes one had to keep evil close for the sake of good.

'I suppose you thought I was some silly young girl, hungry for power, traumatized by the Red Blooded world, desperate to find out what I am. Looking for connection, for someone who understands. Is that right?'

Shay's eyes sharpened, his confused expression clearing into something else.

'Astrid, what are you –'

'Quiet. I'm talking,' she commanded. 'You're not like me. Whatever Jonas and I are, you're not the same. You don't know what it's like to fight for someone else, wholly and truly.'

In the rippling light, Shay frowned. His pale face, usually so considerate, so thoughtful, began to morph. Like a sheep becoming a wolf, a sharp-toothed grin spread across his face.

'It appears I've underestimated you,' he purred.

'You have,' Astrid said frankly, then she gestured to the blade again. 'This sword. Am I to understand it's infected with the Grim in a way that will transfer to me should I touch it?' Shay frowned again, eyes narrowing, and Astrid laughed. 'Don't worry, I still plan to take it.'

This, as Astrid had expected, confused him in a way that gave her a stab of gleeful satisfaction. It felt so good to trick someone when they thought they were winning.

Shay spoke again, his voice harsh now, trying to regain a modicum of control. 'If you know all this, you must also know that this is a dead end. The Shadowling is coming, and he will have you. You will not be able to resist.'

Astrid rolled her eyes. 'I'm aware.'

At this, Shay chuckled, but it wasn't that lilting laugh from before, it was poisonous mirth.

'Humour me, then,' he said. 'Why?'

Sighing, Astrid contemplated the boy in front of her. They were both likely to be stuck down here until one of them took the sword. There was no harm in a little gloating.

'OK, then,' she acquiesced. 'I realized after I used a Cursed Melody for the first time that we simply knew nothing. One taste of this strange, ancient power and I felt the world opening up in my palm.' Shay nodded, like he understood. She supposed he did, but the next part baffled him. 'And if I am to help Gwen in any meaningful way, I have to know everything. It will be hard, it will hurt her tremendously, but she is right: if we are to win, we must know all that happened in the past. Which means we need the Shadowling's knowledge, too.' Her voice softened, remembering who she was doing this for, her body light with her faith as she spoke. 'I only have to trust that in the end Gwen will save me.'

Shay scoffed, shaking his head as if she'd just said the most astonishingly stupid thing in the world.

'You might have resisted before, when Seraphina used her . . . primitive methods. This will be different,' he assured her. 'No one can be saved from the Grim.'

'*I* will be,' Astrid retorted, entirely unwavering, sure to her very bones. Then she looked up through her lashes at the boy in front of her, her expression darkening. 'I'm just sorry you could not be saved too, Quin Larkspur.'

Shay flinched at the name, and then he began to laugh, a strange, almost pained sound. As he laughed his face and body undulated. There was a pop of bones moving, his skin reforming in front of Astrid's eyes until what stared back at her was someone else. Same dark hair and grey, sunken eyes, but now they were set into the features of the boy from the photos Magnus had shown them. She could only wonder how Magnus would feel, when he realized the truth. That one of the Rapscallions was somehow still walking the earth, and that he had betrayed them all.

'So, what are you – a ghost?' Astrid asked, half mocking, half curious.

Shay looked like he was about to laugh again. 'I prefer the term *phantom*,' he answered, crossing his arms. 'His power keeps me tethered to the earth. I cannot leave, and I cannot be killed.' He didn't sound particularly thrilled with this. 'I am simply stuck in this form he gave me, waiting, following his mysterious whims.'

Astrid hummed thoughtfully.

'Sounds like torture.'

Shay didn't comment, and that was answer enough.

'How did you stop Magnus from realizing?'

This time Shay did laugh, the sound almost fond.

'Oh, Magnus.' He said the name like he was referring to an old beloved pet. 'Just like before, when we were young, Magnus sees whatever I want him to see.' His misty-grey eyes became distant for a second, his expression almost regretful. 'It was only Rupert who ever understood my true nature. That my thirst for knowledge and control could not be sated. I think *you* understand a little something of that.'

Now Astrid didn't comment, and this too was answer enough.

'Rupert – he sacrificed himself to the Grim to know too, didn't he?' she asked. This was what she'd come to understand. That the Grim did not just give you physical power, but power in knowledge. That's why the Shadowling rarely infected Bloom Bloods. He didn't want them to know the truth.

Shay, for the first time since they'd started talking, looked away.

'Yes. He held on valiantly to his humanity.' He spoke softly, almost to himself. 'But you can't overcome the Grim. No one can.'

Having received the information she had come for, Astrid decided it was time to wrap it up. She had terrible, heartbreaking things to do, and the others would soon notice she was gone.

'Do you know, then, what Jonas and I are? Why Rupert wanted Magnus to find us?'

'I do, yes.'

'And I'll know too, when I touch this sword?'

He nodded.

'Very well. I suppose I'd better turn into an evil witch now.'

He laughed. 'Why does this not feel like I'm winning?'

She smiled at him, a genuine smile. 'Because in the end, you won't. Eventually Gwen will save me – and the world.'

Shay looked at her, and he almost seemed impressed, until his expression turned to something that could have been pity.

But Astrid wasn't afraid. She knew what she was doing. Sometimes you simply had to get your hands dirty for the people you loved.

She grabbed the sword.

26

Nemesis

Fire and ash, steam and smoke. The Great Celestial Hall was in ruins, and this was not regular fire: it screamed with rotten Bloom, burning bright crimson and eating through the debris like acid.

Ears ringing, Gwen tried to make sense of the world around her. Her arm twinged when she tried to stand up, her eyes and throat stinging from the smoke. The entire left-hand wall of the hall had caved in along with the roof. The cold rushed in, puffs of snow flying around them.

Magisters Beatrice and Ragnar were calling orders as they ran out into the tundra. Beatrice held Prince Teddy's arm, pulling him with her protectively.

It was the wrong way, Gwen wanted to shout. But she couldn't. She'd lost her voice.

Someone screamed in pain.

'They're coming from the sea!' someone else cried. 'They're destroying the boats!'

As the dust settled, Gwen saw the devastation. Custodians were strewn across the marble floor, trying to pull themselves and one another out of the ice and rubble. Near the door, Gwen saw her sister and Thomas singing spells to push or lift the debris, trying to help the injured while the rest fled.

Gwen gasped and looked away when she saw Ambassador Lunaris impaled on a glistening spike of ice.

'Gwen, quickly now.'

Magnus. He grabbed her under the shoulders. Her injured arm protested, but she let him lift her up. And then they were running.

'We have to go, Gwen.' Elijah's soothing voice came through.

Catching a glimpse through the dust, Gwen saw Lorelei helping Captain Kane, the two of them running through the broken wall out into the snow.

'Biscuit!' a boy's voice cried – Eddie. He chased the otter-dog out into the snow too. Gwen wanted to tell them all no, to go back, because that direction was where she could hear the searing sound of the Grim growing.

'Jonas . . .' She uttered his name. Reached out, feeling for him.

'I'm right here!' he said, running alongside them.

Gwen gave one look back at the hall as the black smoke cleared. Above, light pooled through, the sky bright . . . and then a shadow passed overhead.

A shadow with wings.

He was here.

They ran, fast as lightning, chests heaving.

'We need to get the book!' Gwen shouted. The fog in her brain was melting, the severity of the situation becoming clear.

The Shadowling was here, and he had an army of Grim-possessed creatures that were about to swarm the sanctum from the surrounding waters. She could hear it: rot in the form of a melody, the Grim.

It felt like the end of the world.

The rest of the sanctum was in a state of chaos. People injured, people running to help, or to escape. Books and papers were abandoned, as were the still bodies. Their group kept running, until they reached a moment of calm on the mezzanine level.

Suddenly they were alone – just Magnus, Elijah, Jonas and Gwen. The shouting and chaos seemed to recede into the distance, and the reason was standing right in front of them.

'Hello, Magnus.'

A man was perched in the centre of the mezzanine, the ice mosaic under his feet bleeding tendrils of darkness. It seemed he'd put some kind of shadow ward round the space the moment they'd entered. It flickered like purple flame at the edges of the room.

'You?' Jonas choked the word out, his expression shocked, then his face contorted in fury. 'Where is my sister?' he demanded. He looked ready to charge forward, his hands poised to call upon the earth. Elijah held him back, eyeing the man with an expression of equal alarm.

That was when Gwen noticed Magnus, too. The look of utter horror on his face as he took in the mysterious man in front of them.

'Astrid's fine,' the man said, chuckling to himself. 'Better than fine, actually. She's a genius, that one.' He looked up, his misty eyes locking on to Magnus. 'I suppose I should have expected as much from Rupert's little chosen ones. Tell me, Magnus, how did it feel when you drove my knife through his heart?'

Magnus gasped. For the first time in Gwen's life her mentor looked truly disturbed. His usually stoic features morphed, black hair sticking out. A crow ruffled.

'My god, Quin – or should we call you Shay?' he said, hardly able to get the word out. 'You were right under our noses all this time.'

Elijah spoke now, his voice filled with compassion even under the terrible circumstances.

'Quin, what happened to you?'

Gwen's heart skipped a beat. Jonas held his breath.

Quin Larkspur. Another Rapscallion. This was who had been manipulating Astrid all this time.

For a moment his expression darkened. Then he shrugged, smiling, snake-like.

'Oh, you know how it is when you don't heed the warnings,' he said breezily. 'You might unleash an ancient evil, or you might become tethered to the shadows for all eternity.'

Elijah winced, clutching his heart. But Magnus only watched him with bird-like attention, his head cocked. Subtly, so subtly they could almost have missed it, Magnus pulled Elijah closer to him, and moved in front of Gwen and Jonas.

'You two, go get the book,' Magnus instructed. 'Stay together and bolt the door. Understood?'

Gwen shook her head. 'What about you two?'

Elijah smiled at her, the look on his face utterly heartbreaking.

'We're going to have a pleasant reunion with an old friend.'

Jonas looked uncertain for a second, not wanting to leave them, when Shay spoke again.

'Your sister is waiting for you,' he said, almost bored.

Jonas's breath hitched. Gwen felt her heart torn. Without another word, they nodded to their mentors. They had to leave. There was no other choice.

'Stay safe,' Magnus told them, beaming down at them fondly. 'And have faith in each other. Like I have faith in you.'

The moment they stepped past the purple flames, the noise of the fighting and chaos flooded over them. Shouts, war cries, spells in dizzying numbers. Through the windows, they caught glimpses of creatures spilling from the water, dripping ooze. Gwen recognized many of them – mermaids dragging themselves across the ice, capricorns bloated with rot. Some were so rotten she could not tell what form they had originally taken, a twisted chimera that had once been a magical creature. Custodians in furs and cloaks fought back, creating shields of ice and fire. Most wielded melodies, but others, like the special force Magister Beatrice had brought with her, were wielding weapons.

Swords met marred flesh. Charmed arrows flew through the air. Every command led to more bloodshed.

The snow was stained red and black.

Pulling themselves away, they ran up the staircase to the Researchers' Quarters. There were more abandoned belongings tossed about. People had either hid, rooms barricaded, or they had gone out to join the fray.

Reaching Gwen's room, they pushed the door open.

And there she was.

Gwen felt her heart shatter just looking at her. Her hair was still golden, her face still sharp with intellect. Reclining on Gwen's bed, flicking through the book of Cursed Melodies, she had stripped down to just her nightgown, the long black fabric pooling over her legs.

It was still her. Almost.

'Don't worry – I can't read it, of course,' she trilled, putting the book down. The pages were blank. 'Clever little spell Rupert put on it.'

Then they saw it. It was not just her hands that were stained black any more. Like cracks of lightning, black and purple lines bled from her eyes. The Grim crept over her, framing her face, delicate, almost beautiful. The sight of it had Gwen holding back a sob, her eyes stinging.

'Astrid, you fool! What have you done?' Jonas shouted, marching into the room to stand protectively in front of Gwen.

Astrid stood up before he could grab her, flitting to the window.

'I've opened Pandora's jar,' she told them, grinning. 'Maybe you should have a taste of what's inside. It's delicious.'

Jonas shuddered, pain strewn across his face. Gwen could not imagine what he was feeling.

Slowly, Astrid stepped towards him, coming in close to trace a finger along his jaw.

They'd always looked the same, a near-perfect reflection of each other. Same hair, same eyes, same skin, same smile. Now Astrid had changed. She'd broken the mirror.

'My vengeful nature has been sharpened to a fine point,' she told him. He batted her finger away, and she chuckled, stepping back. 'I wonder who I shall cut first? I was thinking of paying our dear Doctor Harris a visit in the old psych ward. Perhaps you'd care to join me, brother, as I liberate him from his own skin?'

Gwen could hardly believe the words coming from Astrid's mouth. And yet, they were still so . . . Astrid. Same humour, same voice, only now steeped in shadows.

'The Shadowling – he's going to kill you in the end. Like he did with Seraphina,' Jonas told her, standing his ground, trying to get through to her. 'He hates all of humanity.'

Now Astrid's dark-tinted eyes narrowed, the look both menacing and mischievous.

'Oh yes, he does,' she agreed. 'I can feel how much he does. We're linked now, all the time.'

And suddenly, Gwen knew. She'd seen it in the temple at Runefjord. In the statue of Merlin. The truth had been right in front of them. The twins had been called *'changelings'*. They'd been treated differently everywhere they ever went; they *felt* different. Because they were.

Astrid smiled at Gwen. She knew she'd figured it out.

'But brother, dearest,' she said, 'turns out, we are not human.'

Jonas paused, looking paler than ever. His legs wobbled under him, and Gwen ran forward to help him stand.

'We're not human,' he breathed, as though tasting the words, confirming the truth to himself. He almost sounded relieved. Perhaps he had always known, deep down.

Gwen let go of Jonas as he sat down on the bed, then turned to face Astrid head-on. She could feel it, warm inside her. The truth.

'You're fae, like Merlin, and all the old kings' advisors. Because we're not just seeing the memories of King Arthur and Merlin. We are them, reborn.'

Astrid looked genuinely proud, tracing a lock of Gwen's hair that had fallen loose through her fingers.

'That's my clever girl,' she purred. The words made Gwen's breath catch.

She twirled around the room again, humming the story. 'Once upon a time, a man called Rupert Faymore sold his humanity in exchange for knowledge. He found two babies in a tree, a tree that had split in two.'

Jonas gasped.

'One soul, two bodies.'

Astrid laughed, the sound deadly.

'So, you learned all this when you became possessed?' Jonas asked. He looked up at her, his expression torn, like he might start laughing or screaming. Like his sister was the most infuriating thing in the world.

'*Someone* had to get their hands dirty.' She shrugged. Those same words. For some reason, they sparked inside Gwen. It felt like a dangerous thought, too naive and hopeful to be true. That, maybe, this had all been Astrid's plan.

What had Shay said – that Astrid was a genius? Gwen went over the conversation and had to wonder, why would he say that if Astrid had been so easily fooled?

Humming, Astrid twirled back to the window to stare out at the horror below. She licked her lips. Bloodlust. Like she was thirsty to join in, and yet she didn't . . . why?

Gwen had to stop her hope from lighting up on her face, realizing that Astrid was, in fact, stifling her new instincts. Somehow, she had a crumb of control over the Grim. Gwen's heart raced at the thought, that maybe, possibly, there was a part of Astrid that could still be saved.

She just had to have faith, like Magnus had told her.

'What happened to us, Astrid?' Gwen asked slowly. 'What do you know?'

Astrid leaned back against the windowsill, her hair pooling over her dress. When she looked at Gwen, it was calculating, like she wanted Gwen to know something she couldn't quite say.

'We failed, I'm afraid, not just each other, but the whole magical world. Cursed forever to repeat our fetid history.'

Gwen's eyes widened, then she took a deep breath. The words of the past kings echoed in her mind.

Look what he did to us.
Cursed forever.
He did this.

Glancing at the book on the bed, Gwen nearly laughed. She felt it, the past rushing up to meet her, the truth of it all so clear and bright. The book seemed to glow with it, like she could hear it. Jubilant, elated, because finally, *finally* someone understood what it was. And there was great power in that knowledge. Power that could change history.

It wasn't a book of evil magic.

It was all the magic that had been cursed.

'I understand,' Gwen said to Astrid, because she did. Astrid had done all this, had succumbed to the Grim, just to get this knowledge to Gwen. 'Thank you.'

Astrid smiled at her again, almost sad.

'I knew you would. I imagine you're going to go face the Shadowling now. He told me to tell you that he'll be waiting for you at the small dock. No creature will attack you on the way. Strict orders. Your path is clear.' She jumped up off the sill, tapping her chin as if pondering while she stared down at the battle. 'Now, I think I'm going to go kill Magister Ragnar. I don't like how rude he was to you.' She made a childish face of disgust, thinking about him, then twirled back to Jonas's side. 'Jonas, take care and have fun with your little princeling. I'll be back for you.'

Jonas, still in shock, could hardly move as she wrapped her arms round him and squeezed. When she was done, she skipped over to Gwen.

Gwen didn't move as Astrid reached out, cupping her face in her hands. There was a reverent spark in her eyes.

The dark wispy tendrils of the Grim almost looked like they were moving under her skin.

'Gwendolyn, my glorious king,' she said, and for a split second Gwen thought she felt something soft in the words, something the Grim had not been able to touch. 'Don't die yet.'

Then she leaned in and kissed her goodbye.

27

Have Faith

Gwen could taste Astrid on her lips still. Like honey and ink, sweetness and darkness. At the window, Jonas called out her name, trying to stop her joining the battle and satisfying the Grim's bloodlust.

'She's gone, Jonas,' Gwen said, her eyes stinging.

'She can't be. She seemed so . . .'

'Like herself?'

Jonas nodded.

Gwen did not want to speak it out loud yet; she didn't want to give him false hope. But she had faith that there was a part of Astrid she could still save. Right now, though, Astrid was right. It was time to face evil.

'Come, Jonas. I'll need you.'

He took a deep breath, readying himself. Although his eyes were red-rimmed, his soul torn in two, he stepped forward, ready to serve.

They ran through the sanctum, their feet echoing on the marble. The halls were mostly empty now.

'Remember, I'm not going to kill him,' Gwen reminded him, eyes firmly ahead. 'I need you to promise me: you must not let me, or anyone else, kill him.'

Jonas gritted his teeth, displeased. But he nodded.

'Hey!' a voice shouted at them as they ran past the medical bay. They paused, and Prince Teddy rushed out to greet them. He was filthy with the rot of the Grim, and blood, most of it presumably not his own. Inside was pandemonium, spells of healing ringing true from songs and charms.

'Where the hell have you two been?' he huffed. His face was haunted, and Gwen dreaded to know what he'd witnessed. Past him, Gwen saw Eddie and Biscuit rushing around, assisting as best they could.

Jonas grabbed the prince and held him, squeezing him into his chest. Pliant to his touch, Teddy put a hand on his head, deciding not to ask any more questions.

'How are they faring out there?' Gwen asked instead.

'It was a bloodbath at first,' he confessed. 'But my mother's forces are strong. I think they can hold off the Grim.'

'My sister and Thomas?'

'They were like assassins. I've never seen anything like it.' Gwen tried to picture this: her sweet sister, cutting through the Grim like butter. 'Where are you two heading now? We could use help here.'

'No,' Jonas said, his voice cold as he pulled away. 'We need you to do something. We're going to go face the Shadowling.' The prince looked thunderstruck, but Jonas went on. 'You need to get your mother and some of her best fighters and come to the back of the sanctum by the docks. We can keep the Shadowling distracted while she finishes off his forces of the Grim.'

'No . . . no.' Prince Teddy stumbled over his words. 'Wait until they're done. You two can't face him alone.'

'We have to,' Gwen said coolly. 'We can't kill him, so we need him to retreat with as few casualties as possible.

This is the only way. We need to get out of here and to safety so we can go away and figure out how to actually defeat him.'

While Prince Teddy stood there in shock, Jonas kissed him on the cheek, then he and Gwen headed back out on their mission.

While the battle continued at the front of the Borealis Sanctum, the main dock now a wreck of destroyed ships and the lifeless bodies of Grim-possessed creatures, the back of the sanctum was eerily peaceful. They saw Shay's purple fire again, which had spread across the doors they'd left through and round in a huge circle, the area somehow warding away the uninvited.

Outside, it was freezing, the wind chapping their cheeks. Even through their fur-trimmed cloaks, Gwen could feel it.

The Grim was louder here, whispers of rot crawling through her ears. The Shadowling was close.

Ahead of them, the small dock was empty, the skiffs and propeller boats bobbing in the water under the boathouse. This was where Astrid would have come when she'd run away last night, Gwen realized.

'Where is he?' Jonas asked. There was a frantic air to him, the fury at what had happened to Astrid evolving into a thirst for vengeance.

Wings flapped above; the sun was blotted out.

They turned, looking up, and there he was on the roof of the sanctum.

He had nearly doubled in size since the last time they'd seen him – a terrifying, god-like presence. White scales shining celestial, gold eyes cruel and calculating. A monster in angel's skin.

His wings stretched out, then he jumped down. The world shook where he landed, his nostrils huffing smoke as he prowled closer.

Gwen refused to cower. Refused to take a single step back as the heat from his breath caused sweat along her face. Behind her, Jonas was poised, hands held low, ready to call upon the earth beneath the snow.

'This belongs to you, I believe,' the Shadowling said. His voice rattled through Gwen's bones.

At her feet, he dropped the sword. Arthur's sword. *Her* sword.

She did not reach for it.

The Shadowling laughed, a dark, cruel sound.

'You need not worry. The curse is gone, taken by somebody else.'

Jonas sucked in a breath at her side, and Gwen held a finger up to keep him back.

'I know what you did.' Gwen spoke clearly as the Shadowling began to circle them. 'You are the reason Red Bloods turned on Bloom Bloods; you're the reason magic is but a shell of what it once was.' She felt her Bloom burning under her skin, fear and power at the same time. 'You cursed it, didn't you? You put a curse on magic itself. The book of Cursed Melodies is not evil: it's a warning. It's all the magic that you defiled.'

The Shadowling made a low rumbling sound, flames spitting from his lips as he laughed at her. At the whole world.

'What we have left of magic are the only things Arthur and Merlin could save,' she continued. 'You caused the magical dark age.'

Jonas, strong as he was, remained stoically at her side, but inside he was a quivering mass of rage. He wanted vengeance so terribly. But, like a trained guard dog, he did not move; he waited for his master's command.

Still circling them like a predator, the Shadowling's throat rumbled again.

'They failed to kill me, so they failed to cure the curse. You will also have no such luck in defeating me.'

'I don't believe you,' Gwen spat back. 'You're trying to trick me.'

For just a second, the Shadowling paused, his features shifting. Furious.

'Then you are doomed again!' he roared. This time he lunged right up to Jonas's face. Flames spilled from his lips with every word he spoke. 'I took one half of your soul, Merlin – aren't you upset? I can see her right now: she is licking blood off her fingers. She's laughing. Her humanity melted away so easily, like flesh off bone.'

Jonas's fists balled at his sides, yet he did not strike.

'Quiet!' Gwen shouted. She had to focus on her Bloom, make sure it didn't spill into her voice as she spoke.

The Shadowling chuckled, circling back to Gwen.

'She cared for you deeply, Arthur. I suppose she was the one who held that side of Merlin's soul. The part you tricked into loving you. That part is dead now.'

Gwen bit her tongue. She wouldn't give in. She wouldn't let Astrid down like that.

'I won't fall for this. I won't try to kill you,' Gwen growled back. Her vision was shining gold at the edges, her Bloom near overflowing. 'I don't know why you are so determined to goad me into using this sword to strike you, but I won't. You've failed.'

The Shadowling simply smiled, his claws curling into the snow.

'Oh, I think you will,' he said, stretching tall. 'Quin, bring me our companions.'

Confused, Gwen watched as Quin materialized from the darkness, and with him, trapped in ropes of shadow, were Magnus and Elijah.

'No,' Gwen barked. Jonas had to reach out, grabbing the hem of her cloak before she rushed forward.

'Ah yes, this is the reaction I was hoping for!' The Shadowling cackled now, delighting in their misery. 'You are the same as you were back then, a slave to your emotions.'

'Let them go!' Jonas hissed at Quin. 'You can't possibly do this. You were their friend!'

Ignoring him, Quin had his prisoners kneel in the snow right in the centre of the purple ring of fire. He was devoid of emotion, unflinching at the injuries strewn across Magnus and Elijah's faces from their fight with him.

'Gwen, Jonas, it's OK. We're OK.' Elijah smiled at her. He looked serene, accepting. Somehow that scared Gwen even more.

Gwen and Jonas chanced running forward to get to them, but the Shadowling only roared, launching fire in a deadly line across their path.

'Do not move,' the Shadowling growled, 'or I will burn them to death slowly. Pick up the sword, Gwen. Pick up the sword and strike me and I will stop this.'

Gwen felt utterly helpless. What could she do? The voices from the past had begged her not to kill the Shadowling. She couldn't give in to these feelings of desperation, no matter how much it hurt, and yet . . .

She could stop this. She could save Magnus and Elijah.

Her fingers twitched, her body leaning towards the sword.

'Gwen, no.' Magnus called her name, stopping her in her tracks.

The Shadowling growled again, fire frothing at his lips, but Magnus went on: 'I need you to remember to never lose sight of what you love. That you must always do what you believe is right. No matter what. Trust yourself. Do you understand?'

Gwen nodded, her eyes running with tears. She couldn't let her fear or hatred win.

'Let them go!' she shouted through gritted teeth.

'Jonas, we love you,' Magnus called now, his words soft even as the cuts on his face streamed red. 'We are so happy we got to meet you, that you and your sister came into our lives.'

It hurt, the need to rush forward, to do something. It was physically painful.

Then Magnus and Elijah turned to one another.

'Goodbye, my love,' Magnus cooed.

'Goodbye. I'll see you soon,' Elijah replied, smiling back as if they were simply saying goodnight.

'Kill them,' the Shadowling ordered.

Quin leaned down and whispered something in Magnus's ear. There was no way Gwen could hear it, but whatever he said, Magnus nodded, smiling, like everything was going to be OK. Gwen had a flicker of hope, that perhaps Quin had fooled the Shadowling, that he was switching sides.

Then he hummed a dark tune to the shadows, creating a sharpened tendril of darkness . . . and with it he slit their throats.

Silence. Crimson pooled into the snow. The world filled with the sound of Gwen's tortured scream. The sound ripped from her like a severed limb.

Bloom burst in every cell of Gwen's body. It burned in her throat, something ancient. A spell to destroy. A spell of rage.

She picked up the sword. The world turned gold.

28

Never Lose Sight of What You Love

White-hot rage. Screaming. Fire. The world was a blur of white and gold, blood and snow. There was a song on Gwen's lips. It vibrated through her blade. This had happened before. This monster – it had stolen from them. Taken everything. The song burned molten-hot in her throat.

Look what he did to us. To the world.
He destroyed everything.
He had to suffer. He had to die.

Someone was screaming, begging her to stop. But Gwen was floating, her power so profound she was hardly present in the human realm at all. She was within the vibrations of magic, the melodies of life, of love, of hatred.

The sword was glorious in her grasp. She was whole again. And this time, she would kill the beast. For Merlin. For magic. For all of humanity.

'Yes. Do it!' the white dragon roared, fire in his words. 'Strike me!'

The sword rang in her hand. A thing crafted by the magic of the fae, built from ancient Albion steel. The blade that was meant to end this madness and yet was cursed to make the same mistakes again.

Gwen lifted the blade and prepared to strike.

In the chaos of Bloom, the searing light of Gwen and her sword, and the blood spilling into the snow, Jonas saw Prince Teddy through the circle of purple flames. Teddy had kept his promise and brought Magister Beatrice and her forces. Just in time for them to see their mentors slaughtered.

Jonas felt his knees weak beneath him. The power of the song from Gwen's lips was shaking the very ground. It sent a tornado around them, snow and Bloom and blood.

With just a huff of breath, the energy surrounding Gwen pulsed, the purple flames around them extinguished. Yet no one could step forward, for fear of the power radiating off Gwen. They were trapped in a nightmare.

Jonas wanted Astrid. He needed her. He felt so lost, the world ajar, not making a lick of sense. But he couldn't stop to cry, he couldn't fall into the snow and scream. He had to stop Gwen. He'd promised.

'Gwen!' Jonas shouted. The song was no longer spilling from her lips, but all around them. Swirling, the music glittered in the air. Formidable as the apocalypse.

She seemed not to hear him, marching onwards to the Shadowling, who grinned, teeth bared. He was waiting for her to strike.

'Gwen, you have to stop!' Jonas pleaded, grabbing her arm. 'You need to let go of the sword. It can't end like this.'

She went still, her head turning sharply to look at him. Jonas gasped at the sight of her face. Fury – pure, and white hot. Her eyes burned with it, gold light pouring out. This was not Gwen the girl they'd met in an abandoned underground station. Not Gwen whom Astrid had fallen in love with. This was the shining power of a king. A demi-god.

Yet, Jonas would not give in.

'You made me promise, and I won't break an order,' he said, refusing to let go.

'Don't listen to him!' the Shadowling roared. 'I will burn everything you love to ash. Strike me, let all magic fall under my shadow!'

Jonas's breath caught at the words. That was it. If Gwen struck him, the Shadowling would win. Somehow, this was all part of his plan to curse *all* magic and doom the world.

Eyes blazing, Gwen opened her mouth, the sound that came from it like a million furious gods. All the kings of the past talking through her.

'He must pay for what he did to us.'

Jonas could only watch in awe as Gwen began to float into the air. She hovered over the Shadowling, and as he laughed, she threw an arm up, and threw it down again. A spear of shining gold materialized out of the air and stabbed him through his haunches. Then she did it again, and again, until he was pinned to the ground.

For a split second, the Shadowling quivered, fear appearing in his eyes at the power before him. All Jonas knew was that he could not let Gwen try to kill him. No matter what.

She raised the sword above her head, ready to bring the blade down into the dragon's head. Jonas called on the earth, what little there was beneath him. Roots flew from the ground, wrapping the blade tight. They snapped and groaned at her strength, pulling back against it.

'Let her kill him!'

Jonas nearly lost his focus at the voice of Magister Beatrice. When he turned his head, he could see Teddy pleading with her, telling her to hold back. But she was watching with enough rage to match Gwen's.

She didn't understand. They couldn't. This was what the Shadowling wanted. Hatred. Vengeance.

It seemed hopeless. There was nothing more Jonas could do.

Then he heard another voice. A man shouting, reckless. Two figures jumped off the roof of the building, one grabbing Gwen's ankle, the other landing on the Shadowling. Lorelei and Captain Kane.

Gwen went crashing to the ground, the golden spears shattering like glass and freeing the Shadowling. Lorelei landed on top of Gwen, seizing the sword. Taking the opportunity, Jonas sang to the earth, holding Gwen to the ground as Lorelei threw the sword out of reach.

Gwen roared.

So did the Shadowling.

'Traitors!' Magister Ragnar shouted.

The Shadowling stumbled backwards, Captain Kane digging his knife into the back of his neck. Then again, and again. Then he jumped off, rolling along the ground.

'Filthy pests!' the Shadowling growled at the captain, then he reared back, his throat rumbling as he let forth a ferocious jet of fire.

The captain ran, just in time, grabbing Jonas and pulling him out of the way of danger.

'Changeling boy,' the captain called, huffing. 'I was wrong. I was wrong about Shay. I was reckless in my search for vengeance and missed what was in front of me. I will put it right. If Gwen says she is not to kill the Shadowling, I will do all that is in my power to uphold her wish.' He pushed Jonas forward. 'Go to her.'

As he spoke, with the Magister's forces now gathered, ready, finally Magister Beatrice shouted the order: 'Attack!'

They charged, and so did Jonas, running desperately to take Gwen from Lorelei. The Shadowling swiped at the forces, falling back. Quin had disappeared into the shadows. Astrid was missing. The Shadowling's Grim-possessed creatures lay defeated. He was outnumbered. He had no choice but to retreat.

While they forced him back, Jonas clung to Gwen, Lorelei with him. There were unspilled tears in her eyes.

'Gwen, come on, girl,' Lorelei cooed. 'Come back to us.'

Gwen's eyes continued to glow gold, a spell forming on her lips.

Jonas couldn't stand it. He shook her desperately.

While the world around them erupted in pandemonium – the barrage of spells, the Shadowling beating his wings, snapping and biting at anything that got near him – Jonas pleaded with Gwen. She had to be in there somewhere. Through the hurt and anger and pain. He felt it too. He understood.

Above them, a winged shadow disappeared into the clouds, the Shadowling retreating. It was only them now. The world still, watching.

'Gwen, listen to me,' Jonas begged her. It hurt to even speak, the pain of all they'd witnessed nearly unbearable. 'You can't kill him. I know it hurts, I know what he did was unforgiveable, but Astrid told me she thinks your love can save her. Don't prove her wrong.' His voice cracked. 'I need you to save my sister. I need you to save the girl you love.'

Finally Gwen blinked, a single tear rolling down her cheek.

The gold light faded, and she collapsed into his arms.

When Gwen awoke, her cheeks were wet, and her throat hurt.

She'd been crying in her sleep.

At first she told herself it had been a nightmare, that she was in her bed at Faymore Manor, that at any moment she would be pestered by Astrid and Jonas about getting ready for their lessons.

But this was not her bed, and Astrid was gone.

Gasping, Gwen curled over, the pain of the memory like a stab wound.

Astrid was gone, Magnus was gone, Elijah was gone.

Through the blur of tears in her eyes, she took in the room. Old stone, a single bed with crisp, lavender-scented sheets. There was a fruit bowl next to her and a window looking out over a lake. She felt numb to it at first, tears spilling silently down her face. Yet, wherever she was, it was beautiful. The lake was peaceful in the winter mist, birds darting across the surface.

The door opened.

'Gwen!' Jonas came rushing in. 'Thank god you're awake. I've been pulling my hair out.'

He was followed closely by the prince, who was sporting a bandage across his cheek and another one round his wrist. Something about him had changed, his ever-smooth edges somehow rougher, hardened.

'Where are we?' Gwen asked, as Jonas wrapped his arms round her.

'That is Lake Geneva,' the prince explained. 'And we

are, quite incredibly, in the headquarters of the Order, the Shadow Library.'

Suddenly awestruck, Gwen looked out over the lake again. She was in the oldest Order stronghold on earth. The place *The Cursed Melodies* had been hidden all those years.

Jonas sat back on the bed. Up close, Gwen saw how worn his eyes had become, and the shadows beneath. She wasn't sure they'd ever truly recover from what they'd seen. She swallowed the thought down, knowing she would be a ruin if she dwelled on it. There would be time for that later.

'What happened to everyone?' Gwen asked.

The prince helped himself to a cherry from the fruit bowl as he explained the situation. 'Thomas and your sister are here; Eddie stayed at the sanctum to help with the injured; Astrid and Shay . . . or Quin vanished with the Shadowling; and, well . . .' He glanced at Jonas, who had a bitter look on his face.

'They've locked up Lorelei and Captain Kane for *treason*,' Jonas hissed.

Teddy frowned. 'They're being kept in the cells below.'

'Because they stopped me killing the Shadowling?' Gwen probed, and they both nodded. 'They might very well have saved the world, and they're being kept in a cell.' She couldn't help the spark of her usual fire that crept into the words. She clutched Jonas's hand, squeezing it, as she allowed another tear to fall. 'You saved me, Jonas. I don't know what would have happened if I had struck him with my sword, but I know it would have been devastating. If not for you . . . I could have cursed us all, just like I did long ago in the past.'

Jonas squeezed her hand back, a reflection of what he would usually do with Astrid, when they'd hold one another, finding comfort in their touch.

'We'll figure it out, Gwen. We'll find out how the Shadowling cursed magic and how to fix it.'

Her resolve hardened. 'And then we'll save Astrid.'

'You two really believe that's possible?' Teddy asked. He seemed concerned, like he didn't want them to have false hope.

'I have to believe it,' Jonas said, scowling up at him.

Teddy held up his hands in surrender.

'Magnus,' Gwen said, choking on the name. She squeezed her eyes shut, forcing herself through the rest of the words. 'Before he . . . before he was taken, he told us to have faith in each other. To hold on to what we love. All I know for certain is we can't kill the Shadowling. We have to find out exactly what Arthur and Merlin did in the past and what these curses are. We won't make the same mistakes again, whatever they were.'

Jonas nodded his agreement, his gaze distant, thoughtful.

'I'm with you both. I'll help you in any way I can,' Teddy declared. There was something so earnest in the way he spoke now. No bravado. A real prince.

'That's good,' Jonas said, attempting a chuckle as he stared up at Teddy. 'With my sister turning into an evil witch, we have an opening for a third in our doomed little trio.'

The prince smiled down at him with a melancholy look.

'We're going to get her back,' Gwen said firmly. 'She promised –' Gwen swallowed down a sob that threatened to overtake her as she remembered what Astrid had said on the boat. 'She promised she'd never leave me. I have to trust that she knew I could get her back.'

A soon as she spoke the words, the door opened again. This time, it was her sister.

'Gwenny!' Jan stepped in, her face contorted like she was about to cry. 'I'm so glad you're OK.' Rushing to her side, she cradled her like she used to when they were little. 'How are you feeling?'

Gwen swallowed, trying not to cry again.

'It's all right – I know,' Jan cooed. 'It's going to be OK. We're going to make him pay for what he did.'

Confused, Gwen sat back in the bed.

'What do you mean?'

Jan held her at arm's length, her face deadly serious. She looked so different from the sister Gwen used to know. More severe, a wrath in her that had never been there before.

'We got the sword, Gwen. We have it, and because Astrid removed the curse on it, you can use it. The Magisters have decided that they're going to pool their forces to trap the Shadowling so you can kill him.'

Gwen was too shocked to speak, her heart thudding in her chest.

'I'll go tell them you're awake now so they can bring you some proper food,' Jan said, then kissed her on the head and left the room.

Heart hammering, panic began to rise in Gwen as she registered the full extent of the situation. This was all wrong. This was everything she'd been pleading with them not to do.

The door slammed shut behind Jan, the air heavy.

'Ah yes, there's just one little problem with our plans,' Prince Teddy said, grimacing. 'We're going to have to escape first.'

Acknowledgements

Before I run away to hide after that diabolical cliffhanger I've left everyone with . . .

Thanks to my wonderful team at Penguin. I adore working with you all so much; you make even the most gut-wrenching stories a joy to write.

Thanks to my agent, Richard, and manager, Mark.

To all the people working behind the scenes on all the big moments in my life.

And, of course, to my readers, viewers and supporters. THANK YOU.

Connie Glynn lives in London with three charming but mischievous cats. She studied film at the University of Sussex, where she started her YouTube channel 'Noodlerella', which amassed over a million followers across social platforms. She has since parted ways with her pink-haired alter ego, but has kept her whimsical approach to life and the search for magic in the everyday. In her spare time, she can usually be found rewatching golden-age Disney movies or taking long naps outside with a book over her face.

You can find her on YouTube at Connie Glynn for video essays and pop culture content, and on Instagram and TikTok at @ConnieGlynn.

The following is an extract from an Order of Pendragon spell book. These are eight of the twelve basic melodies that, once understood and memorized, can be conjured at will to perform any number of magical feats. If you would like to try playing one, please do so with caution and far away from any breakable objects.

AN EXCERPT FROM

THE BLOOM BLOOD'S BOOK OF SPELLS
~ FIFTEENTH EDITION ~

CHAPTER 1: NOVICE LEVEL

I.   CALM

II.   HEAL

III.   PULL

IV.   PUSH

AN EXCERPT FROM

THE BLOOM BLOOD'S BOOK OF SPELLS
~ FIFTEENTH EDITION ~

CHAPTER 2: INTERMEDIATE LEVEL

I. EARTH

II. WATER

III. WIND

IV. BIND

This ancient spell wheel shows how all magic is interconnected and should be in perfect harmony. Bloom Bloods must study it to understand the Twelve Spells and how they relate to one another.

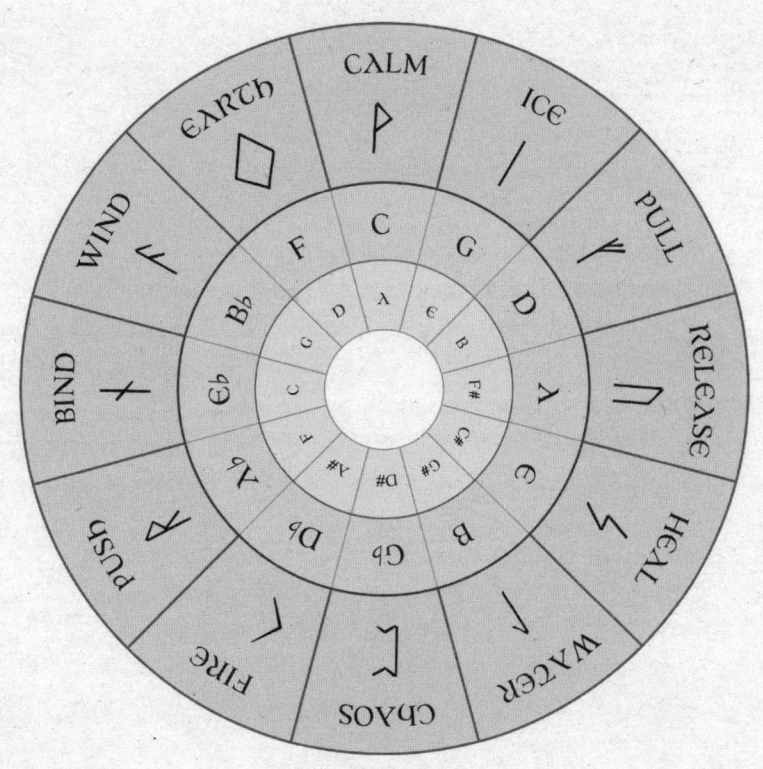

With darkness closing in, the world doesn't just need a hero.

It needs all three of them.

Keep an eye out for the epic conclusion to the Cursed Melodies trilogy, coming soon . . .